CLEAR LAKE PUBLIC LIBRARY

1 6102 00136 6513

S0-AFN-444

LP
LICKEL

14

Lickel, Lisa J., 1961–
Meander scar

12/10   30.99

Couet 04/17

MEADOWS 4/11

MEADOWS 9/15
                PLZ8/11

                APPLE 1/12

PUBLIC LIBRARY
CLEAR LAKE, IOWA 50428

OAWOOD 5/12

DEMCO

Meander Scar

PUBLIC LIBRARY
CLEAR LAKE, IOWA 50428

This Large Print Book carries the
Seal of Approval of N.A.V.H.

MEANDER SCAR

LISA J. LICKEL

THORNDIKE PRESS
A part of Gale, Cengage Learning

GALE
CENGAGE Learning™

Detroit • New York • San Francisco • New Haven, Conn • Waterville, Maine • London

GALE
CENGAGE Learning™

Copyright © 2010 by Lisa J. Lickel.
Thorndike Press, a part of Gale, Cengage Learning.

ALL RIGHTS RESERVED
This is a work of fiction. All of the characters, names, events, organizations and conversations in this novel are either the products of the author's vivid imagination or are used in a fictitious way for the purposes of this story.
Thorndike Press® Large Print Clean Reads.
The text of this Large Print edition is unabridged.
Other aspects of the book may vary from the original edition.
Set in 16 pt. Plantin.

LIBRARY OF CONGRESS CATALOGING-IN-PUBLICATION DATA

Lickel, Lisa J., 1961–
    Meander scar / by Lisa J. Lickel.
        p. cm. — (Thorndike Press large print clean reads)
    ISBN-13: 978-1-4104-3194-3 (hardcover)
    ISBN-10: 1-4104-3194-0 (hardcover)
    1. Abandoned wives—Fiction. 2. Large type books. 3. Domestic fiction.
I. Title.
PS3612.I248M43 2010
813'.6—dc22   2010031529

Published in 2010 by arrangement with Black Lyons Publishing LLC.

Printed in the United States of America
1 2 3 4 5 6 7 14 13 12 11 10

For Mary and Paul, and Deidre and Dave,
whose own special love stories inspire.

AUTHOR'S
ACKNOWLEDGEMENTS

I gratefully thank faithful friends Attorney Mary B. Williams and Attorney David E. Wells. Mary developed Mark's family background and set up his professional character. Dave answered my many questions and vetted the manuscript. Any errors are my own. Readers Deidre, Ann, and Susan, members of the Moraine Writer's Guild, and Andrea made valuable contributions to the story.

Meander Scar. (Mē-án-dər skär) is healed earth alongside a waterway that skewed from the boundaries of its naturally straight course. Whether rushing or dribbling, waterways want to flow straight. When a river runs into a barrier, such as a large rock, its course begins to bend. The river circles until it meets up with its original boundary. The reunited waters abandon the circular path to run true again. The abandoned meander is first a small lake, then a swamp, then a scar.

CHAPTER ONE

"Place me like a seal over your heart, like a seal on your arm; for love is as strong as death, its ardor unyielding at the grave. It burns like blazing fire, like a mighty flame. Many waters can't quench love; rivers can't wash it away. If one were to give all the wealth of his house for love, it would be utterly scorned." Song of Songs 8:6–7.

Ann Ballard jerked awake, shaken by a rumble she felt clear to her bones. A dazzling flash of light burned her retinas when she glanced through the living room window. She jumped and felt her heart stutter at the roll of thunder that rattled the panes of glass.

At least she'd been saved from sinking into the nightmare again. Three times in a row, whenever she'd closed her eyes she dreamed of being trapped in a swampy pool on the banks of the winding Black Earth Creek, helplessly watching her son Ritchie and his friend Trey struggle against a current. The fact that the creek was not that big in real life didn't seem to matter in her dream.

Ann tossed aside the afghan that had been covering her feet and stood. Only little old ladies took naps in the afternoon. What was the matter with her? The magazine she'd been reading slipped to the floor, sending the photograph she used as a bookmark spilling out. She snatched up the picture before it bent. She knew what sleeping during the day would lead to: wandering her big empty house at night, wide awake and scaring herself silly at every creak. Probably another headache, too. One that would take two days of head-banging and nausea to get over.

Another crack of lightning sent her scurrying to the kitchen. Dinner. Make dinner. Anything to distract herself from the storm. Speaking of which . . . Ann stopped in front of the cupboard and rubbed her arms. Where had she stored the battery-operated lantern? Were the power cells charged and ready? She hadn't swept the basement all summer and hoped she wouldn't have to wade through curtains of cobwebs if the severe weather forced her to take shelter down there.

Long ago, her first thoughts in inclement weather went to protecting her family. Since she'd been alone, wondering who would come to her rescue if she became trapped like those Chinese earthquake victims was turning into a sour hobby — especially on weekends when her niece Maeve was gone.

One thing she knew for sure: her mother-in-law wouldn't be the first in line to save her. Maybe Ritchie would care. After a few days anyway, when she was due for supper at his and Colleen's house in Portage and didn't show up with the casserole.

The doorbell rang. Ann walked down the hall, grinning at the thought of Donna, her mother-in-law who hadn't liked being a grandmother, becoming a great-grandmother. She fingered the colored square of paper in her hand while she pushed aside the filmy panel covering the sidelights to check out her visitor.

Bonus. A beautiful, dark-haired man stood on her step. Almost any company would be a welcome interruption. Ann opened the door to a gust of chilled wet breeze. Goose bumps rose at the sudden drop of temperature the coming storm brought. A scurrying rustle of dried leaves swirled on the unswept deck of her pillared front porch. Rain slashed at his little car on the brick drive.

Did she recognize him? Something about the nose . . . the photograph! Ann resisted the urge to compare her picture with her guest.

The man's lips tilted into a practiced smile as he held out a hand. "Mrs. Ballard? Ann? Do you remember me? Mark? I'm Mark Roth. Trey's brother? We lived next door."

Yes, yes. That was it. He squatted at the edge of the frame in her photograph of Ritchie and Trey in fifth grade with a catch of bluegills. How could she have forgotten Mark's eyes? Even when he'd been a high schooler, those eyes had been the talk of the neighborhood ladies. Arresting blue, the iridescent color of bluebird feathers, Patricia from across the way used to say. Patricia always had been a bit of a nature freak.

Ann put a hand to her mouth and held up the picture with the other. "Well, this is amazing. I was just cleaning Ritchie's closet and thinking about the boys and their fishing and found this photograph." What on earth made her say such a ridiculous thing? "Oh, you don't care about that. Please, come in."

Ann pulled the door wide and gestured. He'd filled out from the wiry athlete who took the basketball team to a regional championship. How many years had passed

14

since she last saw him? Ritchie's high school graduation. Mark had gone east to college and stayed except for an occasional visit. After Trey's accident a few years later, the Roths moved away from Wisconsin.

When Mark's broad back was turned, Ann smoothed her hair and tugged her blouse straight, took a deep breath and prayed her deodorant was still working.

Mark preceded her into the living room and, with sweet attentiveness in his enchanting smile and raised brows, waited until she'd taken a seat before he settled into a place of his own. Wow — no one had manners like that anymore. She perched on the edge of one of the oxblood club chairs on either side of the formal brocade sofa. "Well, how are you? It's been a long time. Are you visiting friends?"

"I'm fine, thank you. I've moved back to town. Just a week ago, as a matter of fact."

"You moved from Virginia? So, you quit your job? I'm afraid your parents and I haven't kept up much, just a note once in a while, since their . . . retirement."

Out of the corner of her eye, Ann saw the rumpled stack of newspapers she'd left on the end table and a cobweb hanging from the lamp shade. Unexpected company rarely happened. Shame! How could she have let the place go? She looked back at her guest before he answered. "I've accepted a position with Jung and Royce."

A tingle of surprise made her raise her eyebrows at the name of the well-known private law firm here in Clayton. Unfortunately, she and Gene had required their services more than once to yank Ritchie out of some scrape. That, besides their general legal business. "Todd Royce was a golfing partner of my husband Gene's. I hope it works out for you. They must think highly of your abilities."

Mark turned his head toward the cold gas fireplace. He shrugged and faced her again. "I've had a few successes. I hoped to catch up on news from the old neighborhood. I heard Ritchie and Colleen are expecting a baby. And I wondered how you were doing."

Ann nodded and smiled. "I'm well. It's nice of you ask. And excited for Ritchie, even though that will make me a grandmother." Ann jumped back to her feet like some excitable rabbit. "Forgive me. Why don't I find us a something to snack on?" She started down the hall only to hear him follow her.

Her kitchen, with its seldom used gleaming copper-bottomed pots and dark flecked granite countertops, felt small and cold. She flipped a switch to light the sink area and the swag over the breakfast table set in front of the patio doors. She and Gene used to do a lot of entertaining. In fact, Ann used to do a lot of things, but it seemed that no one wanted half a couple in the spotlight. Maybe they thought her circumstances were contagious.

Snacks. Right. Ann checked the chrome refrigerator, although she knew exactly what she had in there: a quart of skim milk three days past the due date, some yogurt, old tortillas, and leftovers from the church guild lunch meeting a week ago. Drat. The refrigerator fairy hadn't visited. Cooking for one didn't call for a stockpile of food. Maeve always ate on campus. Ann closed the door with a grimace. Stalling for time she asked, "How do you like being a lawyer?"

Mark settled back against the counter and folded his arms.

Ann let her eyelids half close as she studied him. She tried to keep her breathing even, to direct her heartbeats to remain steady. Mark was definitely no longer the sweet polite young man from next door, but an adult in his . . . let's see . . . thirties? He was nine years older than Ritchie and Trey; which made him nearly thirty-five. Eleven years younger than she. And he didn't resemble any of the staid lawyers she did business with at Ballard, Gorman and Wicht, Gene's company, where she worked as a CPA two days a week.

Eleven years . . . not so many. Men married much younger women all the time. In fact, just last year . . . *Stop it.* Where did that come from? Ann watched Mark's lips move, answering her question, while she stood there like a smitten idiot. Thinking ridiculous dreamy scenarios. Watching him like a lusty lonely widow — which she was not. A widow, anyway.

But he was pleasant to look at. His smooth face showed more character lines than her son's. His deep chest and flat stomach under the soft gray dress shirt and dark pleated slacks hinted at regular workouts, something the swimmer in her appreciated. She tuned back in to his words.

"I love helping people solve their problems, especially the folks who've been victimized. You know, the easy targets. I worked for a grassroots group last year who represented landowners over an abandoned mine land property dispute with a reclamation company."

Ann tore her gaze away and hunted for clean glasses in the cupboard to his right.

"So, you sound like you're settling in." He wasn't likely to find too many victims to help at Todd Jung's prestigious firm, but she kept her mouth shut. "Is it hard to change firms? Or does everyone do business pretty much the same way?"

Mark took the two tumblers she grabbed and turned on the tap. "The work I do, estate planning and business law, has to work across multiple states, but every firm has its own way of handling clients."

Ann looked for ice cubes, hoping they hadn't evaporated since the Fourth of July, the last time she knew she had any. They took their glasses to the kitchen table. Lightning crackled outside her patio. She gasped at the immediate report of thunder.

Mark pulled her chair out for her. "Close one."

Ann focused on his calm expression and relaxed. "Seems like this has been going on for long enough already."

"I listened to the radio on the way over here. Sounds like a quick-moving storm. Should be out of here soon."

They watched the play of cloud-to-cloud lightning for a few minutes. Like Mark said, the clouds scudded along. He told her about some of the spectacular storms he'd witnessed in the hills around Lynchburg. Ann circled the rim of her glass with her finger, trying to think of something witty and mature to say. It'd been years since she'd had a personal conversation with a man to whom she wasn't related. "You must have liked it there in Virginia to have stayed so long."

"I always planned to return to Wisconsin. I consider it home."

"And now you're moving up the ladder."

"Mr. Jung knows I want to spend a certain amount of my time doing pro bono work. He thinks it'll be good for the firm's image. Plenty of folks need help around the Madison area."

Ann read the tautness of her guest's expression. Touchy. Okay, time to change the subject. "So, you're back in Clayton. It's really good to see you. I'm sure Ritchie and Colleen will be happy to know you're nearby. And, um, your other friends. I thought you were engaged?" Ann looked for a wedding ring. Nope. Well, not all men wore one. "Did you get married? Is she with you?" Ann tried to recall the name Tiffany Roth linked him with in one of her Christmas cards.

"We'll have time to catch up. I hoped you were available to celebrate my new job with me. You were one of few people from my past who always believed in me, supported me."

Ann's back went straight with surprise. "Me?" She shook her head, brow furrowed. "I didn't do anything special."

Mark smiled. "More than you know. How about we talk over dinner? I'm hungry."

One of the few people from his past . . . in her opinion, Mark's father and stepmother had shamefully neglected both Trey and Mark while they spent all their time on their Internet business. All Ann had done was attend a few of Mark's games and make sure he'd been welcome in her home.

This grown man was different from the boy next door. Ann knew Mark Roth, and yet she didn't. Exciting? What was the matter with her? This nice young man simply wanted to be polite and touch bases with people he used to know. And maybe he was lonely if his wife had stayed in Virginia to wrap things up. The least she could do was eat a meal with him, for old times' sake. She knew better than anyone that eating alone wasn't much fun. And he was obviously proud of his new job. "Of course I'll celebrate with you. There's a new buffet place we could try."

Ann didn't protest when Mark ushered her to his newer model metallic blue Mazda.

Not that she embarrassed easily, but the little Ford she'd traded for her Beemer showed its age.

She knew she'd chosen wrong when they entered the crowded lobby of the restaurant. The place was a madhouse decorated in fake Wild West. Had the storm made everyone crazy to get out? Mark smiled grimly as he folded his wallet back in his pocket after paying the cashier. He picked up a cafeteria tray with their soft drinks in chipped plastic cups and flatware wrapped in a paper napkin. The cafeteria din made her clench her jaw.

Mark led the way into the main dining room and indicated a far corner with his elbow. "I think I see a free table." They seated themselves. Ann wished the place would wash away and take her along. At least she wasn't trying to make some kind of impression on him, as if he were a prospective client. Or a candidate for a romance. She looked at him, hoping he could see how sorry she was for choosing such a raunchy restaurant. Mark mouthed something she couldn't quite hear.

"I'm sorry, what did you say?"

A young waitress with a nose ring arrived, setting a basket of greasy-looking rolls on the table. She lingered, eyeing Mark as she might the dessert table while reminding them to take a clean plate whenever they visited the buffet. Ann wondered how Mark's wife would have treated the girl and sat up straight, squinting with what she hoped was a disapproving frown. Now she felt more like a mother protecting her naïve son. She lost the frown when he spoke.

"You must enjoy the food here," Mark said after the young woman left.

"I've never been here. Ritchie and Colleen said they liked it." Ann took a deep breath and risked a sip of the cloudy iced tea she'd ordered. She couldn't see Mark bringing his wife here. What kind of person was he married to, anyway? "So, um, Allison." That was her name! "Isn't she here with you? Did you leave her to settle things in Virginia before she comes?"

"I'm sorry, I can't hear you."

Ann was pretty sure he'd heard, but no way was she going to shout her question again. She already sounded like a busybody grandma. "Do you . . . do you —"

Mark cut in. "Let's see what they have to eat."

Ann scavenged without much success through the commingled aromas of steaming platters and bins of canned and diced and fried-looking bits. Mark did not appear to have fared much better, she noted, when they returned to their table. Mark looked around, as if waiting for something.

Ann turned her head, too, but did not see anyone she knew. When she faced him again, his eyes were closed. Ah. Praying. That church youth group he'd attended in high school must have left a lasting impression. She briefly copied him. When he looked up at her again with a peaceful expression, she picked up her fork. Dare she ask about Allison again? Ann decided on a safer topic. "How are your parents?"

"Parents?" He cocked an ear toward her. "Dad and Tiffany are well as ever, if that's what you asked. Golfing every day."

They gave up trying to converse through the ruckus after that. She couldn't think of anything to say to him on the way home. Since her ears were still ringing with the noisy chatter and clank of dishes, she appreciated the quiet. Within an hour after they left Ann's, Mark drove back into her driveway. He stopped the car and went around to open the passenger door for her. Another of his quaint mannerisms few practiced anymore.

Ann hesitated after he closed the car door. "Thank you. I . . . I can't recall the last time . . . well, anyway, I apologize for tonight. You must let me make amends."

Mark accompanied her across the driveway to the dark front door. "Yes, I'd like that. Soon." They arrived on her front step. "But I think I'll choose the place."

"Would you like to come in?"

What made her ask that? She stopped mid-reach with her key. "I'm sorry, never mind me. You're tying to make connections with people you knew before. Not that I remember everyone, but maybe I can help if you're trying to track down someone in particular." She felt his long stare. Maybe he was just as embarrassed as she was, caught at trying to flirt. Flirt? Oh, goodness. A little old married lady chatting up a nice married young man. If there couldn't be a flood to swallow her, how about an earthquake? Could things get any worse?

"Thank you, that's kind of you," Mark said. "I'm slowly finding my way again. But I'd like to have some coffee, if the invitation's still open. We didn't get much of a chance to talk back there."

Ann clutched the key so hard she knew she'd bear the impression of it for hours. It squealed, metal on metal, as she tried to insert it into the lock with nervous fingers. She opened the front door and turned on a light with a shaky, yet defiant, flip. She could have a harmless little talk with her former neighbor's son. Do something more exciting than her usual trip to the Y, the monthly guild meetings, and working at Ballard, Gorman and Wicht, reminding Gene's partners, Howie and Tim, that Gene could walk in the door any day now. As if he could. "Coffee?"

"Yes. Can I help?"

She led the way to the kitchen, and let him fill the carafe at the tap while she ground beans. Mark flashed a smirk. "You like fresh ground, too?"

"Ah, don't tell me you're one of those coffee snobs," Ann teased back as she started to measure the grounds and promptly lost count. How many scoops was that?

"I have been contemplating how an espresso machine would fit in my apartment. That was four, by the way."

The heat of embarrassment crawled up the back of her neck. How had he known? She looked at him out of the corner of her eye.

He leaned against the countertop, arms folded the same as he had earlier. "Ann."

Other than when she'd answered her door to him earlier, she'd never heard him call her anything but "Mrs. Ballard." Did that make him a contemporary? Or her less formal? She looked up at him after ensuring a steady trickle of dark liquid entered the glass pot. "Yes?"

"There's never been any word, no new reports or information about him? About your . . . about Mr. Ballard?"

Ann blinked heavily and shook her head. "No. There's never been any more than false leads. Nothing at all now, for —"

Seven years. Sunday would mark the seventh anniversary of the disappearance of her husband.

CHAPTER TWO

Thoughts of the days when the Roths lived next door bubbled up in the following days. Ann sifted through old memories. Mark had been a senior in high school the year they moved in. He'd acted like the perfect model for his half-brother, taking Trey and Ritchie to their various sports practices and church events and especially fishing.

Why did Mark say she'd always been there for him? He'd done much more for Ritchie by taking him to do the fun things Gene rarely had time for.

One long ago Sunday night when Mark dropped Ritchie off at home after their church youth group meeting, he'd mentioned he had a basketball game the following week and could he take the boys? Ann agreed and asked how Mark's father, Edward, liked to watch him play. Mark had shrugged and mumbled about how his folks had been busy with the new addition to their catalog company and hadn't been able to go.

Ann had closed her mouth over the nasty thing she thought about Edward. Still thought. Maybe if they'd paid more attention to Trey, he'd be alive.

Gene . . . Gene hadn't been that much better. How often had he cut out on Ritchie's activities?

After Gene disappeared, Ann did nothing right in her son's eyes. Gene instantly became the hero he could never have been in real life. Only after Ritchie's marriage did he look back with a more rational perspective. Yes, Colleen helped.

Ann picked up the phone Saturday evening to hear Mark's morose-sounding voice. "This might sound strange, but I'm at loose ends. When I was busy in school and out east, having time on my hands wasn't an issue. I wondered if there was anything I could do for you tomorrow."

"What's the matter? I thought lawyers worked at least a hundred hours a week." Ann shouldered the phone to her ear while she inspected her kitchen table bouquet of brown-eyed susans and purple asters. She suppressed a heated, tingly shiver at the thought of feeling his warm breath in person against her face. She could think of a lot of

29

things he could do. For shame!

"Even working a hundred hours gives a guy Sunday afternoons. Can I mow your lawn, or something? I haven't had time to join a fitness club yet."

Ann laughed, glad to be back to mundane topics like fitness. "If only I could have heard that ten years ago. Thank you, but the young entrepreneur who takes care of yards in this neighborhood wouldn't be pleased." She looked out of the window to the swaths of grass along the sweeping brick drive. She paid the boy out of her meager wages to keep the acre of lawn in good shape.

"How about leaves? I recall a lot of trees. Don't tell me you hire someone to rake, too."

"Blow leaves. Nobody rakes. I think there's some ordinance. Actually, I do that myself, and yes, I really do like to do it. It's good exercise."

Ann smiled to herself while she wandered the kitchen, wiping the already shining countertops. "But I wouldn't mind some company. Maybe you could come over and help me."

"I could use some exercise, too. How about I come by after church?"

"Sure. We can order pizza or something later."

Mark's voice sounded soft in her ear. "That sounds good to me."

After they arranged the time and hung up, Ann tapped her finger against her lips. With her stomach churning in nervous anticipation, the idea of pizza made her nauseous. When she felt the frown, she sighed. She hadn't exactly lied to Mark, for she did enjoy taking care of the lawn and reduced gardens. Her precarious and humbling financial state was her own fault. All she did was growl over her monthly expense report to Donna. The woman already blamed her for Gene's absence. Arguing over every cent that went into keeping up appearances was a forever struggle.

Ann had married into the Ballard family, only guessing at the source of Gene's wealth. That battleaxe controlled everything. But soon Ann would make another attempt to break free. Surely by now a judge would agree with her that Gene must be dead. Mark's question the other night reminded her just how long it had been. Time she settled up his part of the estate and at least collected his life insurance. That money wouldn't come out of the precious Ballard Trust, so Donna shouldn't have a reason to object to letting Ann have what was right-fully hers. And the old bat never thought Ritchie good enough to ascend the Ballard throne anyway, so they were clear on that subject.

Ann decided to skip the service at Clayton Presbyterian on Sunday morning. She hardly went anymore, anyway. The guild meeting was enough to cover the bases, in her mind. Today, making sure the leaf blower was ready to go and picking up around the place was more important. Mark drove in while she was unwinding the cord. A bounty of mature red maples and oaks and an island of birches rained down a colorful quilt on the lawn.

She returned his wave and watched him approach, chiding herself at the quick skip-beat of her heart. Her directions for running the leaf blower came out in a rush, as if she were a nervous teenager reading a "how to" report in English class. He was smart. He could probably have figured out how to run the thing himself, but he graciously never said a word.

Mark, dressed in faded jeans and a comfortable plaid shirt rolled up to the elbows, seemed to enjoy the power, swinging it with ease after a few practice runs. She watched him covertly while she filled trash bags with the leaves he sent in her direction. The movement of tendons and muscles in his forearms and his fingers created an instant comparison to her memory of her husband. Gene had preferred to spend his time doing other things, usually related to business. She couldn't remember the last time he'd rolled up his sleeves.

As the sun began to fall below the line of trees at the edge of her yard, Mark shifted his cap backward, pressing curls around his ears. He rewound the cord and stowed the machine, and after a look in Ann's direction, pulled off the billed hat and brushed his head. "Do I have leaves in my hair?"

Thank heavens for the brisk air and exercise to justify rosy-feeling cheeks. She cleared her throat. "I just noticed your hair. It's longer than the last time I saw you."

Mark approached within an arm's length. Ann willed herself not to back up.

"I could use a cut, I guess," he said. "I haven't taken the time yet. But, in my advanced age, I don't need to worry about it slowing me down. You know, let your hair down? Let it all hang out?" He flashed a dimple that probably turned his secretary's knees into pudding every morning, and kept up the terrible puns all the way into the house. "How about we order that pizza?"

Ann reached for the phone. "Sounds good to me. What do you like?" Mark had propped himself against the counter again. Gene had never looked that comfortable in the kitchen. In fact, he'd rarely gone into the room, except for coffee. The breakfast table hadn't been used much back then. Gene breakfasted in the dining room with several newspapers. "On your pizza, I mean?"

"Mushrooms." Mark turned abruptly and filled a glass with water.

Ann excused herself to wash her hands and examine the quivery feeling in her shoulders. She let the water run while she directed orders at her reflection in the mirror. "Are you nuts?" she asked the pale oval-faced woman who stared back with green-flecked eyes. She ran her fingers through her chin-length mostly dark hair. Ann plucked a couple of grays at her temple, narrowing her eyes at the sharp prick of pain when she yanked. "Mark's married. You shouldn't be attracted to his manners. You can't think of him making himself at home in your house. You may not make up reasons about why he wants to spend time with you. You shouldn't wonder if he thinks of you only as a mother figure. Grow up."

She splashed water on her face and patted

it dry. She returned to the kitchen and made small talk, which included her Thursdays and Fridays job at BGW, the high-end financial investment and counseling firm her husband had founded with his friends, until the pizza came. Mark took the warm box from her hands and placed it on the table. He waited until she grabbed napkins and sat. Ritchie would have had it half gone.

After they had eaten a first piece, Mark surprised her. "You've been patient." He leaned his elbow on the table and rested his jaw in his palm. "I should tell you about Allison."

Oh, boy. Ann maneuvered her lips into what she hoped was a polite smile. "Only if you want to."

"I just want to clear the air. We broke up."

Ann's heart made a double beat. He must want some advice, then, on how to deal with being alone again. "I'm so sorry to hear that. Getting divorced must have been a horrible experience."

Mark's eyebrows rose, then furrowed. "We weren't married, but we'd been engaged for three years. She was a lawyer, too, at the same firm."

How could anyone stand being engaged that long? Of course, "dating" and "engaged" were often euphemisms for "living together." But Mark didn't strike her as being that kind of man. He was churchy, or something. Of course, she didn't know him at all. Still, poor guy. Who dumped whom?

Mark stared at the pizza. He reached for another piece but made no effort to eat it. "We weren't right for each other, really. She didn't want to move to Wisconsin, hated fish, and told me she'd rather live in a condo than have a house of our own. We didn't even see each other enough to talk about whether we wanted a family, or travel, or maybe even open up our own firm together. That probably would have been a big mistake, too. In the end, I think we were both relieved to call it off."

Did he think she and Gene had been all wrong, too? That she was relieved Gene was gone? Maybe he wanted to hear everything was okay, that there would be someone else eventually who would love him again. Not something she could promise. "Still, you must have both felt bad."

She reached for the glass of water with her left hand. Gene's heavy platinum bonds of matrimony clinked, audibly reminding her that their circumstances of being separated were nothing alike. He probably just wanted to reconnect with anybody from his former life, see if she knew anybody he could go out with.

"I'm not looking for another girlfriend, if that's what you're thinking."

Ann crossed her fingers under the table. "The thought never occurred to me."

"I just didn't want you to think I might want you to introduce me to anyone else."

"Of course not. You want time to get over . . . her. And I'm sure you'll make your own friends soon enough."

Mark's smile lifted just the corner of his mouth. Ann felt melty, watching.

"Thanks." He straightened and turned on the chair to look around the kitchen with its restaurant quality appliances and wide countertops. "Ann, don't you find this place too much to keep up? I mean, since you're alone?"

She appreciated his change of subject, if not the inference she was getting decrepit. "It's our home, Ritchie's home." Her reply was automatic, but she felt the hesitation in the pit of her stomach. She no longer believed Gene would come back, and Ritchie had his own home now, so why did she stay here? "And my niece, my sister's girl, Maeve, is living with me during the week while she has classes at the university." Ann cocked her head at him, squinting in speculation. Maybe she could introduce them. "She's the ultimate new-age co-ed, coloring and piercing anything visible. I blame Sesame Street."

Mark laughed. "What's she studying?"

"Marketing." Ann smiled at the memory of their e-mail exchange that morning. Maeve went home to Sauk City on the weekends to work as a waitress at the Blue Spoon, but Ann knew her niece spent every other moment in cyberspace.

"No, thanks," Mark said, as if he read her mind again.

Ann pretended to look startled. Then she raised her brows at him, testing the waters. "She's a little young for you."

Mark pursed his lips and nodded. He looked off toward the patio doors. "Age isn't necessarily that important in a relationship, you know." He brushed his hair from his temples. "Stage of life means more. So, you like to keep your hand in, working at the business?"

Ah, another deft change of subject. He must get a lot of practice with clients, steering them expertly in the direction he wanted to take them. How much should she reveal about the true situation with the Trust? "I like to eat."

Mark leaned back in his chair, frowning. "What do you mean? Gene's estate must

38

keep you — never mind, that's none of my business."

Ann rose to throw away the pizza box and make a plate of leftovers to send home with Mark. Smart young business lawyer would know all about the Ballard Trust. What did he really want? He mentioned setting up his own firm. Maybe he wanted a stakeholder. It wouldn't take long to burst that bubble. "I've never settled Gene's estate."

Mark slid his chair back as well. "It's been years. You don't think he's still alive, do you?"

"I'm not the only person involved in this, Mark." Ann stood still in the middle of her kitchen. The blackness of the night seemed to seep through the windows into the room. Mark touched her shoulder from behind, making her shiver. Why? She wrapped her hands around her elbows in defense against her sudden vulnerability.

"Look, there's no statute of limitation regarding a finding of death in missing persons cases in Wisconsin. Let me help you."

Ann closed her eyes, feeling thankful for an instant to think someone else cared about her horrible limbo. Until reality stuck out its tongue with his next question.

"Didn't you sign any kind of agreement

with Gene? A marital property agreement, or anything? You could at least claim —"

"My lawyer understands all that." She had to put a stop to that kind of interrogation. She couldn't let him think she needed anything from him. He couldn't, should not, get involved with her personal problems. And she had nothing to offer in return. "I can't help you. There's nothing I have to give you — no money, no promise of clients sent your way, no Ballard secrets, or even an introduction at BWG."

"Ann!"

She jumped at the anger in his voice, but wouldn't turn around. His hand tightened on her shoulder. He took a step closer so she could feel his warmth all along her body. "Ann, come on. Is that what you think?"

Pressure, gentle yet determined, didn't let up until she shifted to stare at his throat. He let go. "May I remind you that Roth Enterprises was quite successful? And I invested the money my father gave me for my education when I won that scholarship to Georgetown. I don't even have to work if I don't want to. Jung and Royce already does business with BWG. Ann, why are you acting like this? I just thought you could use some help."

Ann blinked, embarrassed at the remorseful tears. But did she understand him? "So, that's why you're here? To help me?" She steeled herself to look at his face, hoping she hadn't driven him away completely. Having him on her side to fight Donna might come in handy.

"We've both had bad things happen to us in the past, like Gene's disappearance and Trey's death," he said. He dropped his arms from his defensive pose and tilted his head. "I think maybe we can help each other."

Was it compassion or sympathy she read in his expression? Both emotions used for someone needy and pitiful. A sharp pain began to pulse behind her left eye. Great. Headache coming on. "I'm sorry," she said. "I can't even tell you I've been the target of scam artists or men wanting to date me thinking I was a wealthy widow. I don't know what I can do to help you, except offer encouragement and a shoulder. I do know what it's like to be alone, especially when you think it'll never happen to you. You'll see. You won't stay single forever." She took a deep breath and let it out. "And I am determined to settle Gene's estate. I could use some professional advice."

Mark nodded and flashed a smile. "Fair enough. How about we start over?"

Ann crinkled her nose, then bit her lip

when her vision blurred. He needed to go. Quickly. She had to take her meds and curl up in a dark, quiet place. It wasn't what she wanted, but maybe she could get him to come back another time. "All right."

"Hi, Ann. Remember me? I'm Mark Roth. I used to live next door."

She played along. "Of course I do. How are you? Are you visiting your old neighborhood?"

"I've moved back home. I missed . . . Wisconsin."

"Well, maybe there's something I can do to help you reconnect. Ritchie and Colleen are coming for dinner next Saturday. Why don't you come, too?"

CHAPTER THREE

Ann scrambled to the bathroom medicine cabinet after Mark left. Annoyed at the headache, she wandered along the hall, straightened a picture that always tilted on its hanger, checked the locks and closed the drapes on the way to the couch. As she closed her eyes and relaxed, she allowed herself to think of next week, when he would return. She had to make sure Ritchie and Colleen knew he was back. Routine. Keep this visit in its proper perspective. It had nothing to do with her personally and there was no reason to attach any kind of shivery romantic nonsense. Maybe now the boys were older, they could put the past behind them and be friends again. And maybe, just maybe, once she was really a widow with some stability, she could start going out again.

Ew. Not with anyone from the office, though. Stop getting ahead of yourself, girl. Sleep.

Ann woke with a clear head at four-thirty in the morning. An energizing litany of how she could reinvent herself drove her to shower and change as the sky lightened. Maybe she could get herself a condo. She walked up and down the hall again with a feather duster, brushing at the picture frames. The only thing of value she owned was this house. It drained her emotionally and financially, for her mother-in-law's purse covered only physical wear and tear. Why did she cling to it? Taxes, updating the furnishings, lawn care, most of the utilities, all came out of Ann's small salary — the only money of her own. For years, Donna had thwarted her. A divorce would leave her nothing and sale of the house would probably not even cover the legal expenses.

Going into substantial debt to battle the Ballard Trust wouldn't give her a good foundation, and probably would wreck her credit. Crawling from under that rock would take years, but it could be done. Maybe Tim or Howie would give her full-time work. With Mark to help her get a settlement, she had a better chance of working things out. Maybe he could set up a case that wouldn't make Donna feel threatened. Maybe if Donna saw just giving her the value of the life insurance would free them both from having to deal with each other. Donna could keep her dream and Ann could — do what? She would still be tied to Gene's name. So? She had nothing else brewing in her life. She'd been married and had no need to do it again. But she wanted to be careful not to let Mark think marriage was bad. With all he had going for him in caring manner and wealth, he'd make good husband material. And his good looks should definitely be passed on to the next generation. But what did she know of marriage? She thought back to her own. Gene took care of many of BWG's national accounts. Ann had never minded his absences and even went along on business trips occasionally when her mother could keep Ritchie during his summer vacations. She didn't mind until the September day she'd driven to Madison's airport to pick Gene up after a trip out east and heard the news about the attack on the twin towers. She had to pull over. Ritchie, with a brand new driver's license, went instead to collect his father.

A year later, just when things were starting to settle in the world, Gene never returned from a routine trip to New York City to check on a client.

The first six months of not knowing what happened to him had been like trying to use a faulty GPS tracker. Had he been kidnapped or hurt or worse? Did he have a midlife crisis and run away? No note, no ransom demand, no news. She had to keep outwardly confident for Ritchie's sake, but waffled daily between panic and anger in private. Just when a tip came in that someone had seen Gene, that an unidentified person had been brought in to a hospital, or a body had been dredged up, it would seem the clues all matched up. Ann flew to New York City three times to attempt to identify Gene's body. The second victim had been found with Gene's driver's license and wallet nearby, but the body hadn't resembled Gene. The third one had been a younger man, thin and, after a month in the Hudson, not close to the description of her fifty-year-old husband. She told the nice detectives she'd need a lot more evidence before coming to do that again. Gene's aristocratic mother said she'd hired private detectives, but Ann heard no reports.

That fall Ritchie started his senior year of high school inside that same cloud of unknowing, but with all the energy and anger of youth. He took it out on her, relentlessly begging to go to New York to look for his father, picking up speeding tickets and even smoking pot with Trey in his backyard. Tiffany had sent Ritchie home, reeking, with a warning she'd turn him in if she caught him again. Ann thought Tiffany was more likely to join them, but thanked Trey's mother all the same.

At Christmas time Ritchie and Trey flew to New York City. When Ritchie came back, he brought a new sense of recklessness resulting in the loss of his driver's license, and came close to not being able to graduate. Donna soothed things over with his college application. That spring, Trey died and the Roths left Clayton.

Even before high school was over, Ann let Ritchie go to weekend training sessions for a summer sports camp job at the University of Wisconsin in Green Bay. The day after graduation, he moved away.

Ann turned forty years old in the spring, all alone.

Had she loved her former life? Or merely lived as an extension of Gene and the influential circle he drew around her? Since he'd been gone, she was nobody, nothing, just a placeholder who waited for Gene to come back. Definitely time to crawl from under her load of self-pity. After the get-together with Ritchie and Colleen, she'd schedule a time to meet with Mark and discuss strategy for another court date.

Maybe for lunch. Then, maybe he could help her find a good roofer. And a new car. While she considered possible dates for him.

She shook her head and went to turn her computer on. Maeve had left a message for her.

"Anything happen while I've been gone? What's nu with u?"

What's new with me? Ann felt as if she rode an out of control Tilt-a-Whirl. What could she tell her impressionable twenty-year-old niece, just starting her junior year at the university? Maeve had been the little girl she could borrow from her sister whenever she needed a daughter fix. She let Maeve shamelessly manipulate her into buying barrettes and makeup and pretty undies her mother refused to purchase. Ann could safely say "nothing much" to the "what's new" and not expect a third degree like her sister Rachel would give her for being a boring old recluse. But this time . . . dare she?

"You know nothing new ever happens to me. Except for Mark Roth coming back to Mad Town. He's a lawyer."

Maeve had replied. "A lawyer? Who is that again? Is he hot?"

Ann typed back. "No flames I could see."

"Don't play coy. Is he cute, or what? I don't remember him. Is he related to Trey

Roth? Did I meet him?"

"Edward Roth's son with his first wife. Trey's half-brother."

"So, how did you hook up?"

"We did not hook up." Ann decided to change the subject. "What color is your hair this weekend?"

"Silver spikes."

And so on for another few minutes until Maeve signed off to go to bed.

Still not sleepy, Ann clicked open her computer diary and typed more of a poem she'd started a week ago. *Fall people realign the year. In spring, the riot of life goes so out of control. In fall, the achievements and mistakes of spring and summer burn in a blaze of glory like changing maple leaves. In winter, they curl and die before the tranquil dormancy of winter. Fall people can start new.*

She added an entry to her diary: *Mark Roth is back. He makes me remember what it's like to be alive.*

Gene's mother and son were the only ones who still believed Gene would turn up someday. She didn't have to live according to their dreams any more. Mark helped her see she still had plenty of life left. But first she had to step off the curb, where she'd been orbiting the "Do Not Walk" sign long enough.

Ann's week flashed past, faster than she could remember time passing during the blur of the last several years. She looked forward to her morning laps at the YMCA for more than a routine regimen as she acknowledged a fresh dedication to fitness. Because you hope Mark thinks of you as something besides a nice former neighbor who needs his help? No, because if Mark could make her feel like more than the other half of Gene, maybe the opportunity for a more suitable relationship would come up in the future. Uh-huh.

She and Maeve passed each other in the hall or the garage at home, but with the admittance of a new acquaintance and her ferocious tiger-striped hair-do, Ann had backed away from prying any deeper into her niece's life. Maeve hadn't slept in her room for three of the four nights the previous week, but had left a note that morning on the kitchen table, telling her goodbye.

Ann turned her attention to Ritchie and Colleen's upcoming visit. This meal would be special. Mark deserved nice home cooked food, especially now that she knew he was a bachelor and probably ate out a lot. He'd been generous to offer to help her settle Gene's estate. But how would she explain his presence today? Ritchie wouldn't be happy to know that she planned to go to court again over his father's case. But Ritchie was an adult now. He might see things in a different light. Even so, she wouldn't discuss the subject.

The farmer's market had squash and late tomatoes and herbs. Back at home, she consulted the shadowy shelf above the built-in desk and grabbed a copy of "Entertaining Made Easy." She blew dust from the top before opening it.

Mark arrived early on the appointed Saturday, as she secretly hoped he would.

"Mmm, smells good. Just like I remember." He handed over a gallon of fresh cherry cider.

Ann placed the cider in the refrigerator. "You don't even know what I'm making."

"Doesn't matter. I never had a meal here I didn't like. How about we wait for Ritchie and Colleen outside? It's nice for October."

Ann adored the way balmy late afternoon sun washed the lawn and trees outside her front door in clear white gold. Most of the late maple leaves had fallen, while the oaks curled brown and hung on. Mark sat on the top step of the wide veranda and leaned against a painted pillar. Ann parked herself on the second step and basked, leaning against the rail. "I love fall."

She closed her eyes and inhaled, his spiky scent overriding the musk of the season. She opened them to find Mark watching her.

"You remember that story you used to tell the kids? About why the oak leaves fall last?"

Ann shook her head. "I don't even remember you were here when I told stories."

"Just once. Trey liked it. Anyway, this was about the daughter of a chief who fell in love with an enemy brave, just like Romeo and Juliet. Seems like every culture has its ill-fated love story."

He recited the tale while Ann let her mind wander. Mark had dressed for the occasion in crisp jeans, a tan turtleneck and leather jacket with a new-leather scent. He had his hair trimmed, though it still curled along his temple. She would have liked to brush it back from his forehead.

"And so the brave asked the chief to wait to give his daughter in marriage to another until all the leaves had fallen from the trees."

Ann relaxed, lulled by the cadence of his voice. Out of the corner of her eye she saw Ritchie and Colleen pull up the drive. Ann blinked with the realization she and Mark had been staring at each other. She hadn't noticed when his words stopped flowing. She wished, much too late, she hadn't invited the kids.

Ann felt the heat on her face and, unfortunately, her son leaped to the top step in time to catch it. Narrow-eyed, he helped her up and hugged her. Ritchie turned to Mark next. "Well, if this isn't a blast from the past! Mark, it's good to see you, man. What's been going on?"

Ash blond Colleen, about five months along, had let her coat part around a slightly protruding belly. Ann took her hand and kissed her cheek. "I hope you weren't too uncomfortable on the ride."

"No, of course not. Thank you for having us."

Always polite with round-eyed sincerity, Colleen managed to simultaneously let Ann feel necessary and tolerated, like the worn teddy bear missing an eye and trailing its stuffing. Despite their arm's length relationship, Colleen was sweet and even-tempered, and Ann was delighted that Ritchie found her. Especially since she convinced Ritchie his mother was not the wicked witch of any particular direction.

Ann pulled the door open. "Come in, everyone. Sit for a minute and have something to drink. Dinner's almost ready."

Mark hung coats in the front closet and then offered to help set out food. Colleen echoed, and Ritchie followed. Conversation began with the biggest news.

"Congratulations on the baby," Mark told Ritchie and Colleen as he carved the tenderloin. Colleen flushed a pretty pink and Ritchie became animated with talk of fixing the baby's room.

"And of course, Grandma, here —" Ritchie flashed a sly grin at Ann, "— has already offered to babysit."

"When the baby's older," Colleen put in firmly.

Ann passed the plate of buttery squash. "Of course." She smiled at her daughter-in-law, then caught her breath at the gleam in Mark's eyes.

Once Mark finished carving, he sat. "Mind if I say grace?"

Ritchie set his fork back on his plate. Ann caught the look of pleasure on her daughter-in-law's face and knew she'd missed the custom in their home. Church should be important when they had kids. Hadn't she always taken Ritchie when he was little? Maybe Mark's actions could still influence her son, despite the loss of Trey and the time lapse since they'd been friendly. She closed her eyes and listened to Mark's voice asking a blessing on this family and food.

Ritchie took squash and passed the dish to Mark. "So, are you back for good, now, or what?"

"Yes. I'm renting until I decide on a house."

"Still a lawyer?"

"That's right." Mark passed the squash to Colleen.

Colleen helped herself, then filled in the lull. "This is so good, Ann. Thank you. What kind of lawyer are you, Mark?"

"Mostly business succession, some estate planning right now," Mark said. "Not all that exciting. Todd Royce, one of the senior partners, is setting up a legal aid clinic where we'll do some work pro bono — that means for the public good, like for people who can't afford to pay — once in a while. How about you? What do you do?"

Ritchie answered. "She's going to stay home, take care of us after the baby's born."

Ann hid a grin at Colleen's acid look in her husband's direction, accompanying the bread basket. "I work in the fourth grade room with learning disabled students. I feel really good being able to help them. Some of the students come from broken homes and many of them have multiple medical issues to deal with."

Ritchie passed the basket to Mark. "So, run into anyone from the old crowd yet? Have to bail anyone out of the clink?"

Mark chewed and wiped his mouth with one of Ann's linen napkins before answering. "I'm not a criminal defense attorney."

Ritchie tossed his napkin on the table, sat back and launched into a series of memories from the years he and Mark's brother were close friends, until that last year of high school, after Mark's time and before Colleen entered the picture. Neither Mark nor Colleen appeared to pay rapt attention, Ann thought. Colleen had cleared the plates during what must have been the fifteenth time Ritchie said, "Hey, remember when . . ." to no one in particular.

Colleen went to stand behind his chair, rubbing her tiny belly bulge. "Ritchie, I'm tired. Remember, Mother's coming tomorrow."

Ann got to her feet. Mark tossed his napkin beside his plate and pushed back his chair.

"Sure, sweetheart." Ritchie reached back to pat the hand Colleen placed on his shoulder. "We were just having fun reminiscing, that's all. I didn't realize how long we've been sitting here."

Ritchie hesitated at the door after Mark handed him and Colleen their coats. "Mom, thanks for supper." He offered a hearty handshake to Mark who hung back, out of the family circle. Ritchie lingered. Finally he asked Mark, "Coming, man?"

Ann looked quickly from one to the other, not able to read Mark's expression. Why was he hanging around, anyway?

"In a couple of minutes." Mark did not explain and Colleen eventually got her husband out the door and into their car. When Ann closed the door, Mark offered to help her clean up.

So, Mark must not have wanted to embarrass Ritchie or Colleen by making them feel guilty about not sticking around to wash dishes. "Thank you, but you don't have to stay. I'm sure there are more fun places you could go. It's not that late."

Mark followed her back to the kitchen without comment. Ann didn't want to push him out the door yet, anyway, so did not renew her protest. If he was lonely and wanted to talk, she'd listen.

They worked together in silence, Ann putting leftovers away while Mark loaded her dishwasher. He started the machine whooshing before speaking up. "That's nice that you have family close by. I suppose you visit them, too."

Ann dried a pot that wouldn't fit in the full dishwasher. "Once in a while. Ritchie likes coming back to his old house, I think, even though they're not that far away."

"Portage, you said?"

"Right." He started to dry the crystal water glasses she handed him. When he said nothing else, Ann said. "So, how's work going?"

If she thought he'd open up and chat freely about everything and anything, she was mistaken. He didn't answer in monosyllables, but neither did he bend her ear.

"I'm settling in. They've given me a good case load. I'm nearly up to speed on procedure. Going well."

"Are you glad you made the change?"

Mark hung his towel and rolled down his sleeves. "I had peace about it before I even got here."

Ann wondered why he used the word "peace," but couldn't come up with a reasonable question to ask what he meant. When the kitchen sparkled and there was no more reason for Mark to stay, Ann accompanied him to the door.

"Thank you for inviting me." Mark stood on the veranda with her. Moonlight illuminated the pillars where they'd sat companionably while waiting for Ann's son.

"I'm glad you could come. You were always good to the boys when they were growing up."

Mark touched a chipped spot on the pillar. "Not good enough to Trey, apparently."

"Trey was old enough to know better."

"Maybe. I still wish I'd been there for him. I'd better go."

"Mark? Could we make an appointment to talk about Gene? I'll treat you to lunch."

He smiled. "I have to look at my calendar. I'll call you, okay?"

"Sure. And thank you." Ann locked the door behind him, but stood by the side window long after his taillights faded.

Mark studied the tickets in his hand while he punched numbers on the phone. When she answered her extension, he willed his voice not to crack.

"Yes?"

"Hi, it's me, Mark." His throat went dry.

"I thought I told you never to call me here."

The sound of his own heartbeat in his ears drowned out the rest of the office noise. How should he respond?

"Mark?" Her voice broke the rhythm of the pulse. "Mark, I was just kidding . . . you know, um, like in the movies or something. Mark, I'm sorry, I didn't mean it. Did you check your calendar?"

"Ann . . ." Mark took a deep breath. "Ann, I should have thought about this. I didn't mean to embarrass you. I'd better let you go."

"No, wait! I was — it was just silly. I don't know what came over me. Really, are you ready to discuss my case?"

"I can talk to you later. At home."

"Really, it's all right. What do you want?"

Everything — but mostly for you to see me for who I am. When I became a man, I put childishness behind me. "I just have these tickets for tonight. The symphony. Nice seats. It's so last minute I know, that's why I wanted to call you right away."

"Wow. Is that the performance with Stella Lombard? The one where they accompany her to the show tunes? That's been sold out for a while. How did you . . . never mind. You want to take me? Mark, really, there must be —"

"I'm sorry, I'm late for a meeting. I'll pick you up at seven, all right? We can talk then. 'Bye." He hung up before Ann could find another excuse. She must be starting to guess by now . . . about how he felt about her. Sometimes when she looked back at him, he could see her confusion, her curiosity and maybe a hint of her willingness to believe that she could be loved again.

"Mark, old man! I knew you wouldn't waste time finding a date. Who'd you call?"

Mark whirled in his chair at the voice of Jim Parsons. Jim specialized in estate planning, Jung and Royce's bread and butter, and had worked at the firm for the past eight years. He was happy with the tasks he accomplished and had no desire to ride the career rocket to partnership.

Jim's grin was comical. "I couldn't help notice how Janice in reception has her eye on you. Was it her? Or how about Sharon, the new clerk? I'm married, so of course I don't look, but —"

"Yeah, I know. Thanks again, though, for the tickets. You're sure I can't reimburse you?"

Jim shook his head, but paused in the door of Mark's office, arms folded and an expectant look on his face. Jung and Royce had set up their floors like a castle, with offices in a ring around the outside walls, the assistants all guarding their bosses' doors. Smaller conference rooms anchored either end, and equipment was in the middle with notes about who could and who couldn't use what machines, apparently according to past sins. Two huge formal conference rooms and the partners' offices were on the floor above. Mark ranked a corner office as a rising associate.

Mark got up and came around his desk. "I'm sorry about Katie. I hope she feels better soon."

"The wife's more upset about missing the symphony than Katie's fever. Frankly, I'm not all that heartbroken. So?"

Mark glanced beyond Jim to where his legal assistant, Jennifer, waved at him from her desk. "Just hang on a sec, will you? I have to talk to Jennifer." Mark brushed past the stubborn Jim and signed some faxes. He faced Jim from Jennifer's desk while she went to send the pages. "Well, thanks again." He tried the handshake routine, which Jim didn't fall for. The man did not move from his lounging position in Mark's doorway.

Mark heaved a sigh and put his hands on his hips. Looking Jim in the eye, he said, "I'm taking a friend, someone I've known for a long time. Okay?"

Jim straightened. "So you do have a girlfriend? Is that why you came back to Madison?"

Two loud phone hang-ups and the sound of one dropped stapler from the assistant array made Mark cringe. He hustled Jim inside the office and closed the door. "It's not like that. Will you keep your voice down?"

"I get it. Keeping all the options open." Jim made the universal eyebrow wag.

"I came back here because of someone special, that's true. It's just complicated. Can we leave it for now?" Mark wasn't sure how a romance with Ann would appear to his new co-workers, even if he could get her cooperation. Their responses would be a quick and deadly way of finding out who'd support him and who wouldn't.

Jim winked and punched his shoulder. "My lips are sealed. Say, by the way, a bunch of us go out after work once a month. Unwind, you know? Next time's on Friday. Think about it. Later." He opened Mark's office door and left.

Mark swallowed and took a breath. He walked out to where Jennifer sat at her desk. Her kindly little smirk made him understand that Jim's outburst had already been heard and discussed, but not enough. Mark cleared his throat and straightened his tie. "Jennifer, could you pull up any records we have about the Ballard Trust, please? Let me know when you get them. Thanks." With a cautious glance around the room, he went back to hide in his office.

He did not have to wait long to get the information he wanted. He whistled at the cart Jennifer wheeled in two hours later. He looked at his watch and decided to give his lunch hour over to sorting through a few files. By one-thirty, he thought he had a fair insight of the web that entangled Ann.

On paper, the Ballard Trust looked solid, profitable and a perfect shelter for the millions Ballard, Gorman and Wicht generated. Donna Ballard had things shrink-wrapped. He didn't recognize LMS Enterprises, which appeared to be some kind of hedge fund. Regular deposits and payouts were made, but at this brief glance, he couldn't tell where the profits landed. At least Gorman and Wicht hadn't been suckered into letting the Trust handle their own shares of the business revenues. Gene's father, James Fitzgerald Ballard, set it up when he decided to make a run for the United States Senate. The original assets included extensive holdings in oil, fledgling airline industrial stocks, real estate, and corporate bonds. Upon her husband's death, Donna became the trustee.

Mark wondered how much Ann understood of the control the elder Ballard woman had over Gene's finances. Given

Ann's background as an accountant, probably quite a lot. What could he do to help her? Donna Ballard fought the two times Ann petitioned for a finding of death in her husband's disappearance. Why? Gene's life insurance settlement wouldn't mean a thing to the Ballard Trust and could only help Ann. Ann had hinted about cash-flow problems. Who owned the house she lived in? Taxes and insurance and upkeep had to be a drain.

Mark tossed the last folder on his desk and turned in the swivel chair to look out the window. He threaded his hands behind his head and leaned back. Family. They either nurtured or ate you alive. Although he was thankful for the comfort his father's business acumen brought first his mother, then the rest of them, he knew the toll it took. Absent for most of the important events in a kid's life, never taking a vacation, hardly aware that life was passing him by. Mark shook his head. Seemed like Donna wasn't much different from his father. Mark knew Gene Ballard hadn't been around home much, either. How had Ann dealt with raising Ritchie almost single-handedly? Having wild Trey around probably hadn't helped much. Mark tried to spend time with his brother, but he had to get out when it came time for college.

Mark sat up and packed the folders back in their boxes. If he were ever blessed with a family of his own, he'd do what he could to make time for her. Them.

A rain-slush mix made Mark's drive home a glaring hazard. He usually left the office much later, too, and had forgotten about rush-hour on the beltline. Mark buzzed around his condo, ignoring the message light blinking on the answering machine, grabbing a quick cup of left-over coffee and changing clothes. He mentally reviewed the parking situation at the theater, considered the huge cement tower and wondered if he should offer to drop Ann at the entrance and meet up with her after he took care of the car. He looked at the ticket stub again. Ah, valet parking was available. Nice.

A couple of deep breaths later, Mark headed for Ann's house. He left the motor running while he knocked on her front door, wondering if she would be ready. Recalling her frantic expression during the thunderstorm when he first went to see her, he hoped she would still want to come out with him.

"Hello, Mark. Are you set? Did you want to — no, I see you left the car running."

Ann pulled the heavy door shut behind her. "I hope you didn't have to rush around too much tonight."

Mark swallowed again before he could make his tongue work. "Ann. No, it was good to get out of there, actually. I have an umbrella, although the weatherman promises this will stop soon." He unfolded the nylon circle and held it over them during their walk to his car.

The speculative look on Ann's face when he sang along with the crowd to a number of the old show tunes set his heart beating out of time. The music, the program, the company — all led to a fantastic evening. One of his favorite parts, besides his first glimpse at beautiful Ann in a stunning teal dress with beaded flowers, was keeping her close to him as they worked their way out of the theater. Symphony people were more polite than concert rabble. They tended to respect personal space, or at least beautiful clothes.

Mark reclaimed Ann's coat from the check-in window and handed his valet ticket to an usher. While they waited, Mark kept his hand at her back. She hadn't seemed to mind, and once, stayed pressed against him several seconds, much to his delight, while they stood aside for the lobby doors to clear.

Ann had agreed to have supper with him after the performance. He took her to a place on the square by the illuminated Capitol building. They had to walk a couple of blocks past the waning riot of gardens on the government grounds. He didn't dare take her hand for fear of rejection, but occasionally clutched her elbow when they passed gaggles of rowdy university students out for a late night stroll. He felt like a tongue-tied teenager and couldn't think of anything to say.

Fortunately, Ann rescued him from making a panicky comment about the weather. "You surprised me tonight."

Mark feigned innocence. "I did?"

"Yes. Did you know I liked musicals?"

He had, in fact, peeked through her music and movie collection, although he'd also remembered Ritchie groaning about the type of music his mother listened to. "Who doesn't like musicals?"

"And what about Stella?"

So, he'd also noticed Ann had a number of recordings by the popular singing star whose solos the symphony accompanied. "What about her?"

"She's my favorite singer."

"Oh, good." The cover of dark hid Mark's unfortunate tendency to blush when nervous. Why did he have more self-confidence in a courtroom with an unhappy judge and belligerent clients fighting over a will than with this woman? "Here we are. I made a reservation." He opened the door of the bistro to the chattering people eating from dishes wafting garlic and lemon or basil and pine nuts.

When they had been seated and faced each other over a flickering candle, Mark studied Ann's expression. Talk to her. "You look happy."

"Is that okay? I'm having a good time. Thank you again for inviting me, but —"

"Wasn't the background they showed for 'America' inspiring?" He continued to comment about the parts of the performance he could recall until their waiter came to take their order.

In the quiet after the waiter left, he couldn't stop watching her — even seeing her take a sip from her water glass made his toes curl. She picked up the napkin with her left hand to dab her mouth. How had he missed that little detail earlier? The toe curl sizzle moved all the way up his trunk. It had to be a sign.

When she caught him staring at her hand, she tucked it back on her lap and looked around the room. "I don't think I've been here at night before. Just for lunch."

"Different crowd." The two of them shared comfortable memories and observations until their meal arrived.

The point at which Mark finally had to call the evening over did not occur until he prepared for bed. Even then, he allowed himself to replay parts of their time together. Her laugh. Yes, she'd laughed tonight. The joy of the sweeping music and even his terrible out-of-tune singing voice made him glad Jim had given him this opportunity, this excuse, to spend more time with her. Ann . . . Annie. He would have to thank Jim again, send something to his wife Glenda, who had to miss the concert to stay home with their sick daughter. Maybe Ann could help him.

The perfume she wore reminded him of . . . what was it? A sweet, light scent. Lily of the valley. It bloomed in the spring in the ditch between her house and his. He turned over and punched the pillow and made a mental note to call a florist in the morning. Annie. Her beautiful dress made her eyes glow like the Austrian crystals his mother used to set out and hum her strange hocus-pocus to. What Ann hadn't worn was just as prominent in his mind. Neither of them mentioned it. But hope for a future ratcheted up a notch. Once Gene Ballard was out of the way. Jim Parsons just happened to be Ann's attorney. How convenient was that?

He felt his lips curve upward at the memory of saying good night to her. He had a hard time turning down her offer of coffee, but knew his self control would be tested. Spend much longer in her company, and he'd be blabbing about how much he wanted. . . . Better to go home. Another dinner invitation, though — that he'd been eager to accept. He decided his favorite part of the evening, after all, had to be the end, where, on her doorstep, he'd almost kissed her mouth. At the last second, sanity surfaced and he simply let his lips rest on her soft cheek.

CHAPTER FOUR

Ann held her hand to her cheek as she watched Mark's taillights disappear. She pinched herself hard, their last words echoing.

"Can I offer you coffee?" she'd asked, reluctant to let him leave after the enjoyment of being with him.

"Thank you, but I should go home."

"You must let me pay you back for this lovely evening. How about you let me cook for you again? On Friday? Come after work." Did she sound too desperate? "If you can, that is."

"Thank you." Mark bent his head. "I hate to turn you down for such an irrelevant thing, but I already agreed to meet some guys after work on Friday."

"That's important, too." Was their time together over? She would be gracious. "You need to —" do things with other people sounded proprietary. Do things with people your own age sounded defensive — "make connections, meet people." One last plea for his company. "Maybe another time?"

"The week after?"

Ann's heart thudded with pleasure and relief. "The next Friday would be perfect. See you then."

Her breath caught when he'd leaned toward her. A kiss? What should she do? Turn her head? Slap him? Kiss him back? She was not disappointed to feel his lips brush her cheek. Was she?

Ann laughed at herself, her absurd notion that maybe she wouldn't wash her face tonight. Even more absurd was this developing habit of standing in the front hallway and watching out of the window, either waiting for him to arrive, or waiting until she could no longer sense his presence.

Mark Roth.

Ann touched the corner of her mouth, where the smile started. A week from Friday she would see him again. Too far away. Too soon.

Ann turned off the outside light and, trailing her wrap, headed for her room. The dress she'd chosen tonight came out of another lifetime. People wore anything to the symphony and she hadn't been surprised by the college students in jeans. Ann rubbed the empty third finger of her left hand. She'd removed the wedding rings she'd worn for over twenty-five years. Somehow, it just seemed the right time. Only a pale circle of skin under the heaviness of the platinum and diamond settings reminded her of their absence. Without them, her whole body felt lighter. Maybe she would float.

Gene had attended social functions as a matter of course, to make those invisible business contacts and let the world know that Ballard, Gorman and Wicht was well and prosperous. Gene had been tone deaf and wouldn't be caught dead humming anything in public, let alone show tunes he despised.

Gene! Ann had forgotten about the proposed discussion regarding her case. Well, they could talk when they got together again. It's not like Gene was going to show up anytime soon after being gone this long.

As she reached behind her back to tug at the zipper, Ann thought about how many years it had been since she'd gone out to a place she could wear something besides a business suit. She could still feel the ebbing tide of being socially acceptable. Having a missing husband was worse than being the fifth-wheel at an all-couples party. In her circle, no one remained single long. Partners were quickly replaced and the world of attachment barely hiccupped. People tired of getting the same answer to the same questions, of not knowing how to commiserate, of trying to seat an even number for dinner parties. Ann couldn't blame them as they gradually dropped her name from their invitation lists. She didn't know what to say when she ran into them at the market or church.

Mark had seemed to enjoy himself. And had he known she had every recording Stella Lombard made? Of course he hadn't. Did any children of her circle of friends like that kind of music? She slid the dress onto a hanger.

Ann put Stella's music on now, low and vibrant, while she pulled off her earrings and necklace and placed them in their velvet boxes. She studied her face in the mirror of her dressing table.

The crepe skin under her chin she would do nothing about. Lines fanned toward her temples from her eyes. She couldn't justifiably call them laugh lines, for laughter had been rare in these past gray years of not knowing. She pushed the hair back from her temples. Strands of white showed. Should she color it? Maybe Maeve would help her. Maeve had a lot of experience with dyeing her hair. Ann considered the last color she'd seen on her niece, a royal purple, and thought again. Maybe not. How much would a professional job cost? Fern might know.

Was this dating? How was she supposed to feel about a date? She couldn't, naturally, date a child from her past. But maybe she could use this as practice, in case someone eligible ever asked her out. Her friendship with Mark could work both ways. Maybe Donna Ballard would never give up Gene, but Ann needed to move on. Mark showed her that much. Gene. Drat. She'd forgotten to set that appointment with Mark. Oh, well. Next time.

Still not sleepy by one-thirty in the morning, she booted up her computer. As she suspected, Maeve was home from work and online from her room in Sauk City.

"I'm confused, Maeve. You'll never believe this, but I think I just had a date."

"U never said a word all week! How come I didn't know? About time. What did U do?"

"He had symphony tickets, with Stella Lombard."

"I know kids who went. What else happened?"

"We went to the show and then had supper at the Bistro."

"Candlelight?" Maeve asked.

"Everyone had candlelight."

"Kiss good night?"

"On the cheek."

"R U touching your cheek now?"

Ann dropped her hand and stopped smiling.

"Sorry. Couldn't resist, Auntie. Can U tell me his name? When do I meet him? Or do I have to call Mom?"

"Blackmail isn't nice. Besides, I told you, it couldn't have been a date. I don't know when you'll meet him. You would have to show up here once in a while."

"Ouch! What's got U so riled? Auntie Ann? U still there? Wait! Don't leave! I won't say a word to anyone. I promise."

"LOL"

"Is he handsome?"

"I think so."

"Where did U meet him?"

The first time she'd met Mark Roth, he'd come from next door through the gully that separated their homes. Ann saw the delivery van and knew the new neighbors were moving in. She'd held Ritchie to the yard the first two hours until he broke loose and scampered to meet the new people. Barbara, the real estate agent who also was a friend of Fern Wicht's, told Fern the Roths ran a home business. There had been some deal with the zoning board that let them use their home as their distribution office for their catalog service.

"Mom! Mom! They have a boy, just my size!" The boy Ritchie dragged home was named Trey. When a teenager came across the gully an hour later looking for Trey, Ritchie carelessly introduced him as Mike.

"It's Mark, Mrs. Ballard. Mark Roth. Trey's my brother."

"Half-brother," Trey said.

"And their dad said I should call him Edward, not 'Mr. Roth,' " Ritchie said.

Ann made no comment. Gene wouldn't like that informality. "Hello, Mark," she said instead to the tall young man with sparkling blue eyes.

The boy held out a hand to shake hers. "I'm pleased to meet you, Mrs. Ballard."

Where had she met Mark? Just five weeks ago, when he stood on her doorstep and reminded her that she was so alone?

"I met him a long time ago."

"I understand. I love you, Ann."

"Thank you, darling. I love you, too. Good night."

Ann yawned. She wandered around her dark house for a time, double checking the

78

locks. She stopped in the front hall and looked out of the window, chiding herself for even thinking about headlights or tail-lights. She eventually wound her way back to her bedroom. She checked the luminous dial of her bedside clock. Two-thirty. If Maeve had asked how Ann had met Gene, the story would have been soporific. Gene Ballard helped found Ballard, Gorman and Wicht, a firm specializing in businesses that traded overseas. They employed twenty-five accountants, one of whom was Ann, a newly graduated and tested CPA. That's all. Love at first sight? No, not really. Ann supposed Gene had been ready for a wife. Ann was available.

Ann slipped under the spread, rolled on her side and pulled the blanket under her chin. Maybe now she could sleep.

Mark couldn't shake the desire to belong to someone, to be part of something that had nothing to do with business, all during work on Friday after the symphony date with Ann. Date. Friends. Family. His father tended to roam, spending no longer than a few years in this town, that neighborhood, before moving on to the next business opportunity. No time to form lasting friendships. College and law school had passed in a heartbeat. The seven years he lived in Georgetown were the longest he'd spent in one place up to then. He hadn't taken the time to do more than hammer facts with the study group. He couldn't even remember most of their names or faces.

After school, Mark never planned to stay at his first job experience in Virginia. Though the time stretched into a career after Georgetown, then a few more years with Allison, he kept his hunger for Wisconsin. That period of his life seemed fractured when he looked back, as though looking through a kaleidoscope. All he'd accomplished there led to these moments back in Clayton, the one place he'd been happy. On the day Allison returned his ring, she told him she'd known his heart belonged some other place, with someone who knew how to connect with the joyful places he'd buried deep inside. She'd been right, and he'd mourned more for the time he'd stolen from her than for losing her as a mate.

The Friday night outing was held at a restaurant not far from the condo. When he arrived, he met Jim near the door and followed him to a private back room. "A little calmer," Jim shouted over the clink of glasses, called orders, whooping of a birthday bunch and a karaoke machine just cranking up.

Jim made introductions. "John Moseby." Mark shook Moseby's hand. "John's at BGW." Mark gave the man a second look.

Moseby nodded. "That's right."

"And Ken, here, you already know." Mark clasped hands with their fellow attorney. Ken Windom worked closely with Jim in estate planning. Mark knew the man was going through a second divorce, but he didn't act too shook up about it.

Moseby took a seat at the table and waved Mark to join him. "So, you been with Jung and Royce, what, a couple of months?" He crunched some potato chips. "Where were you before?"

"In Virginia working with corporate liability, stuff like that, for the past couple of years."

"Where you from, originally?"

"Everywhere. But I graduated from Vilas and always planned to return."

Moseby laughed. "Catching up with the past, eh?"

Jim and his brother-in-law gathered around the table and broke out a deck of cards. Jim hadn't mentioned that. What games did he remember, anyway? It had been awhile since he'd played.

"Just for laughs," Jim said. "Loser buys pizza."

Jim had been right. The men who gathered played for something to do. After the fifth round, the arrival of pizza halted the action. During the break, Mark learned about how each of them got involved with the others. Jim started the group with his wife's twin brother, Glen Carlton, a few years back. Windom from the office joined up, as had various others from Jung and Royce.

Jim grabbed two pieces. "Now our buddy, Moseby, had to take last year off with his wife being so sick."

Mark studied Moseby. The man's leathery face was etched with melancholy, though Mark suspected he'd once purported a healthy sense of humor. "I'm sorry."

Moseby nodded in acknowledgment. "Cancer. She's in remission."

Windom reached for another slice of pizza. "We let him in because of all the time we spend trading files with Ballard."

Mark shifted and cleared his throat. "Oh?"

"Yeah. He's their chief accountant."

Mark wondered at the stare Parsons laid on him. "That must keep you on your toes."

Jim piped up. "Our pal John works with all their accountants."

"Mm hmm," Mark muttered and turned

to Jim's brother-in-law. "So, what do you do?"

"I have a sales route," Carlton said. "You know all those vending machines at the rest stops along the freeway? I fill 'em. Are you all ready for another round?"

A couple of hours later, Mark was holding his own in the game when Jim brought up the fact Mark had used his tickets for the symphony.

"With that singer?" Carlton asked. "Ah, what's her name? Would have taken Marie, but she had to work."

"That's the one! And, funny thing, but Martina Dixon, who usually sits behind us with her husband, called Glenda the next day for a gabfest, or whatever." Jim set his cards, face down, in front of him and winked at Mark. "You know what she told Glenda?"

Mark could guess, but why spoil the man's fun?

"That you had Ann Ballard with you."

Moseby went still as a deer caught in headlights. Windom coughed.

Mark glanced at his hand, then around at the faces turned on him.

Moseby came back to life, and threw in a couple of chips. "Raise."

"So, how was it?" Carlton asked. "Paper

83

said it was good. Marie cried."

Windom got up and refilled his glass.

Mark cleared his throat. "Yeah, it was a great show."

"So, what were you doing with Ann Ballard?" Windom asked.

Mark assessed Windom's expression before answering. The two people he was most unsure about reaction-wise were Parsons, Ann's lawyer, and John Moseby, Ann's boss. What would they think? He didn't want to hurt Ann's reputation in any way. What would they think of her, not just that she might or might not be a married woman being seen with another man, but a younger man at that? Did they wonder if he was just after her non-existent money? Of course, both of them knew her situation better than he did.

In the meantime, Windom came back to the table. "Bait?"

"You said you had a girlfriend," Jim accused.

Mark gave up trying to figure a strategy for the full house he held and tossed in the hand. He addressed Windom. "It was a good performance. I enjoy the symphony. Parsons, here, offered tickets." He shifted in the chair and stared at the colorful pile of plastic poker chips in the middle of the table. "I used to live next door to the Ballards."

Windom hauled the chips in his direction. "I've met her niece. Maeve, I think. Strange name. You fold? Anyone else? I win." He calculated the piles in front of the other men.

Mark pushed the chair back and stood. "It's getting late. I've still got some papers to look at. It was great meeting all of you."

Windom announced the results of his addition. "Carlton, you're buying next time." He looked up at Mark. "You gonna come back? Or did we scare ya?"

Mark grinned. "Sure. I never turn away free food." Their laughs were reassuring. He grabbed his jacket from the back of a chair. "And I don't scare that easily. Good night."

"Thanks for coming," Carlton called. "See you around."

Moseby joined him. "I'll walk you out."

Mark walked next to Moseby along the restaurant's narrow lane between noisy tables of patrons to the door.

Once on the street, Moseby said his piece. "About getting involved with Ann Ballard, you might want to think that one over very carefully. And it's not just the age factor."

Mark jingled some coins and the keys in his pocket. "What makes you say that?"

85

"There are some pretty strange issues surrounding Gene Ballard's disappearance.
The Ballard Trust holds a lot of power."

"That's the second time I've heard that."
The two of them continued to walk into the
night.

"Then I would make sure I respected that
information. Mrs. Ann Ballard is a nice lady,
still works with us a couple of days a week.
We all like her."

Mark tried to read between the words. If
there was a threat, it was well hidden. "Do
you believe her husband is dead?"

They reached Moseby's car, parked in the
lot across the street. Mark was a row over.
Moseby opened the door and hesitated. He
looked past Mark's shoulder toward the
direction of the pool of light cast by the
outdoor fixtures. Then he glanced at Mark
as he tossed his jacket into the passenger
seat. "For what it's worth, yeah, I believe
the man's long gone. Time enough to bury
the guy already. I'd leave the dead alone, if
I were you." Moseby got into the car and
drove away.

Why were they concerned? What did it
matter if he was polite to his former neighbor? Lord, Lord, are you listening to them?
Loving Ann is the right thing to do. I know
it is.

Mark tried to remember just what he'd said to Parsons when he accepted the tickets. That he'd come back for someone special — that was it. Mark had taken Ann to the symphony, a public place, surely. And to dinner, of course. He was having dinner with her next week, too, at her place. Mark looked back at the restaurant. There were complications, he remembered saying. In his mind, those issues were related to the current state of Ann's marriage, not her dead husband's family secrets. Now he supposed he'd created the mother of all complications by not talking to Jim about Ann's case before making it look like he was trying to date her.

CHAPTER FIVE

On her lunch break, Ann took her parents to the Veteran's Day ceremonies at the high school auditorium. Gene's father had served in World War II. Her father had been stationed overseas during the Korean conflict. He wore his faded service cap today, and pins on his food-stained plaid shirt. She and her mother helped him climb the four steps to the wide front doors, joining the dozens of vets and citizens who had come to honor them and all for which they stood. Ray Michels was only seventy-four, but years of hard labor and arthritis stiffened his knees and bent his back. Difficulty hearing and poor eyesight left her father a sheltered world from which they had to coax him. Alice, Ann's mother, at seventy, was in great shape. Ann marveled that although her mother was physically capable of going out and meeting new people and finding things to do, or taking the day trips scheduled by

Honors Manor, she refused to do anything without her husband. Was that love, or devotion, or fear? Maybe all three. Were all those ingredients necessary for a healthy relationship?

"You're looking good today, Dad," Ann shouted into his good ear, the right one.

"You, too. You got that spark I used to love to see."

Ann exchanged puzzled looks with her mother. Her mother shook her head. "We started a fitness class. Maybe he's getting too much oxygen."

Ann laughed. If her mother could get her dad involved in something like that, there was hope yet.

Ann recognized very few members of the weekday lunchtime audience. Geared toward those who had memories to relive, the program was more attractive to the retired. The retired of her former acquaintances did not usually remain in Wisconsin, so Ann was not surprised to see few she knew. A color guard of proud flag-bearers made their way on stage and stood as straight as they could during the pledge and salute. Tolerable renditions of the usual poems were recited by grade school children. A young woman with a soaring voice sang God Bless America, followed by a speech from one of the always ready and available politicians, and the program was over.

On the way out of the auditorium, a group of elderly men stopped her dad. Ann sorrowed at the painful concentration on her father's face as he struggled to understand them. She finally stepped in to interpret. "Do you want to go have lunch with Terry and Sam? Reminisce?"

Her father shook his head, moist eyes to the ground as he leaned on her mother and continued to walk to her car.

"I'm sorry, Mr. Wallace. Dad isn't feeling too well today."

Mr. Wallace patted her shoulder. "That's all right. We'll catch up in the great by and by."

The thought of losing her parents made her own eyes water. At least they still had each other. She had only faded memories of Gene to provide a cold comfort. She hurried after them to drive back to Honors Manor in Sauk City, a nice place set on the banks of the Wisconsin River where folks could sit on a bench and watch canoeists in the summer and the eagles in the winter. And wait.

Ann dropped her folks off, then drove home to Clayton.

Maeve sat on Ann's living room floor in a pool of sunlight. Her back was plumb with the wall, her legs twisted and her eyes closed.

"Maeve! I wasn't sure if you lived here anym—"

"Shh! Ohm."

Ann slowly turned and hung her coat in the closet. With one more glance at Maeve, she went into the kitchen to make some tea and stare out the window. She should refill the bird feeders. Ann jumped when the kettle shrilled.

Maeve wandered in, looking half-asleep. "Can I have some, too?"

"Were you just meditating?"

Maeve's little smile was both grave and sheepish. "Yeah. Chandra, she's into Enlightenment, you know? And she's teaching me. Anyway, how are you?"

"I'm fine." Ann chose not to ask about Chandra. "I was just with Grandma and Grandpa."

"Oh. How are they?"

The women took their cups to the table. "It's Veteran's Day, remember? We usually go to the program at school. Dad seemed slow today," Ann said.

"That's right. Grandpa was in the army, or something. Was Uncle Gene?"

Ann shook her head. "No, not him. But his father served in World War II." She changed the subject, not wanting to talk about Gene or the Ballards. "How are classes? I seem to remember some kind of marketing project you wanted to talk to me about."

Maeve shrugged and evaded her by looking at the empty bird feeders. "Yeah. I've got to get to that. I want to meet your man friend."

Ann sipped her tea, a jasmine blend that provided a balm to the tingling sense of warning. Once she'd wanted to introduce them. Now, she wasn't so sure. What should she say to Maeve? The girl was sure to tell her mother — probably already had. Ann was surprised her sister hadn't shown up already, with instructions on the propriety of older married women in the company of younger single men. "We seem to get together on weekends so far, when you're gone."

Maeve spooned sugar into her cup and clanked it around. "Do I have to worry about you?"

This time her niece searched for some sign

Ann couldn't understand. "No more than I worry about you. You could tell me about your own social life, you know."

Maeve grinned. "I could. But then I'd have to shoot you. I haven't said anything to Mom about you, by the way. If I tell you nothing about me, then you can return the same favor, right? I'll go fill the bird feeders. Then I have an appointment. I'm sorry I'm not better company."

"Do you need me to do some laundry?" Ann sent a pointed look at Maeve's stained scruffy blue sweatshirt, bandana and lack of socks. If she couldn't reach inside her sister's child, the least she could do was make sure the outside was cared for properly.

"Nah." Maeve bent to kiss her on the cheek. "See you probably next week. Be good!" She hesitated at the garage door. "And thanks for everything, you know."

"I know."

Ann woke from a restless sleep. She reached out to switch on the bedside lamp, then sat up, pulling the extra pillow behind her. She'd dreamed of Gene's memorial service, which had been held years ago, not long after Trey Roth's memorial and shortly before Ritchie's high school graduation.

In the echoing Clayton Presbyterian Church, Ann stood in a receiving line with her parents and Aunt Elle after Reverend Bolls gave Gene a majestic eulogy. A stream of rushing water gurgled across the floor, winding around boulders that jutted up at random. Ann only now thought it odd, in her wakefulness. Donna Ballard hadn't responded to Ann's message inviting her to the vigil, much to Ann's relief. At what point the simple prayer service had turned into a coffinless funeral, Ann couldn't say. Gene had been missing for over a year and Ann had been to New York twice to look at homicide victims. There had been no leads for three months and Ann was frustrated and still afraid of what would happen to her and Ritchie in the future.

Reverend Bolls had approached her in the spring with the offer to have a service in the church. "Think of your son. He needs some closure to this . . . this matter. It would do you both good. And it would give the rest of the congregation a way to support you in your time of grief."

Ann never heard of a vigil for the missing and/or dead. She wondered irreverently whether the little black book with all the words to all the rites inspired the reverend. She'd reluctantly given in. Maybe Ritchie did need something to help him deal with the loss. She'd been so caught up in icy fear wondering if Gene had been kidnapped or killed or simply found another woman, then expectant to find Gene's body, then battling Donna, that she hadn't had the time or the energy to have a nervous breakdown, or whatever it was women whose husbands went missing were supposed to feel.

Her son's rage caught her off guard.

"He's not dead." Ritchie's too-flat tone signaled a cyclone of anger. She'd been prepared to give Ritchie a lot of leeway, especially after Trey, but she also felt guilty for the relief of knowing that he planned to spend the summer working in Green Bay before he began classes at the university. He refused to come for the service. Reverend Bolls had called to talk to him, to no avail.

As the reception line wound to a close, Ann heard shouting through the glass of the enclosed sanctuary that separated her from the wide gathering area. She picked out Ritchie's characteristic high-pitched rant and, alarmed, excused herself from the last of the well-wishers to go and see what he was up to. She faced Mark Roth first. Ann remembered that she'd felt pleased to see him, although puzzled at his somewhat slaphappy choice of dress. He wore an unusual Hawaiian shirt, white with red flowers. He must have grown a mustache. His face looked puffy, probably from tears. It must have been hard for him to come, after being at his brother's funeral just a couple of months ago. She was touched that he allowed himself to appear vulnerable in public. She smiled at him, then froze in incredulity when her son's fist slid, slow motion, across Mark's cheek. Mark's head snapped to the side and he staggered before righting himself and facing his young friend.

"Ritchie! Stop that! What are you doing?" Ann willed herself through the door with long strides of her high-heeled pumps to grab her son. At the same time she realized in horror that Mark hadn't grown a mustache and that his shirt hadn't been decorated with red flowers.

On the Friday Ann invited Mark for dinner, minutes inched. When she returned to her desk after delivering the stock inventory report of one of their holdings in Japan, her message light flashed. Absentmindedly, she pressed the button while clicking her computer screen back to life.

"Annie, it's Mark. I just want you to know that I'll be a little late tonight. I have to catch up on some research. It shouldn't take that long, just a half-hour, forty-five minutes. I'll see you later."

Annie! Nobody called her that. She hated it. She hadn't even let her mother call her that and whenever Rachel tried, Ann had pulled her sister's hair or punched her.

Annie.

She waited for the usual passion to stir up. Annie Oakley. Annie, Annie, pants on fire. Annie, Annie, all come free! Annie Banannie. Annie Bo-mannie.

Annie.

Mark's voice sent a trill of pleasure up her neck, even if he called her . . . Annie.

Could she be an Annie? Could she become that kind of woman Annie represented? Annie was a baby name, a nickname for a person who was . . . what, carefree? Unconcerned. Young at heart? Annie — Any, anyone. Ann never wanted to be just anyone. She was Ann, mistress of her own life. Well, that's what she had, the past seven years. Her own life. The woman who was Alone. A woman who took naps in the middle of the afternoon. The woman who waited, as if occupying one of those benches on the shores of the Wisconsin River at the retirement home.

She knew, then, that she didn't need to be Ann anymore. Straight laced, alone, too

97

secure, too demure, waiting for something to happen to her, waiting for someone to come and fix her problems for her. Gene's absence was problem number one. After she dealt with putting his memory to rest, she could find someone to have fun with. She would show everyone that she was more than just plain old mopey Ann. She could be fun Annie, the woman who could have a good time. Maybe she would even get herself a boyfriend. Her palms turned clammy as she thought of touching a man again, feeling warm smooth skin under her palms. A man who had muscled forearms like Mark's, whose strength she could lean against in a crowd and know he would keep her safe.

Gretchen Tomlin, Howie Gorman's assistant, stopped at Ann's desk. "Howie's looking for you, Ann. Are you all right? Not getting one of your headaches, are you?"

"Oh, no, I'm fine. Here's the report." Ann handed her the folder and began to roll back to her desk. She stopped. "Gretchen, just a sec." The other woman's eyes widened in her surprise. "Do you think I look like . . . an Ann? Or could I be an Annie?"

Gretchen folded her arms, the report clutched in one hand, while she tilted her head and pretended to study Ann through twinkling eyes and a mock frown. Gretchen, who had known Ann since she married Gene, couldn't hold back her wide smile for long. "Ann, woman, you can be whatever you want. You don't need anyone's permission."

Ann lowered her face to her folded arms on her cubicle's work surface after the other woman left. "Maybe just a blessing."

Just for fun, Ann Googled "older women and younger men." Thousands of results popped up. Once she got past the sleazy-sounding sites, it did not ease her mind to see that even Oprah had done a show on it. The word "experimental" came up often. It was not comforting. There were even whole books on the subject. Other unflattering names flashed on the screen. "Cougar." Ann wasn't after a man, was she? Mark had come to her. So, what did that make her?

"Wow. One-third of women over forty are dating younger men. I can't read this anymore!"

"Hi! What have you got there?"

Ann jumped when Fern, Tim Gucht's current wife, appeared at her side. The woman leaned forward and peered at the screen. Ann hit the button to shut down the display. "Fern, you scared me!"

Fern sat back in the chair and crossed her

legs. She tossed a lock of her red-blond hair and crinkled her eyes in a familiar kindly smile. "Research?" Fern wasn't any kind of marriage-wrecker or gold-digger or anything else that came up when people whispered about the realignment of couples in their circles.

"Um, sort of. Aren't you in school today?"

Fern taught fourth grade at Clayton Elementary. "We have conferences later, so it's like a split shift. I'm so done with curriculum consorting! Tim can't do lunch. Let's go out, grab a bite and talk."

"Yes, let's." Ann shut down her computer and locked up her cabinets before tugging her coat on and following Fern.

Ann swam at the YMCA every weekday morning. It got her out of the house and forced her to keep in shape. When Fern found out, she asked if she could join, and so their friendship began.

Today they visited Reggie's, a pizza bar they both liked for its family atmosphere and decent homemade crusts.

Fern studied her after the waiter had taken their order and went to place it. "So, mind if I ask why you were reading up on unusual relationships?"

Ann blinked and decided to confide. Maybe it was the music, maybe it was the sight of couples and their children who had a day off from school, enjoying each other's company. "I'm going crazy." Fern did not laugh. The waiter dropped off their iced teas. Fern held hers up. "To love."

Ann did laugh, then. "Is it so obvious?"

Fern tossed her head. "I think you're still thinking about it, sister."

Ann dropped her gaze to the shiny faux wood tabletop and bit her lip. "I don't know what to think."

"If it's love, you shouldn't have to think about it."

"But what if everyone thinks it's wrong?"

Fern snorted and took a sip. "Tell me about it."

Ann tried again. "Not like — well, if people bothered to stop and get to know you, they'd . . . This isn't like that. And how can I be in love? With — oh, I'm just thinking out loud, of course. When I'm not getting out the phone book and looking up the number for the nearest psychiatrist."

"Do you want to talk about it?" The waiter brought some reprieve with their pizza and Ann took her time considering her words. Fern graciously allowed her the space.

"His family lived next door," she finally said, half-way through their meal. "He went away and came back. Now he's a lawyer, doing well for himself."

"Good looking, too, I bet."

Ann slumped. "And nice, nice as ever. I'm sure he just wants to talk to someone he used to know, until he gets settled again. I don't know what's happening to me, why I. . . ." The last came out as a vulnerable whisper. She felt sick and closed her eyes, the lights and talk mingling psychedelic in the background. She reached for the pill bottle in her purse.

"Ann. Ann, honey, are you all right?"

"I don't know."

"Here, let's go."

Ann watched the woman toss some bills on the table and gratefully accepted Fern's help with her coat. They passed the waiter and Fern said no, everything was fine, her friend just wasn't feeling well. In the car, Fern turned on the heater while Ann swallowed a couple of her migraine pills. She was not getting a headache tonight. No way. They buckled themselves in.

"You know, Fern, in all of this, I can't forget."

"Forget what?"

"That I'm still married. To Gene."

Ann picked up the kitchen extension on the fourth ring. "Hello."

"You really should get caller ID, Ann."

"Hello, Mark. Thanks for the advice, as always."

"I wanted to let you know that I'm on my way."

Ann stirred her simmering tomato sauce. "Very thoughtful of you. I'm nearly ready."

"What are you making?"

"I'll leave it a mystery. See you in a little while." Ann hung up, whipped off her apron and plunged into the powder room tucked under the staircase to comb her hair one more time. She stopped in the vestibule to look out the window and breathe deeply while shivery tingles caressed her rib cage.

When Ann saw his blue car turn and halt in front of her house, she scrambled to the kitchen in order to let him know that, when he rang the bell, she'd been busy with important things. Certainly not standing around, waiting. For him.

She walked sedately down the front hall to answer the door. "Hello, Mark, come on in." His pallor and the lines under his eyes made Ann want to rush him to a warm beach somewhere, to relax. She hung his overcoat in the closet and watched while he set his briefcase by the bamboo table that always held a vase of flowers and her key ring and phone. Gene's side, where he'd deposited his wallet and keys, was empty.

"I'm just finishing the sauce. Why don't you come, have something to drink?"

Mark shrugged off his jacket and loosened the tie. "Do you mind if I use the powder room first?"

"Of course not."

When he joined her in the kitchen, Ann looked up from folding napkins by the two place settings on the table. "What can I get you to drink?"

"Don't let me be a bother, Ann. I can help myself."

Ann stirred and tasted her sauce. She reached for the basil while she listened to the homey, comfortable sounds Mark made with a spoon in a cup of coffee.

"Do you go to Ritchie and Colleen's for Thanksgiving?"

"They'll be with her family in Green Bay." She was distracted by sprinkling the right amount of basil. "Are you going south to be with your dad and step-mom?"

"No, we haven't gotten together in years. I don't have that much time, anyway, with my new job and all."

Ann smiled at him over her shoulder. "I'm having my family here. Why don't you join us? It'll just be my folks and my sister . . . oh, and my aunt. I think my niece has other plans." Maeve left a note stating that she would be at the Buddhist retreat center over the break, but Ann wasn't going to start worrying about that. "We have a small turkey and my parents go home right afterward. They usually don't even stay for football."

Ann turned and stirred the pot some more, waiting for Mark to say something. When he didn't, she continued her nervous chat to fill the empty air. "Sometimes my aunt hangs around. She's different. Esoteric. I suppose I should say eccentric, but that wouldn't be fair to her spirit. We pretend to understand her, and she really does understand us. She'd like you, I think. You must come, at least for dinner."

Having decided she was chatting to herself while testing the sauce's piquancy once more, Ann whirled to quench her burning tongue. She hadn't realized how closely Mark stood behind her and bumped into him, sending some of the contents of the spoon flying against his white dress shirt. The fragmented memory of blood decorating a white shirt much the same way the sauce did froze her in a time warp of confusion. When she found her voice again, she said, "I'm so sorry. Look what I've done to your shirt."

"It's okay, Ann. I should have warned you. You didn't know I was right here. Ann? Ann, are you all right?"

Ann shook her head. "Just something I remembered." She touched a spot of sauce on his shirt. "The last time I saw you, after . . . before you came back, you had blood on your shirt. Here, let me."

"It's okay, Ann," Mark repeated. "No harm done. I'll take it to the cleaners."

She continued to stare at the stains, memories of shouted words echoing. Spaghetti sauce bubbled behind her, the heat of the burner on her back mingling with the warmth that shimmered down her front.

"Ann?"

His voice came from far away. Ann replied from the same plane. "You were fighting. With Ritchie the night of Gene's memorial."

Mark's voice sounded muffled. "Yes. I'm sorry."

Ann felt his hands on her shoulders and shivered. "Ritchie never said why." She didn't really care why. She just wanted to stay in the warm circle of Mark's arms, afraid to leave, afraid to stay.

"It was about you."

Ann raised her face, eyeing the column of his throat, his shadowed chin and the sweeping lines of his mouth, then into his eyes to see the thing she'd feared and dreamed. "Me?" Her breath choked her. She was drowning, mixed up with the out of control springtime flood churning against a riverbank, gouging new channels through soft stone.

"He said terrible things about you." Mark's fingers slid down and tightened painfully in the soft skin above her elbows. "I told him to stop but he kept going on and on. I knew he was upset about his dad being missing. The memorial service made him mad, because in his eyes, his father wasn't dead like Trey. Just not here, and he'd be back."

"Mark." The rest of what Ann wanted to say, to apologize and to thank him for defending her to her son, stuck in her throat. She felt him take the wooden spoon from her hand. He reached just past her to turn the burner off while his other hand slid up her arm. "Ann? Ann, don't you know? I've loved you forever. For years, since I was old enough to know how a man can feel about a woman. Everything I am, all that I've done since he left, it's all been for you, so I could come back to the one place I always felt like someone cared." His hands slid up to cup her cheeks. "Ann."

Her eyelids fluttered as Mark's face closed in. His lips were soft and cool, not demanding. Ann could have pulled back any time she wanted. She shivered despite the warmth she felt through the layers of her shirt and sweater. Her hands ran across his back, the firm layers of muscle flexing in response to her touch. She could feel his fingers tremble against her ears. Knowing that he was as nervous as she comforted her.

Or was his reaction lust? Had she led him on, made him think she wanted him to . . . What about hormones? Maybe he just needed her for his reputation in the business and was actually grossed out, kissing a woman old enough — What was she doing? Did she even have a conscience? The childhood friend of her son! She pulled away, breathing hard. "I don't —"

Mark let her go. Ann stepped away, folding her arms about her waist and grabbing her elbows. He didn't move. "I love you, Ann. With everything that goes with it. If you tell me to go, I will. Because I love you, not because I want to. I love you, and I hope that someday you will accept that, and maybe you could find it in your heart to love me back. I don't want anything from you. I just want you to think about me, get to know me a little, get used to the idea of having someone around who adores you. We're both adults. You have to know I would do anything for you. I want to be with you all the time, not just when it's convenient."

Ann hunched. Gene had been home when work allowed. He had to travel and Ann went into their marriage knowing that. How could Mark, the boy from next door, know that all Ann wanted, all she needed, was to feel necessary in more ways than what Gene allowed?

We are both adults, Mark had said. Would accepting this man's declaration reveal her to be some kind of woman who preyed on younger men? Did it matter what anyone else would think of the two of them, mismatched, in a forever kind of relationship? Ann couldn't even pin down what it was she wanted. What about Mark? What did he want from her? And Ritchie would have a fit.

Ann felt her smile crest. She straightened and returned to Mark's fierce embrace. "Call me Annie."

Chapter Six

Ann answered Mark's call the next night, well after eight o'clock even on Saturday. Ann began to get a feel for what a lawyer went through with his tough schedule. "I'm on my way home. Can I stop for a few minutes? Say hello? I don't want to interrupt you if you're busy."

She appreciated that he gave her an out. She was as anxious as he seemed to be to make sure last night wasn't just some accident of witless bad timing. "I'd like that."

When he arrived, Ann noted the care with which he stepped around her, the way he watched her for signs to give her time and space if she needed it. What kind of man would put another's emotions first, especially after a long, tiring day? The kind you don't let get away, Aunt Elle would say. Ann guessed she would find out from Elle herself on Thanksgiving. Mark probably assessed a jury the same way, looking for agreement, misunderstanding, the "aha" moment. The glow in his eyes reassured her, delighted her, when she lifted her face for a swift kiss that quickly turned deep before he cut it off.

"It was real? I didn't just imagine last night?"

"Depends." She wrapped her arms around his waist and listened to the pace of his heart. "What part of last night?"

His arms wrapped her shoulders, cradling her in delectable warmth. "Annie."

"Just please don't call me your dream girl."

"Dreams are done. Now you're real — more than real. Ann, I love you so much."

Ann forced her lungs to fill and empty in regular rhythm. Still, those troubling words Ann couldn't yet form. *How do I reply to 'I love you'? It hadn't been an issue with Gene. And did she? Dare she admit it?*

"Are you hungry?" Ann asked him. *Good move, girl. Feed him something, anything, so he doesn't miss it.*

"No. But I've been wondering about . . ." Mark swallowed.

Ann watched his Adam's apple move in his throat. "Yes?"

"What you want me to say, um, how to act, that is, around your parents. You know, at Thanksgiving dinner."

Ann moved reluctantly out of his arms and touched his cheek before she led him to the sofa. "You want to put on an act around my parents?"

"Annie, I just — I just wondered what you're going to say, what you plan to tell them."

Ann drew him down next to her and wrapped his arms loosely around herself so she could fit against him. "About what?" It's not mean, not really, to make him say it.

"About — you know — about me."

She picked up one of his hands, his right one, to examine his fingers and watch the way the tendons moved inside his wrist. "I plan to introduce you."

"As what?"

"As an attorney. Or what? As a former neighbor? Or do you have any hobbies? You can tell them that yourself, you know. Small talk. Oh! I should warn you, my father's hard of hearing." She cupped his warm hand around her ear to muffle sound. Perhaps this was all her father could hear through his damaged eardrums.

"But what are we going to tell people?"

Ann dropped his hand and turned to face him. She took a deep breath and closed her eyes for a moment in silent petition. "Mark, what do you want?"

"I guess I want to know how we define . . . us."

"Us? We're just Mark and Ann. What more is there?"

A line appeared between his eyes. His mouth turned grim. "Are you embarrassed?"

Ann wanted to say the right thing, the thing she knew would alleviate his anxiety, but her fear during the lonely time locked those comforting words away. "Of what? Mark, you're not making any sense. You told me you weren't looking for another girlfriend."

"I told you that I didn't want you to try to introduce me to anyone. I want to know how I'm supposed to think about our relationship."

Ann got up and walked unsteadily to the fireplace and back, to watch him from the relative safety of the other side of the coffee table. "Mark, I spent the last seven years trying to define myself. I'm not a widow, I'm not divorced. I'm married, but I have no husband. I'm tired of trying to explain things to other people. I'm just Ann. You're just Mark. Isn't that enough?"

"What will your parents think when they see us together?" Mark pushed himself up from the cushions and raised an eyebrow.

She wondered, too, what they would think. Hopefully partial deafness and her dad's poor eyesight would make Mark's youth less obvious. Aunt Elle was the more curious issue. Ann never knew what her crazy aunt was going to say. Elle might embarrass Mark with her frankness. Well, if Mark wanted to be with her, he might as well jump into the deep end with the family. Rachel — she wouldn't think about her caustic sister's probable reaction now.

Ann folded her arms. "I'm sure I can't speak for my parents. Of course, if you plan to ravish me on the dining room table, they might have questions. Are you?"

Mark started to circle the coffee table. "What?"

"Planning to ravish me?" Ann sidestepped around the table. "Maybe? Just a little?" She feinted a move to the left, which Mark deflected by hauling her against him.

"I plan to, temptress. Just a little."

Mark let his briefcase thunk on the floor of the condo. The sky had long ago lost the rosy feathers of mauve, which he'd managed to catch sight of between his office and the courthouse. The endless day in court came to a close. He headed for the kitchen first, for he'd taken only the briefest moment to snatch a few bites of a sub his assistant, Jennifer, had brought him while he regrouped with his client at lunch. The client had enjoyed a full plate of take-out celestial chicken while nodding either yes or no at Mark's suggestions.

Tomorrow was Thanksgiving, and if he rose early enough to finish the details on the re-direct, he might be able to put work out of his mind for the dinner with Ann's family. He remembered meeting Ritchie's Aunt Rachel a couple of times, but did not recall talking long. He picked up an arrangement of fall flowers at Ann's suggestion. He still didn't have a comfortable idea of how to greet her, or them . . . or how to act. Just Mark. Just be Mark. The man who loves your daughter, your sister, your niece.

Mark loosened and pulled off his tie and shed his jacket on the way to the apartment kitchen. The phone rang just as he opened the refrigerator door. Mark checked his watch and groaned. "Right on time." How could I forget? "Hello."

"You bag your old lady yet?"

"C'mon, Lace. I told you not to call her that. You have privileged information and you need to use it respectfully."

The gusty sigh at the other end was

calculated just loud enough to let him know she was put out. "Did you at least try to talk to anyone else? How about your secretary? She's got to have some friends who are your age. Or relatives. I'm worried about you. It's not healthy."

Mark pressed the speaker button on the phone so that her voice filled the kitchen with her teen-aged disapproving Virginia mountain twang. He grabbed a slab of cheddar and a tub of margarine from the fridge and started preparations for a lonely dinner. He muttered an "uh-huh" every once in a while toward the phone.

"You're not listening, are you? I can hear you cooking. How come you're just eating now? Or are you eating again? Trying to substitute love with food —"

"Lacy, it's been a long day and I just got home. How come you're up so late?" Mark slipped the spatula under his toasted cheese sandwich and put it on a plate.

"It's not that late."

"It's, what, midnight out there? On a school night."

"Duh — no school tomorrow, remember? It's Thanksgiving. And I had an assignment."

"What on?" Mark breathed a quick word of thanks then took a bite of the sandwich.

He listened while she took the hint and changed the subject. Good kid. Lacy Smith had been twelve years old when he first met her. Defiantly angry and scared spitless at the thought of losing her home, she'd made an indelible impression on the judge during the trial last year. A mining consortium tried to condemn her neighborhood after a vein of poor-quality coal had been mapped underneath the homes. Mark freely admitted that much of the case had been won because of her testimony. Dirty blond hair and freckles that looked more like a rash spreading out from her nose decorated Lacy's narrow face. Watery blue eyes and crooked teeth made up the rest of the picture. She'd continued to call him or show up at the office long after the trial was over, uncannily at just the time he planned to find some dinner.

"Are you listening?" Lacy's voice sounded cranky.

"Of course, Lacy. John Brown and the anti-slavery movement."

"So now it's your turn. Tell me about her."

Mark took another bite so he wouldn't give an evasive answer he knew would irritate Lacy further.

"Mark? Lawman?"

"Let me swallow, please."

"Sorry. So, why don't you want a woman your own age?"

Mark could feel his throat closing before he had a chance to swallow. He reached for his glass of water but couldn't stop the gasp and cough.

"Mark? Hey! Are you all right?"

"Yeah. You just — um, never mind."

"I'm worried about you. It's not natural, you being so hot, and wanting some old woman. Maybe you have a mother fixation, or something. Did your mother leave you when you were young?"

Mark kept eating, mechanically forcing himself to chew and swallow while he listened to her attempts to analyze his psyche. Yes, my mother left me when I was eight. She died. Her boyfriend, Pugs, bought me a black suit to wear to the funeral. Then he told me I had to go live with my father and his new wife. I stuffed the suit under my mattress when I left.

"Hey! Are you still there?"

"Lace, I had a perfectly normal relationship with my parents. I love Ann. Some day you'll find yourself in love, too. Hopefully not for a long time yet, but when you do, I promise you'll understand."

"Bet it won't be with someone old enough to be my grandfather."

"What if it is? Lacy, you can't decide ahead of time what kind of person you'll fall in love with. If you try, you'll only be disappointed, waiting for that dream person to show up. Only he never will. No one will meet those expectations."

"You decided that about Ann."

"I didn't wish up someone like Ann, Lacy. That's the difference. She was already there."

"But weren't you, like my age, or something? That's just wrong."

"I was almost nineteen years old when I first met her. I waited and worked hard to be the kind of person who could give her a good life, be a good husband to her."

"She's an old married lady. That's not right."

"Her husband is missing, I told you. Probably dead. Which makes her a widow."

"She's older than your step-mother. That's gross."

Mark ignored the last comment. He needed someone to understand that relationships sometimes can't be built inside neat little containers. Sometimes they leak or don't fit, or grow outside of their limits. Maybe their debate would help him figure it out, too — how to define his and Ann's relationship. The discussion about how to act on Thanksgiving Day had left him unsettled. "Men and women have different life spans. Don't you think a younger man who doesn't live as long should take care of a woman who will probably outlive a man her own age?"

"But, don't you think there's something wrong with that kind of thinking? It's not normal."

"The only thing that's wrong is that we aren't following other people's expectations of what they think should be normal."

"That's what I said! You're not normal. And I liked Allison."

"Allison is nice, Lacy. We just weren't right for each other. And what's wrong with not being normal? Normal only means some custom that most people follow. That's 'most,' Lacy. Normal isn't about what's right or what's moral."

He heard her gusty sigh, meant to travel over the airwaves all the way from Virginia. "I knew you'd bring religion into it."

"Not religion, Lacy. You remember what I said about how we should live our lives and treat others?"

"Yeah."

"How we treat others shows them —"

"What we think of God. I got it, already." Silence.

"So, Mark?"

"Yes, Lacy."

"Did you tell her?"

"Yes, I did."

"What did you say? Was she all freaked?"

"A little. So was I."

"So?"

"I can tell you're tired. You're getting cranky." Mark smiled at the phone and continued to talk through her attempts to interrupt him to declare that she was not cranky. "Ann is just fine, I'm just fine. We enjoy each other's company and will be having Thanksgiving dinner with her family. How about you? Who's going to be at your house this year?"

Lacy must have been tired, for she took the bait. After a litany of who wasn't speaking to whom, how she felt that her oldest sister should not bring the new baby over to get handled so much, and that her uncle was back in jail so her aunt wasn't coming, he heard a muffled crash in the background. "Gotta go," Lacy said in a hurried whisper. "Dad's awake, tossing his shoes."

"Goodbye, Lacy," Mark said and severed the connection. Lacy had a way to go to achieve her dreams. The one thing he could do was help her with tuition. She didn't know it, but before he moved back to

Wisconsin, he and his fellow Rotarians started a college scholarship fund for students at her high school. Anyone who could hope for a fulfilling future made even a dark moment in today feel brighter. Mark might not be certain how Ann's family would react to him, but he would do everything in his power, with the help of the Lord, to give them reason to accept his genuine love for Ann. Thanksgiving would be the shining start of their new life.

CHAPTER SEVEN

On the morning of Thanksgiving Day, Ann opened the door first to her father's sister, Elle. Aunt Elle handed over a pottery casserole dish and leaned her cane against the receiving table while Ann helped her off with her cape. "No, no, the scarf stays. Happy Thanksgiving, dear one." Elle smooched Ann's cheek. "Now go put that in your warmer."

Elle was the keeper of her grandmother's butternut squash recipe. When Ann had asked her mother about how to make the dish after her own marriage, Alice related the family secrecy regarding matters of food. She told her daughter about the mistake of asking to see the recipe, just once, after she married Ray. Elle's comeback had been that the succession of the recipe collection was carefully denoted in her will. Alice might be in line to get the recipe over Elle's dead body. Ann's mother, married into the Michels family all of six months, did not quite understand the undercurrent of humor and told Ann she could never bring herself to ask again.

Ann returned her smooch. "Thank you, thank you. It wouldn't be Thanksgiving without this."

Elle grabbed her cane and trundled down the hall after Ann. "That young man of yours coming this year?"

For a moment, Ann was awash in guilt. Would they all notice something different about her? Could they detect that man scent when she was supposed to be alone? "Young man?"

Elle's voice was deadpan. "Ritchard, your only son."

"Of course." Ann bit her lip, glad she faced away from her aunt to hide the color she could feel on her cheeks. "I told you, he and Colleen are going to her mother's this year. But one of his former friends is coming. Mark Roth. He's back in Clayton, working with Todd Jung." Ann set the dish on the counter while they waited for the warming oven to heat.

She caught Elle's raised eyebrow. Ann looked away, through the kitchen passway into the dining room and the table set for six with her good Spode and napkins the color of allspice set on a ginger-colored table cloth.

Elle went to peer through the patio doors that framed a bright day that could have been warm. "We've never seated many around the table, have we? Give your aunt a drink, now."

Ann poured her a cup of mulled cider from the crock pot on the island. "You look fabulous today, dear. New scarf?"

Elle preened over the silken fringed square she'd draped around her nut-brown turtle-neck sweater. Her collection of chains jingled, making it easy to track her where-abouts. Her scarves and wafts of patchouli intermingled with the cooking turkey aroma and the cinnamon of pumpkin pie, creating a Casablanca moment in Ann's kitchen. Stella happened to be singing As Time Goes By, piped through the house on the inter-com system, an event Ann couldn't have timed more perfectly if she had attempted to plan it. When the door leading to the garage opened, Ann expected a tux-clad figure to come through.

"Hi, there! Happy Thanksgiving." Rachel greeted Ann and Elle while she and Ann's mother helped maneuver their father over the threshold. Both he and his sister, Elle, suffered from degenerative joints, worse in

Dad, a condition Ann hoped to stave off as long as she could by swimming.

Ann went to greet her mom and take her dad's other arm while Rachel buzzed back into the garage, where she'd parked, to gather a blueberry pie and her traditional broccoli and cauliflower bake.

Ann's mother handed her the bakery bag of hard rolls. "I wonder if anyone else in America keeps to such a rigid menu for Thanksgiving?"

"Thanks, Mom. Some traditions are good."

Rachel and Aunt Elle took Dad into the living room and settled him on the sofa. Mom went to check out the table. "You didn't get a centerpiece, dear. You should have told me. I would have brought . . . oh, you counted wrong, too. There're six settings. You said Maeve wasn't coming."

The doorbell rang as her mother said "wasn't coming." Ann flashed a weak smile in her direction before she barely beat Rachel to answer it. Ann ushered a rush of adrenaline in with Mark, who handed her a beautiful arrangement of colored leaves and mums in a basket shaped like a duck. He kissed her cheek. "Happy Thanksgiving," he whispered in her ear while his cold fingers touched hers when he passed the flowers.

"Thank you." Ann inhaled the freshness of autumn for strength before making the introductions. "Everyone, this is Mark Roth. He's come back to live in Clayton and work for Jung and Royce. Mark, my parents, Ray and Alice, my dad's sister, Elle, and you might remember my sister, Rachel." There, that wasn't so bad.

Aunt Elle reached her hands out first to clasp his, casting a wicked little grin at Ann. Her parents looked confused while Rachel scorched Ann with a glare of smoldering, furious curiosity. Ann withered under Rachel's tense mouth. Her sister preferred to be on the giving end of surprises.

"We're so glad you could join us today," Aunt Elle said, as she took Mark's arm and led him into the living room. Ann watched a moment, shifting from foot to foot, then took the flowers into the dining room.

In the dining room, Ann settled the duck basket on one end of the table. She'd set it so that the six of them lined the sides of the table. The head and foot would be left open for dishes not being passed. Ann thought it would be convenient. She would sit between Rachel and Mark, with Dad across from Mark, then Mom, which left Aunt Elle and Rachel facing off. Ann took a deep breath and checked the turkey and Elle's squash.

Just a couple of minutes longer.

"What can I do?" Her mother's quiet voice made Ann jump and snatch her hand out of the oven. She brushed the back of it against the hot surface of the interior.

"Ow." Ann flipped the door and squinted at the red welt.

"I'm sorry. Here, under the faucet." Ann's mother held Ann's hand. A worried, guilty frown creased her brow.

"I'm all right, Mom." Ann squeezed her mother's hand and turned off the faucet.

"I guess we're not supposed to put anything on that, anymore. I used to smear a burn with petroleum jelly."

"I remember," Ann said. "But you're right. I'll just leave it alone for now, thanks. Maybe it won't be so bad. Where were we? I think we can fill the glasses. I put ice cubes in a bowl in the freezer."

Handing her mother the ice and following with a pitcher of water, Ann shook her stinging hand, grimacing. Wow. There was a blister rising. No time for that now.

She grabbed the last of the dishes from the oven and detoured toward the living room. "We're ready, everyone."

Ann's father struggled to his feet. "Smells so good." Elle took one of his arms, while Rachel flanked his other side. Ann studied

Mark's reaction. He wagged his eyebrows at her, smiling slightly. They walked into the dining room together.

Ann's father waited for the signal to offer the family prayer. He took his wife's hand, who took her sister-in-law's. Rachel and Ann took hands, while Mark hesitated at the look of the raised blister on the back of Ann's left hand. She shook her head at him, then let her hand rest gently on his palm and closed her eyes. Her father's words of gratitude for family and food and welcoming friends washed over them. "We ask your blessing, Lord, on those who couldn't be with us today. Those who rest in your joy, your son, Art Corley and for Gene."

Ann felt the twitch of Mark's hand under hers.

"We think of Ritchie and Colleen and the new life they'll soon be sharing. Keep them safe and well. And bless our dear little Maeve."

Rachel's hand convulsed briefly. Ann squeezed back, wondering if Rachel approved of Maeve's decision to spend the holiday at the Meditation Center west of Madison.

"Amen," Dad said.

"Amen," the rest of them echoed. Ann began to pass dishes.

"Ann tells us you came back to Clayton," Aunt Elle started her interrogation of Mark. "Where have you been?"

Ann busied herself with spearing some turkey and passing the dish to her sister.

"I've been working at a law firm in Lynchburg, Virginia."

Mark passed Aunt Elle's dish to Dad and took the salad from Ann, taking care not to brush against the burn.

Rachel took a turn in the question and answer round. "You were that boy from next door, weren't you?"

Ann frowned at her. She turned to see Mark adjust the spoon next to his plate before answering.

Dad put a hand behind his ear. "What's that, Rachel? What did you say?"

Mom shouted. "She just asked Mark about his parents. You remember, those folks who used to be next door to Ann?"

"Oh! Who is he, again?"

Mom put her mouth next to his ear. "From next door. The Roths. Ritchie's friend."

Ann's dad hollered back. "I wondered where they got to, after that bad business with the other boy." He shouted to Mark. "Your brother?"

Mark nodded yes.

"Where are they? Are they going to come, too? There's not enough people to fill the table."

Ann loved the little smile that played across Mark's lips. He glanced at Rachel before replying loudly. "They moved south. They like to golf."

Dad nodded. "Warmer down there, too, I bet." He looked at Mom. "We should go there sometime."

Mom's eyebrows rose as she halted her fork in mid lift. "Oh? Where are they living?"

Mark answered. "They couldn't make up their minds, so they have houses in Arizona, Florida and South Carolina."

"It's a long way away, Ray," Mom said to Dad, who continued to shovel potatoes into his mouth.

Aunt Elle took back the floor. She raised her fork and pointed it down the length of the table. "So, how long have you been in town?"

"Just a couple of months. I started just after Labor Day at Jung and Royce."

"He's a lawyer," Dad shouted at Mom. Mom just nodded and kept chewing.

Aunt Elle wasn't ready for her turn to be over. "What kind of lawyer?"

Mark held his own during dinner, even

131

managing to eat between the questions. At some point, his foot moved against Ann's. She let her knee rest against his, relaxing at his touch on one side and ignoring the stiff disapproval from her sister on the other.

After their meal, everyone but Dad and Elle helped clear the table. Mark was shooed out of the kitchen by Ann's mother. "Go, keep Ray out of trouble. There's got to be a football game on somewhere, but don't try to turn the volume too loud. He can't hear it, anyway."

Mark agreed, casting one last look at Ann's hand, then at her face, as if to gauge the level of her discomfort.

Once the dishwasher was humming and Rachel had taken the dessert tray into the living room, Ann's mother began an interrogation of her own. "Are you seeing that young man?"

Ann shifted slightly so that she could look through the wide passage into the living room. She stared at the young man in question, who, having given up at shouting at her father, now apparently enjoyed the football game on television, communicating with him through some kind of male hand-signal camaraderie. Her father hadn't sent the "rescue me" look to Rachel or her mother yet. "I'm seeing him right now, talking to Dad."

Mom watched them, too. "They seem to be getting on."

Ann poured them each a cup of coffee and fixed the cream and sugar for her mother. She took the cup and placed it in her hands. Ann's mother fingered her arm to stop her from moving away. "Ann, do you know what you're doing?"

Ann covered her mother's hand with her own. "He's been kind to me, Mom. I don't know what's going to happen, but right now, I'm happy."

"But, what about . . . Have you heard anything? About Gene?"

Ann shook her head and moved from under her mother's hand. "No. It's time to move on, don't you think?"

"Yes, I do. How have your headaches been?"

"Not so bad. Let's join the others."

Ann settled in a chair near Mark, while her mother sat next to her husband on the sofa, in between the men. Elle studied all of them, while Rachel ignored everything in favor of her dessert.

Mark tasted a piece of Rachel's blueberry pie. "This is delicious, Rachel."

Dad noticed their exchange. "What was that?"

"Mark was just complimenting Rachel on the pie," Mom told him.

"Yes, doesn't my daughter make good pie?" Their father continued to eat his piece. Ann watched Aunt Elle sip at her tea, amusement rippling the air around her chair.

Rachel hopped to her feet a few moments later. "Let me take your plates."

Ann got up and reached for Mark's plate. "Stay here, visit with the folks," she told him and headed for the kitchen.

Rachel came back for another stack of plates and cups then followed her to the kitchen. "Are you insane? Are you that desperate that you've taken to cradle robbing?"

"Rach — he's a guest in my house. So are you. And what would I have to be desperate about?"

"I remember him. He's that boy who used to take Ritchie fishing, isn't he?"

"That was a long time ago. He's a well-respected attorney. He's over thirty. I think that makes him no longer a boy."

Rachel jerked the handle of the faucet. "Ha! And how old are you?"

"Old enough to know better than to listen to you." Ann handed her a plate to rinse.

"You never did, anyway." The plates

chinked together in the sink. "Ann, what are people going to think?"

"About what? And take it easy, will you? That's the good stuff."

"About you and your escort. Honestly, have you lost your mind?"

"Since when did we worry about what people think?" Ann told her, handing over a coffee cup. "Be careful with that. And I give it five minutes, tops."

Rachel shook off water drops before setting the delicate cup in the drain. She faced Ann. "No one will want him as a lawyer."

Rachel stoked Ann's fear with icy fingers. Still, Ann snorted. "Why ever not? I'm not cursed, Rachel."

Ann could hear the shuffling commotion from the living room and turned away from her sister. Mark hesitated on the threshold. "I think your folks are getting ready to leave." He looked from her crossed arms to Rachel's stance at the sink while she dried her hands. He went to the pot of cider, poured two cups and offered one to Rachel.

"Thank you," Rachel said, her words low and terse.

Mark took the second cup to Ann, then stood close behind in protection mode. He said nothing, as if waiting for some kind of signal Ann wasn't sure she knew to send.

Rachel's puckering lips met the rim of her cup as her cinched eyes watched their interplay.

Ann swirled the contents of her cup, her thoughts equally dizzying. Rachel was jealous. Why hadn't she seen that earlier? Mark must have noted it right away, with that sixth sense he'd developed from assessing juries.

Ann's mother stuck her head into the kitchen from the hall. "Dad's nearly ready to go. How about you, Rachel? Do you need some more time?"

Rachel shook her head. "No, Mom. I'll just get our things arranged." Their mother nodded and took herself away from the tension in the kitchen. Rachel rinsed her cup.

Ann brushed against Mark before stepping away. "Let me help."

Rachel glared while Mark took the cup from Ann. Her expression melted into nothing as she continued to look in Mark's direction. Ann turned from the refrigerator to see Mark drink from her cup, while he stared back at Rachel.

Ann's parents were dressed for the outdoors, ready to depart. Mark couldn't recall Tiffany bothering with a coat, even in Wisconsin winter. "Why?" she would say.

"We're just going to the car, then inside." She probably never gave wraps a thought in Arizona or Florida, or wherever they were. Ray, helped on either side by Alice and Elle, shuffled into the kitchen. "Thank you, daughter," he boomed in the megaphone tone of the deaf. "Good dinner. Fine company." His cheery farewell acknowledged all of them. Mark nodded, watching while Ray took Ann's sister and his wife's arms and guided them toward the garage door, in a show of independence. "I like to see her happy," he said to Alice. "Did you see that, Alice? Your daughter is happy."

Mark read sympathy on Alice's face. Not disapproval, like Rachel's stiff back indicated, but more of a challenge. Were he and Ann ready for society's reaction? Mark appreciated Ann's mother's acknowledgement of him. What did Ray understand about the two of them being together? Rachel would be hard on her sister.

He heard Ray's voice echo in the garage. "Nice man. Not so young. I like him. He made Ann smile."

"Get in, Dad." Rachel's voice competed with the late November chill.

Ray wasn't finished talking. They could still hear his voice bouncing off the cement floor. "Where was Maeve today?"

Ann's aunt shut the door on them. She bent over her cane with crossed hands, mingled true and false jewels sparkling as she tottered in an unconvincing shuffle. Elle lifted the cane to point in the direction of the living room. "Let's have one more cup of tea, shall we?"

Mark cocked his head, looking at Ann for a hint of what to expect. Ann looked both perplexed and nervous, not unlike a client of his about to be cross-examined despite their best preparation. He followed the women into Ann's living room. Before he fully cleared the entrance, the older woman brandished her cane at him. "You're not hiding anything from me."

Mark raised his arms and folded them across his chest. Ann's aunt was quick. He did not want to act outside of Ann's comfort zone, but neither did he want to act merely on her cues. He needed to prove to others that his love for Ann was genuine. If everyone else believed it, Ann would have to know that being associated with him was nothing to be ashamed of.

Ann stepped in between them. "Aunt Elle, quit the Macbeth routine. No one will believe you anymore, anyway."

Elle straightened, changing character so fast Mark wondered at the depth of her craziness. The dipping cane accidentally rubbed against Ann's hand, the one with the red welt. Mark felt her wince before he saw the expression of pain on her face, the chagrin on Elle's. He grabbed Ann's elbow and led her to the sofa. "Here, sit. I'll get something for that."

Mark ignored Elle and went to the first aid kit he knew Ann kept in the laundry area. He returned to see Elle seated on a chair opposite Ann, the two of them avoiding facing each other. "I should have done this earlier," he said, squatting beside Ann and taking her hand. While he smoothed on antiseptic lotion and taped gauze over her crimson weeping burn, he noted the hint of cerulean beneath the eye makeup she wore. Had she been sleeping well? She looked trembly and frail, although she held her hand still while he tended to her. His heart ached to think she worried about anything and hoped he hadn't caused her this grief. Mark gave her an analgesic and watched her drink. He'd ask her about the other medication he found in her cupboard when they were alone.

Mark was then ready to face Elle. "Can I warm up your tea, Elle?"

"Thank you." The woman held out her cup, which Mark took back to the kitchen along with the first aid kit. He returned to the low murmur of their voices.

"— two-day wonder." Ann was pouting. She raised her eyebrows at Mark, forcing a smile. Mark handed the cup and saucer to Elle, then joined Ann on the sofa.

Elle juggled the handle of the cup and edge of the plate, nearly dumping the hot contents in her lap before she set it on the side table. "While I doubt anyone cares about Gene being cuckolded, I don't think this man can stand being treated like a gigolo. I may have to take him away from you."

Mark, surprised at the slant of Elle's attack, started to laugh and throw an arm around Ann until the glistening distress in her eyes stopped him. He took her hand instead, and raised her fingers to his lips. With his gaze locked on Ann, he told Elle, "I love Ann. I would never demean her. And Gene Ballard is dead. A dead man can't be a cuckold."

"Ah. Is that your professional opinion, mister lawyer?" Elle raised her brows. "What evidence do you have that the woman's husband is dead?"

"No one's heard from him in all this time. None of his accounts have been accessed, a police investigation has revealed nothing.

Anyone can get a legal judgment of death with those criteria." He made himself stop there. She hadn't asked for his personal views, but he had little doubt that would come.

"I wouldn't tell Gene's mama, young man. That woman has held onto her beliefs like a grizzly over her cub all this time. What I really want to know is, what on earth do you think you have to gain? Either of you."

Ann's eyes were closed. Her hair fanned around her head as she lay against the back of the sofa. Mark kept her hand as he settled sideways to face Elle. Ann gave no indication of answering her aunt. Mark let the arguments swirl before they coalesced into a coherent semblance. Elle was as tough as any judge. "Because you obviously love Ann, I concede the point that our personal lives could possibly be considered your business. At least in part." He peeked at Ann for some acknowledgment. Her eyes remained closed.

Elle smirked while the teacup jiggled in her hands. "Son, I'm the least of your worries, and I'm on your side." She set the cup down again and settled back, crossing her wrinkled hands on her lap. "Go on, practice on me. Work up a good defense, Counselor."

Ann sat up. "We shouldn't have to." Mark

noted how deep the lines delved between her brows.

"You saw how Rachel acted." Elle wriggled and pulled her scarf straight. She addressed her niece. "I'm willing to bet Mark's already tested the waters, so sure he is of being in love."

Ann took in an audible breath. "Is that so? Mark?" She tried to pull her hand from his.

He resisted her attempt to free herself from his grip. This wouldn't be the only time he could possibly hurt her. "The gossip started after the symphony. So and so reported seeing us together to the person whose seats we took that night." He took her hand in both of his, not apologizing, but trying to find a firm foundation on which to hold his ground.

"What gossip?"

They conversed in front of Elle, as if she was not there. "We can't stop rumors, Ann," Mark said. "We've been seen together, so people draw conclusions. It's human nature. I'm not going to hide."

"There's hiding and there's being discreet."

Elle coughed. "Discreet? Like you're having an affair?"

"That's my point, Ann." Mark risked a

142

glance in Elle's direction, to find the older woman facing the mantle, pretending to distance herself from the discussion. "You said earlier we are just ourselves," Mark said in a low voice. "But others are going to ask. Elle's right. I don't want anyone to think badly of you."

Ann turned to him after pursing her mouth at her aunt. "And you have your reputation, Mark. Rachel . . . Rachel said, too, that no one would want you for a lawyer."

Mark snorted. "Well, that's a little far out in left field." He stole another glance at Elle, who now seemed to be fascinated by the painting of a covered bridge Ann had hung between her wide front windows. He lowered his voice another notch and was rewarded by the older woman's inclination in their direction. "Besides, being involved with you makes me intriguing. Everyone will want to come to me, if just to —"

Elle crowed. "I knew it!" Her distraction gave Ann enough time to grab one of her pillows and smack his chest. He snatched it, pretending to be wounded and swooned lengthwise on the couch, their laughter in the background. At their silence, he opened one eye. Aunt and niece stared at each other.

Elle reached for the cane and used it to

raise herself. She gathered the scarf about her. "I'd better be going." She turned toward the hall.

Ann jumped up and took two steps toward Elle. "You said you were on our side."

"What good is one old woman?" Elle maneuvered herself to the closet, Ann close behind.

Elle's shuffle no longer seemed feigned to Mark. "Can I drive you home, Elle?"

Ann held her aunt's coat. She patted Ann's cheek. "Yes, he's a good man, dear." To Mark, she said, "I meant it when I said I'd like to steal you away. Some other time I'll let you drive me, but not today. Enjoy the rest of the holiday. I know how you lawyers work. Figure out ways to be thankful."

They walked Elle to the door and watched while she drove off. Alone now, Mark drew Ann to him and kissed her as he couldn't do with her family watching. "Come. Let's sit some more." On the way back to the living room, he pushed the switch that started the gas fire with a gentle whoosh and instant flash. Mark let Ann deflate against him once they resettled on her sofa. Every sigh seemed to make her smaller, weightless. They watched the blue and gold flames pretend to comfort them with projections of light. Ann shivered, curling closer to Mark.

He slowly stroked her arms as she leaned against him. "You want me to turn up the heat?"

"No, this is enough."

Mark felt a sigh and controlled it. He was worried about the other bottle he'd found in her medicine cabinet. Did he have a right to snoop yet? "How is your hand?"

Ann wiggled her fingers. "All right."

"I found a prescription pain med in the bathroom. Headaches? You get migraines?"

"Mmhm. Sometimes."

"Bad?"

"They can be."

Lethargy began to seep into Mark's bones. "What triggers them?" He hoped it wasn't stress.

She rubbed her nose in his shirt, an intimate gesture that made him smile. "Seems like mostly change in weather. I don't know. The pills help."

"You're okay now?"

"Very okay."

He wished they were already married so he could stay here with Ann squeezing his ribcage and melding to his side as if she belonged. He shook his head. "I like your family."

"Even Elle?"

"Especially Elle."

"She's right, I guess."

"About what?" Mark brushed his lips across Ann's temple, only half paying attention to her talk.

"I hoped we could be a momentary distraction and then forgotten with the next scandal —"

"Scandal!" Mark pulled back.

"You know what I mean. News. Anyway, if you've already talked about us —"

"It's not like that." Mark made a rueful frown. "Not exactly."

"What did Aunt Elle mean, then?"

He shook his head. "I don't understand what she was getting at, either. But, I think John Moseby thinks something. I don't read him as —"

"Moseby? At the company?"

"Parsons was talking —"

"What on earth? You are all worse than a bunch of little old ladies." Ann wagged a finger under his nose. "How in the world did you meet John Moseby?"

In all fairness, he probably should have told Ann about the card game night. So much had happened in between. He did not ever want to hide anything from her. "Parsons got some guys together, just for laughs."

"My lawyer, Jim Parsons?"

"Yes, the one who gave me the symphony tickets and works at my office. Um, Ann, I don't think there's anything to be alarmed about. I held them off for now, explained about how I used to live next door."

"So you reduced us to neighbors? Or were you being either nice or hit upon by a lecherous old woman?"

Enough with the guilt trip. He told her he loved her. And she was not what she said. But maybe he was. Mark leaned over Ann to quiet her with a kiss. "None of the above. Remind me to refrain from cross-examining you. The only thing I know about Moseby is that he has a healthy respect for you." He punctuated his statement with another kiss.

Ann returned the kiss. "That's probably good. He and Paula went through a lot over the past year. He's never said anything to me at work about . . . us, I guess." Ann trailed her lips along his jaw.

Much as Mark hated to, he took a deep breath and moved away, faking interest in the fire. Yeah, lecher, give it a rest. Time enough, if Ann agrees with your proposal. But when the time was right.

Ann seemed to accept his drawback and returned to the topic of her family. "Dad and Mom liked you." Ann shucked her pumps and curled her toes under a cushion. "I'm glad you were here today."

Should he ask about her sister's feelings? Rachel had been obviously upset. But why? "Rachel —"

"Rachel doesn't even like herself. Don't let her get to you."

Mark couldn't stay separated from Ann. He shifted her head to his shoulder and brushed the soft strands of hair. "Family is nice. I've spent the last few years so busy that I never allowed myself the luxury of holidays." Mark felt Ann's cool fingers along his throat when she reached back to touch him.

"Wow. What about your friends? Allison? You must have come back once in a while before your folks moved."

"Allison's folks live in Australia. And I did come back."

"Why didn't you come by?"

"It just didn't seem right."

Ann turned to put her lips next to his, teasing him. "That was probably a good idea."

Mark shifted so their mouths met. "Mmm."

"I've got a good idea of my own," Ann said.

Mark tensed. *Oh, please, Ann, please don't ask me.*

"Why don't you stay here tonight?"

He wondered how he would react if he ever allowed them to get carried away with their feelings. Sparks of passionate dreams had been quickly thrust away. He'd barely adjusted to the knowledge that Ann would even consider being with him. Coward. A tremble in his fingers and chest made him hold Ann away so he could face her. Gently. "I want to. I can't lie about that. But I'm not going to."

He caught Ann's hand when she strayed toward his stomach. "Stop that, Ann. You can't imagine how hard this is for me. I want you to know that I respect my faith first, you almost as much, but also myself. I don't need to sleep with someone I'm not married to. I love you too much for that."

Ann stared at him, her eyes dark and wide. "Are you telling me that you've never —"

Mark's mouth felt dry while his stomach churned. Didn't anyone appreciate how hard that had been? All those years of desperately wanting to be close to someone, to be part of someone else, but not hearing God whisper yes? Until now? Even hurting Allison. "No, I haven't. In my mind being married was always worth the wait."

149

"Even while you were engaged to —"

"Allison. And that was part of the problem."

"That you wouldn't sleep with her? What kind of hussy —"

"No." Mark tugged Ann's jaw to keep her facing him. "The problem was I couldn't forget you. You supported me, made me feel as if I could be worth something. Do you know you were the only adult who came to my basketball games to watch me play? Dad and Tiffany showed up late to my graduation. None of them came out when I finished at Georgetown. You sent a card and a gift."

"So, I'm some kind of surrogate mother."

"Ann! No! I'm trying to explain the impact you had — have — on me. It's not just that I saw the kind of home and family I wanted with someone like you — with you. This is where I came to saving faith. This is where my ideals, goals, were set. Nothing, no one, no other place, was good enough, comfortable. I wanted to come back here, to find you. See you. See if you could ever feel that way about me."

He could see her try to comprehend his sentiments as she stared down at his hands wrapped around her forearms. She apparently made up her mind to accept his statement and turned to snug herself against him again, to draw his arms around herself. "Wow. But, okay. Honestly, there hasn't been anyone else, since — since Gene." Ann suddenly thrust his arms away and jerked around to look at him. "Maybe there's something wrong with me. Maybe I'm frigid or something. You're a healthy young man, with needs and desires. You should —"

Mark used his favorite method of silencing her, strengthened now by knowing that she wouldn't test his resolve more than he could bear. When he broke off the kiss, he said, "Believe me, there is nothing wrong with either of us." He filled his lungs. "Despite what society tries to preach, people who share convictions about morality are not out of touch with reality."

"But, Gene. We never got together to talk about what I should do."

"I was thinking about that. With Jim as your lawyer, I could talk to him, find out where he's at with the case. Then you and he could go from there. But I'll be able to advise you, too. If you want." He grinned. "No charge."

"Ha."

Ann seemed lost again as he watched her stare at the flames. Time for a dash of cold water. Was she ready for the next step he planned? "Speaking of conviction, I would like it if you'd come to church with me on Sunday."

"That's very public. We'll probably stir more than talk with a bunch of office guys. Are you ready for that?"

"I've only been waiting for the right time to ask you."

Mark watched her mentally withdraw from stoking their passion. Would she pull back all the way, decide not to risk further involvement? He'd almost convinced himself their relationship could never be mutual when she surprised him.

"I'd like that. Maybe I've just been waiting for an excuse to stop going to my church simply because it's what I've always done." Ann now looked to him as if he held the answers to a question she didn't know how to phrase. "I want to understand more."

Mark debated what to say. "It's been a long time since the days of the church youth group. You didn't seem to mind that Ritchie went with me to my church then. At least, one night a week."

"You were quite enthusiastic, as I recall." Ann smiled with just the left side of her mouth.

Mark could see by the way Ann folded her arms in front of her that he'd pushed far enough. "Let's get coffee. And a piece of pie."

CHAPTER EIGHT

Mark sucked in a deep breath after he exited his car. He parked in the shadow of the great edifice which made up the administration sector of Hope Church. Since Mark had been away, Hope had grown from a rented storefront to a private campus with three buildings, including a main sanctuary that accommodated five hundred worshippers at a time for the five services on Saturdays and Sundays.

He'd called earlier in the week, asking if Gary St. Clare, the pastor from his youth, could see him, catch up the news. St. Clare met Mark at the door to an imposing office suite and greeted him with a hug. St. Clare ushered him into an office which no longer sported a folding table and metal chairs in a room of cement block walls. This room was decorated in mauves by a professional, Mark noted. He'd learned in his law career that atmosphere was nearly as important as speech when making a case.

Gary St. Clare wore a gray suit and tie to work in the commodious office. The senior pastor had influenced Mark's life since Mark first made a profession of faith before graduating from high school, and Mark had simply wanted to talk about his feelings for Ann with someone he liked and trusted. Mark was surprised to see St. Clare dressed so formally during a week day. He hadn't done that in the past. Perhaps he had other meetings lined up.

After sharing prayer, the men exchanged personal news.

"I'm delighted to know you've returned. On your way out, I'll give you the newsletter and some brochures. There are many opportunities for you to step in to help."

"Thank you."

St. Clare sat back in his leather chair and crossed his legs. "You have the appearance of a man with a dilemma."

Mark had considered several ways to broach the subject. A dilemma? Well, that put a label on the reason for his visit.

"I'm not in trouble." Where did that come from? Mark cleared his throat and took another tack. "I'm involved with a woman." At St. Clare's raised eyebrows, he rushed on. "Whom I hold in the highest regard. In fact, she's the reason I returned to Clayton. You know I was engaged back in Virginia to a very nice girl. It just didn't work out. And part of the reason was because I couldn't forget about this woman, and I think Allison, my former fiancée, knew that."

"I'm happy for you, Mark. I was sorry to hear about you and Allison, especially when you seemed so happy at first."

"I'd always planned to come back to Wisconsin. Since Trey died and my parents left, and I don't have any other family here, it might seem strange."

St. Clare smiled. "But —"

"I hoped that if I invited Ann here to church with me, that she would be welcome."

"Of course. Why would you ask a thing like that? Unless you're asking my permission to date someone who has rejected our Savior. You know I can't condone that. 'Be not yoked unequally with unbelievers; for what common ground is there between righteousness and lawlessness.' "

Mark wondered who he was supposed to be: the righteous or the lawless. "Ann hasn't rejected Christ. You can't make that kind of judgment without knowing her. You taught me to look both at context and words, Pastor," Mark responded to St. Clare's quote. "The Apostle is speaking the whole time of reconciliation, not of separation. And not necessarily of marriage in that particular passage of his letter to the Corinthians."

"Many people try to justify their actions by interpreting scripture to suit their needs." St. Clare said. He removed gold-rimmed half-glasses and tapped them in his palm. "If this woman is not saved, you should not be romantically, or otherwise, involved with her."

"I didn't say she wasn't saved, only that she currently attends a different church." He did not want to play the scripture game. "And anyway, doesn't Paul also write 'the unbelieving wife has been sanctified through her believing husband'? Pastor, I don't want to get into a theology of judgment with you." St. Clare opened his mouth. Mark ignored him. "I can't presume to know the state of her salvation. I merely said I'd invited her to attend worship here."

"Why would you worry that she might not be welcome?"

Mark took a deep breath. "I guess that was the wrong way to put it. She has many acquaintances in Clayton. She's lived around here all her life. It might look odd for her to be seen with me."

"Why?"

"She was married."

"Was? Or Is? A married woman contemplating a relationship outside the sanctity of marriage? Mark, you know better."

"Her husband is dead."

"A widow? Mark, there's nothing wrong with having a relationship with a widow."

"Actually, he's presumed dead. For many years."

"Mark, you didn't tell me Ann's last name. I can guess, based on the facts you've shared. You stayed in touch while you were out east. I value the faith you've kept much more than your support of the ministry we do here. But I think you're making a serious mistake, getting caught up in a situation that can only lead to your spiritual downfall."

"Ann would never hurt me."

"Not intentionally, I'm sure. There's a reason behind the saying 'the road to hell is paved with good intentions'. Men of greater wisdom and authority than either of us have tried to rise above the exhortation of God." St. Clare reached a hand to Mark in supplication. "I couldn't stand watching you fall, Mark, especially when you've just returned."

"Can't you see that Ann is poised on the

step? She wants to hear the word, to believe. How can you push us away? We've done nothing wrong, Pastor."

"Having a relationship with a woman who is married to another will always be wrong."

"Is there nothing we can do?" Mark held his breath waiting for the pastor's response.

"What do you want me to do? Turn back the clock? Where would that leave you? Mark, I urge you to put your whole heart and mind into serving the Lord. Don't get caught up in the sinful nature."

"But that's what I'm trying to do. I want our relationship to be honest and in tune with God's will."

"How can you know that?"

Mark exhaled. "She has tried in the past to seek a finding of death. The man's mother opposed that action."

"It is hard to give up hope."

"Hope of what?" Mark stood. "Ann doesn't want to be a burden to anyone. We just want to have the past settled."

St. Clare returned the glasses to his nose. "Scripture also says that younger women should not be put on the widows' list, but should marry." He seemed to study Mark before getting to his feet and coming around the desk.

"I've always liked you, Mark, but I'm

concerned about you. The concepts of love and marriage, and duty and faith shouldn't interfere with each other, nor should they be considered lightly." St. Clare set his hand on Mark's shoulder. "I wonder what I would say if my daughter Sara came to me with a fiancé who was much younger than she. How would I feel? I find myself suspicious of the true nature of the relationship. The Ballards are quite wealthy."

Mark's neck and shoulders tensed. "Ann married into the Ballard name. They keep her husband's money from her. She has to work. And you know I don't need any more money."

St. Clare let his hand drop to his side. "What would you and she get out of declaring Mr. Ballard deceased? That's the question everyone wants to ask, isn't it?"

Mark paced half a dozen steps away, swallowing his anger, before facing St. Clare. "I never thought you would take this stand."

"You feel I'm betraying you."

"Yes."

"If you already knew what you wanted me to say before you came, you could have saved us both time by telling me first. If you just wanted to tell your story, you could have simply sat in your car and shouted at the back wall of the church." St. Clare's stern expression melted into sympathy. "I apologize. I thought you wanted to listen as well as talk."

The tension moved down Mark's torso, making every heartbeat a chore. He blinked his eyes rapidly. "I do want to hear you. That's why I came. I just didn't expect —"

"You wanted to be able to say your pastor agrees with you."

Mark let St. Clare's statement settle about him before responding. "I guess so. I wanted to be right, more than I wanted to hear. I wanted to know that someone else was on my side."

"That's all right, son. For the record, I don't think you're wrong. Just idealistic, which is not a bad thing to be, either. But consider this. If you feel so defensive around people you know and trust, how are you going to react when strangers believe they have the right to offer their opinion?"

Mark's heart took two painful thumps. "You're right, of course. I haven't even told my father."

St. Clare leaned against his desk and folded his hands. "There was a lot of anger there, after Trey's death. Even though there was only the other boy's word about who was behind the wheel, a death is not something forgiven."

"Trey was wild. Everyone knew that."

"Your stepmother may not agree."

"I love Ann, not her son. Dad and Tiffany won't have to see him, if they don't want to."

"Tell me, does this woman return your feelings?"

"Yes."

"And have you discussed marriage?"

Mark shook his head.

"If I could tell you one thing," Mark's pastor said, "it would be tie up those loose threads before you consider permanent decisions. And I have a hard time repeating Paul's dictum that it's better not to be married. I've been blessed for eighteen years."

That Sunday, Ann waited in her customary place in the foyer of her house for sight of Mark's car. Three inches of snow had fallen the previous afternoon. Ann left her coat unbuttoned and tapped a heeled foot, still debating whether to wear boots.

Since Ritchie's wedding, pew mates and guild members at Clayton Presbyterian asked Ann how her son and his new wife were handling marriage and when they might present her with a grandchild. When the news they sought wasn't forthcoming, they gradually drifted away. No one ever asked about Gene or her own life. Overcome with lethargy one Sunday morning, Ann gave in to her desire to stay home.

Until Mark asked her to go to Hope, to worship with him as he put it, she hadn't realized she'd let two months slide by since her last appearance at her own church.

She'd spent two hours last night discarding outfits, trying combinations of clothing she forgot she owned. Ann was not certain how formally people of Mark's church dressed. Would the women wear slacks? Did she have to put something on her head?

Ann hurried out the door, locking it behind her, before he could come to her. "Hello."

"Good morning, Ann. You're ready?" Mark followed her to the passenger side of his car and opened the door for her. His smile made her feel brave. Beneath his topcoat, she could see neat slacks. Hopefully her skirt and sweater wouldn't be too out of place.

He turned to help her with the latch of the seat belt, a chore she made difficult for herself by wearing gloves. "You'll be fine." Ann closed her eyes as his finger drew a straight line between her brows and down her nose. "Nothing to worry over." The gentle brush of his lips over hers stirred nascent love into a harmony of peace and courage. Mark adjusted his own belt before driving. "The snow is beautiful, isn't it? Looks like your plow guy did a good job."

Ann drew in the still-new scent of the car mingled with the freshness of outside that lingered yet on their coats. "You said a lot of people go to Hope?"

"Yes. Many more than before I left. You know the new place they built. They have five services over the weekend."

"Oh. I suppose I remember reading about the building, but I didn't relate it to the church you used to attend. I didn't know there was such a big church around Madison."

Mark glanced her way before turning east onto the beltline. "Hope's not the only one of its size."

When Mark neared the huge complex of buildings that made up Hope Church, Ann realized how seldom she ventured to that side of town. Her world had shrunk to visiting her family to the west in Sauk City, or north to Portage where Ritchie and Colleen lived. Other essential places that made up her routine were in Clayton.

"Looks like I'll have to park in the back rows," Mark broke into Ann's reverie. "Would you like me to drop you near the front door?"

"Oh, no. I can walk with you. It doesn't look icy to me. There sure are a lot of cars here."

"Yes. With Christmas coming up, I suppose people are staying around more, practicing music or getting ready for the program."

Ann let Mark hold her arm. At her hesitation, Mark tugged on her sleeve, offering an excited smile. Stepping through the wide portal into a two-story open atrium, echoing with music and voices, Ann wondered if they had mistaken this place for a shopping mall. Mark took her coat and hung it next to his. When she caught his grin, she realized she'd been staring at the coffee counter staffed by middle-aged women in colorful aprons. A nearby windowed door painted "Gifts of Hope" stood ajar, a steady river of customers entering or leaving. Ann raised her eyebrows at Mark. "Wow. I would never have guessed church would be like this."

He steered her toward double doors guarded by ushers holding stacks of programs. "Things have changed. Hi, Darrin," he greeted the man on the left. "This is Ann."

Ann nodded, but held up her hand against

the proffered papers. "Hello. Oh, no thank you, I'll share." She followed Mark to a row of comfortable padded chairs in front of a curtained stage decorated with poinsettias and small potted Norway pines. Two huge screens flanked the setting, flashing announcements and music and pictures. Mark quietly greeted a few others around them and introduced her. Ann smiled and returned a hand squeeze here and there, filing names and faces away. She recognized no one. The service began with what Ann would consider a concert. She heard few voices following the words on the screens while three guitarists, a drummer and a young lady with a tambourine beat out music. The songs were considerably different from those she sung accompanied by organ or piano at Clayton Presbyterian. Ann enjoyed them, but still wouldn't call her experience so far "church."

A man bounded onto the stage after the curtain closed on the praise band.

Mark whispered again. "That's Pastor Tom Brennan, associate. He'll do some of the readings, then Gary St. Clare, the senior pastor, will give the message."

The older man who took his place at the podium appeared closer to Ann's age. He was jacketless, but wore a tie. She could pay more attention to a man in a tie. St. Clare's voice, magnified through the speakers, purled over the congregation at first, repeating the passage Brennan had read from Luke, but with subtly different wording. Slowly, the rhythm of the message grew into a rushing stream. Ann's fingers clenched her copy of the pew Bible, unable to look away from the disturbing images of international leaders thrown from the screens, punctuating the story of deception, from Matthew's account of Herod, the King who lied in an attempt to destroy the true King, through the ages of European kings and dictators and modern presidents.

St. Clare's voice dropped, drawing all attention back to him. "The worst, however, are those who don't even try to hide behind lies." The screen, blank for this statement, flashed Adolph Hitler, Idi Amin, Nicolae Ceauşescu, and Osama bin Ladin. "They spout beliefs of their own perception, their hearts and souls so corrupted by evil that they can't accept reality, even when they know it. This time of year, my friends, we celebrate truth. The truth of God's redeeming love. The truth of the depth of his riches and grace, that he lived and walked among us as the Messiah who washed away our sins in his blood. The truth that the Holy Spirit now dwells in each of us, and allows us to not only hear and know him, but to live in faith. Christmas is about seeking the Christ — not to reject him, but to know him. When you seek him in the light of sincerity, you will find him, not in your own perception of reality, but in peace and in honesty and in power."

The screen projected "Amen," iterated by the worshippers.

Know him. The concept was so foreign, yet attractive.

Ann jumped when Mark circled her shoulders. "Ann." She focused on the crinkles around Mark's eyes, then dipped to his mouth when he asked, "Are you ready to go?"

The rows of chairs near them were empty, although cliques of people still chatted. "Sorry. I was thinking about all of this."

"I could tell."

The chirp of Ann's phone buzzed deep in her purse. "Oh, my goodness. I completely forgot to turn it off. It's Rachel."

"It's okay, Ann." Mark sat back, waving to someone beyond Ann's line of sight.

"Rach? I'm at — Mom's sick? Okay. At Meriter? Okay. I hear you. Yes, I'll be right there. I have a right to — never mind. I'll be there soon."

CHAPTER NINE

Mark listened to Ann's side of the conversation, picturing Ann's sister, who was obviously agitated. He could even hear an occasional word berating Ann.

"Mark? Mom's in the hospital. Rachel says she has pneumonia. I have to —"

"Which one?" Mark began to lead her out of the sanctuary. "I'll take you." He held her coat, which she accepted on the run.

Pastor St. Clare waved, his head cocked. One eyebrow raised meant Mark would receive a phone call later. Mark waved back. They hurried to his car.

"You'll come in with me, won't you?" Ann asked.

"I want to, if you don't think there will be any problem."

"What problem?"

Mark turned out of the lot onto the street. "I'm not a member of your family. Rachel might object."

"Let her. I'm not planning to fight with her about anything. We both have Mom's best interest at heart."

Mark had heard that sentiment many a time across a conference table between feuding family members. He didn't respond.

At Madison's Meriter Hospital complex, Mark dropped Ann off at the main entrance before winding around the ramp looking for a parking spot.

By the time he was directed to the elevator at 7 Tower, and found them in the Intensive Care waiting area, he could see Ann and her sister had gotten into some arm-waving debate. Ray leaned on his cane, bent as if in physical distress. The women kept their voices low. Mark approached Ray, making sure the older man saw him first, so as not to startle him. Ray's eyebrows met. His glasses were foggy, his lips thinned.

"Sir, I'm sorry to hear about your wife," Mark told him. Rachel and Ann took a pause to acknowledge his presence, then went back at it.

"I need . . . Could you —" Ray turned toward the hall. "Son, could you lend your assistance?"

Mark followed Ray's line of sight to the men's room. "Of course." Mark took up position on Ray's other side, and with a

170

backward glance at Ann, shuffled her father around nurses with clipboards into the hallway. Once behind closed doors of the men's room, Ray explained how his arthritic back and fingers hampered his ability to control the valves to empty his foley catheter.

" 's full. Could you . . . Careful. Ah, thanks. Dad-blamed prostate thing. Alice always helps me, but she's —"

"I understand." Mark emptied the bag at Ray's direction and washed up.

"Them girls. Rachel gets so excited. I had to call her, you know. They came and took Alice right away this morning. Couldn't wake her up. Oh, my."

"Are you all right, Ray? Do you want me to find a doctor?"

"Sakes, no. Just, I need to find out about Alice. Those girls don't pay heed like they should. The doctor should be talking to me first."

"Then let's get you back there where we can see what's going on." Mark accompanied Ray out to the waiting area again, where now the sisters sat side by side. Mark steered Ray to a seat across from Rachel, then lowered himself to a padded bench near Ann.

A physician arrived. Mark watched the

general dance of the doctor trying to speak to Ray, while Ray's daughters attempted to interpret the doctor's tangle of explanation to the deafened elderly man.

Mark was caught off-guard when Ray stamped his cane. "Come here, son, would ya?"

The patriarch stamped again. "Back, now, you girls. Mark, now, will ya listen for me? Doctor — explain it to him."

The white-coated young man of Eastern Indian descent apparently dealt with similar circumstances as a matter of course and switched gears without hesitation. "Alice is responding well to treatment. If her lungs continue to clear, we can release her in a day or two. We just want to be sure there's no chance of relapse and clear the infection. You can see her for a few moments when you're ready." He touched Ray's arm and hurried off.

Mark repeated the doctor's comments, making sure he held eye contact with Ray. That simple measure of making sure he had Ray's full attention helped them communicate. When they turned to the women, Rachel's streaming tears made Mark pause. Ann patted her sister's shoulders, a stiff set to her mouth and her eyes brittle with disappointment. Why?

"I'm sorry, Dad," Rachel muttered. Ray couldn't possibly have understood her. "Mom always said she didn't want any heroic measures taken to save her life. I thought she was dying."

Ray acted like he heard the word "dying," or maybe had become adjusted to seeing it on the lips of his friends. He came to attention over the cane. "You listen! We'll know when it's our time, and that time's not up yet. We don't give up so easily." Ray turned his back and thumped over to the nurse's station, where they could overhear him asking to visit his wife.

Mark watched as Ray was led to Alice's room before focusing on Ann. Was she getting one of her headaches? How bad would it be? Did she have her pills with her?

"He didn't mean it like that, Rach," Ann told her sister. "Come on, now. He can stay with me for a couple of days. I'm closer to the hospital."

"It's so hard, just so hard. I thought, with Maeve out of the house, I would have more time. Instead, everything's just worse." Rachel sobbed on her sister's shoulder. "I'm not mean."

"I know. We know." Ann looked up at Mark, twisting her lips into a smile, eyes now soft. "Thank you for being here. I can deal with this, if you need to go."

Mark moved to crouch in front of them and took Ann's fingers. "I have no doubt you can handle anything. I'll stay as long as you want me to." With a sideways glance at Rachel, he whispered, "Are you okay? No headache?"

Ann gave him a raised brow and a tiny negative shake.

Rachel's tears slowed to a trickle. "He'll want to say here with Mom."

"They don't have time to take care of him, too," Ann told her. "He'll just have to come home with me. I'll tell him that I'll bring him to visit here tomorrow whenever he wants."

Rachel straightened up and scrubbed at her cheeks. "Maybe he'll listen to you. I'll just run to the ladies room. Excuse me."

Mark took her place next to Ann and drew her to him, putting his lips in her hair. "I'm so sorry."

"It seems a relatively minor catastrophe in retrospect. If she really does get better. Pneumonia seems like a death sentence these days. I meant it, though. You don't have to stay if you have more important things to do."

Mark hid his smile as Ann pulled away from the circle of his arms, self-consciously glancing at the nurse's station. He watched as she smoothed her hair and straightened her sweater, ignoring him. When Ray reappeared, he handed the cane to Mark while he struggled into his jacket.

Rachel came in time to hear his announcement. "I'll stay with Ann for now. She can bring me here in the morning." Ray went to hug his younger daughter. "You were here when we needed you, and we are grateful. Now, you both go see your mother and then we'll go."

When Ann returned, Mark told her he'd go and pull the car up to the front entrance.

Rachel called after him. "Wait! I'll walk out to the ramp with you." Mark watched while she snatched up her purse and coat from the chair.

"You don't have to rush," he told her.

"Hospitals make me crazy," Rachel replied. "I have to get out of here."

They rode the elevator in silence. Mark knew Rachel would speak her mind when she was ready. Once in the echoing, cold, cement ramp, she stood on the sidewalk before speaking. "I'm over a couple of rows. Mark, I still think this whole relationship thing is all wrong. I'm sorry. You seem like a nice young man, but I can't imagine why you're after my sister. She doesn't have access to her husband's money, and although she lives in a nice house, she's barely making ends meet. I don't understand what you see in each other, and frankly, I don't want any details."

Rachel turned around. Of all the things Mark had learned as a child, the ability to wait was most useful.

Rachel spoke with her back to him. "Thank you for coming here. Dad seems to like you."

"I like him, too."

"So, what are you doing?'

"Right now, I'm waiting, Rachel. Just waiting."

Rachel offered him her profile, a curt nod. Her heels echoed on the pavement.

Mark chauffeured Ann and her father to pick up clothes and personal items at Ray and Alice's home in Sauk City, then back to Ann's house in Clayton. He helped Ray one more time with his particular need, then whispered about it to Ann. Ann whispered back that her mother had told her about the catheter situation when it first came up in the summer. "He's still thinking about surgery, since medication didn't help," Ann said. "He's a private man."

"I can tell." Mark took Ann in his arms to

say goodbye. "When things settle down, I want to continue our conversation from this morning."

"I thought you might. I just can't think about that right now, though."

"I know. Call me if you need help, okay?" Mark kissed her nose, then her lips. "I'll try and sneak a call in between clients."

"Well, if that's all —"

Mark unlocked the door to his apartment. Good. No messages for a change. He shrugged off his coat and hung it in the closet. A cup of coffee would be good right now. Mark closed his eyes while waiting for the machine to drip through. The echo of Annie's kisses felt soft on his mouth.

The next step was obvious. Ann said she was ready to try again for a judgment in Gene's case.

A thick file rested on the coffee table in the living room. Ann's past attempts had been blocked by Donna Ballard, and dutifully recorded in typewritten legalese. At each hearing, some hint at evidence pointing to the possibility Gene still lived would come to light just as Ann sat in the courtroom. The hearing would be postponed. Five years had gone by.

Mark perched on the sofa in front of the

documents. He settled his cup then folded back the cover of the top file. Gene's keys and empty wallet had been found since the last hearing. That should have been enough evidence to satisfy the older Ballard woman. Mark would make the case so air-tight no one could object. No one.

Jim Parsons had been involved the last time. Mark would talk to him, outside the office. Then Jim could work with Ann.

Mark turned next to the puzzling file on LMS Enterprises. Ann's son, legally named Eugene Ritchard Ballard, had come up as beneficiary on one of the documents. In another twist, a separately funded little trust hidden inside of the larger LLC, someone by the name of Richard Michael Smart was receiving regular payouts even now. If this affected Ann, he wanted to be sure she understood everything about the Trust before she went ahead. Donna might be able to accept her son's death by now and Mark wanted to think ahead. One trump she could play was to force Ann to sign away any rights to the Ballard money in exchange for the judgment. He would figure this out.

The telephone buzzed. Mark checked the glowing green lines on the LCD. Arizona. So, the folks were calling from their place in

Phoenix as opposed to Jupiter or Myrtle Beach.

"Tiffany."

"How are you?" Tiffany Roth never said hello or goodbye. Mark's step-mother jumped right into a conversation as if they had all left the breakfast table together this morning.

"I'm fine, Tiffany. How's Dad?"

"Oh, working on that handicap. Say, I hate to think of you with all that snow up there. Anyway, I wanted to let you know that if you try to call us on Christmas, we'll probably be out of cell range. Your Father and I are taking a cruise, one of those specialty yachts, you know, around the Caribbean. They only take six couples just to golf courses. Nevis, St. Croix, even Puerto Rico. Can you imagine?"

He couldn't. "It sounds like something you'll enjoy. And there's not too much snow up here right now. It's cold, though."

"Oh." The long pause meant Tiffany was searching for another question to ask. It certainly wouldn't be anything to do with asking him to join them, even if she was concerned about the weather.

Mark decided to cut her some slack. "My new job's going well. Madison and Clayton have changed a lot, obviously, since we've been gone. I like the people at Jung and Royce, and my assistant's working out just great."

"Assistant? You mean, you don't work alone? I thought lawyers had their own cases."

"Jennifer helps with scheduling and paperwork, and handles some of the questions."

"So, she's your secretary, then. Is she married?"

"Yes, she's married, very happily. The lights around the capitol grounds are gorgeous. You should see them."

"Perhaps. Your father's calling. I have to go. Call him soon."

Click. Moving right along, following their agenda, as always. Mark no longer had to wait for his parents to keep their promises. Before the divorce it was, "Just one more thing, Mark, then we'll take you to the park." Or, "Just hang on, we'll be there when we get this order out." After Mom died, he was shifted into his father's house. Soon after Dad and Tiffany had Trey. Then it was, "Sorry, Mark. Santa must be late this year. Never mind, we'll take you boys to the mall next week."

Maybe they felt the same. They no longer had to bother with another person in their way as they pursued the next golf course.

He was not ready to tell either of them about Ann. Pastor St. Clare was right. They'd been devastated when Trey died. Neither came right out in public and blamed Ritchie Ballard for the fatal rollover in Ritchie's new Jeep. The fact that Trey had alcohol in his blood and Ritchie did not salved none of their wounds. Ritchie insisted Trey had been driving that night, though nothing could be proven. Tiffany needed a lot of therapy after that. Dad retired and bought her two houses. Mark talked to them only a few times a year. He'd never been to any of their new homes.

So what? He had Annie now. They would spend Christmas together. At least he didn't have to bother tracking the folks down this year for the phone call of false cheer. Mark added coffee to his cup before returning to the living room to pick up the LMS Enterprises file again. After the holidays, he and Jim Parsons needed to talk.

CHAPTER TEN

Two weeks before Christmas, Ann called Mark for help to get her ten-foot artificial fir up from the basement. She hadn't brought it out in the last three years. Since Ritchie and Colleen went to her mother's house, Ann hadn't bothered to decorate much at all for the holidays. Everything had changed.

She handed Mark some glittering snowflake ornaments and watched while he studied the tree, apparently looking for just the right place to hang them. "How long has it been since you've trimmed a tree?"

Mark settled the last snowflake in the soft papery needles before answering. "I guess, never. Not really. The housekeeper mostly did it herself when I lived at home. During college and after, well, I didn't have any reason to."

"Not even when you were engaged?"

"Allison decorated her own place."

Ann bent over the ornament box, thinking. Apathy kept her joy of the season at bay since Gene had gone away. The shock and horror of the first year alone melted like candle wax across the calendar of Christmases since.

"I'm glad we're decorating this year, though." Mark took two more ornaments from her. "Thank you for letting me help you." He hooked them onto an empty wired branch. "How's this?"

Ann wrapped her arms around his waist. "Most worthy of a cookie, I think."

"Just one? I really worked up an appetite."

They walked arm-in-arm into the kitchen, where Ann heated water for hot chocolate.

Mark munched on one of her gingerbread cut-outs while they waited for the kettle to whistle. A rumble and scuffling noise from the garage made her frown. Mark put a hand on her arm in caution as she strode to open the door.

"Maeve!"

Ann's niece hustled in cold air with her swirling cape. "Auntie Ann!"

"Where have you been? I've left messages —"

"This is him? Mark?" Maeve marched toward him, pulling along a dark-haired person attached to her other hand. "Nice to

meet you. I'm Maeve, this is Chandra."
Maeve wore an exotic scarf wrapped tightly
around her head and under her chin.

"What's going on? Did you take over Aunt
Elle's wardrobe?"

Maeve chuckled. "No. I've been busy,
that's all. Finals, the usual. You know. Aunt
Ann, I just came back for my things. I've
accepted an invitation to live at the House
next year."

Ann took a huge breath, forcing herself to
count to at least six before the words rushed
out. "What is going on? Did you talk to your
mother about this? I agreed to let you live
here."

"I know. I will. It's not your fault, or
anything."

Ann finally blinked and looked at the
person named Chandra. A similar silky-
looking scarf wound around her head and
neck. At least, Ann guessed she was a
woman. Chandra stood half a head over
Maeve, but was shapeless, dressed in a
ragged coat with some sort of wrinkled
dress hanging to the tips of beat-up hiking
boots.

"What's the House?"

"Chandra, stay here a minute while I go
pack up, okay?"

Chandra nodded and turned an eager face

in Mark's direction.

"Hello!" Ann was about to start yelling when Mark pressed her shoulder.

"Come, talk upstairs," Maeve invited, as she slipped out to the hall staircase.

Ann stomped after. She stood in the doorway to Maeve's bedroom while her niece jammed a few items of clothing and toiletries into her backpack.

"Auntie Ann, do you trust me?"

"You haven't given much opportunity."

"But you love me, right?"

"Well, of course I do. So does your mother and your grandparents. Just tell me what's —"

"I like him, Ann. Downstairs. Mark. And he's beautiful."

"Maeve!"

"I knew he would be, inside and out. I could feel his love even before I opened the door."

"Maeve, can we please talk about you?"

"Okay." Maeve zipped the bag and plopped on her bed. "The House is the Buddhist Retreat Center. I want to study there. It's my calling. Don't be mad."

"What about your degree?"

"I need to do this. Ann, I need your support."

Ann folded her arms. "How can I do that

when I don't understand why you're dropping out of college and moving in with a —"

"Stop!" Maeve leapt up. "Chandra is a wonderful person. You'll come to love her as much as I do. I promise." The young woman brushed by and thundered down the steps to the kitchen.

Ann followed, trying to check the fear and threatening tears. "Please! Maeve, I just want to understand."

"I can see why people say you look like your aunt, Maeve," Chandra said.

"What?" Ann felt dizzy. "What's that got to do with anything?"

Maeve kissed Ann. "Don't worry. I'll be in touch, okay?" Chandra followed. At the door, Maeve's friend faced them. "It was nice meeting you, Mark. Goodbye, Ann." She pulled the door closed behind her.

The overhead garage door rumbled down. Ann rubbed her arms. "What just happened?"

Mark stirred their mugs of hot cocoa and brought one to her. "What did it look like to you?"

She accepted the warm mug, wrapping her freezing hands around it before sipping. "Rachel will murder me."

"I won't let her." Mark tugged her elbow,

pulling her back to the living room. He plugged in the lights of the tree, turned down the others, then settled next to her on the sofa.

"What am I going to say?"

"What did Maeve tell you?"

"Just that she was dropping out of college and studying to be a Buddhist — whatever. I don't even know. She asked me if I loved her." Ann shivered and leaned forward to set her mug on the table.

"What did you say?"

"I told her that yes, I loved her."

Mark put his cup next to hers. He pulled her against him and bussed the top of her head. "Sometimes, that's the best thing you can do. And pray. So, she's supposed to look just like you? I didn't see it."

Ann sighed out some of the tension. "Yes. I'll show you pictures. It really cooks Rachel when people think she's my daughter." She pushed Chandra to the back corner of her mind for now.

Mark shifted. "Did you talk to your mom today?"

Ann shook her head, welcoming the change of subject. "Yes. She sounded perky and talked about getting back to her exercise class."

Mark chuckled. "Good for her."

"I haven't heard from Ritchie and Colleen yet. You'll come spend the day with me, anyway, won't you?"

He kissed the tip of her nose. "Some of it. I don't want to get in the way."

She put her hand against Mark's raspy cheek. "How long has it been?"

His eyes narrowed for an instant. She could feel the muscles changing shape under her palm as he formed words. "Five weeks and a day."

Ann brushed her mouth against his. "Only thirty-six days since I came to life. What did I do before you? There is no other way for me. Not any more."

Fern had already changed into her swimsuit when Ann rushed into the women's locker room at the Y on the Monday morning before Christmas. "Hi, there! Last day of classes, right?"

"And how." Fern handed Ann a towel. "The kids have ants in their pants. We have a nice family movie and snacks this afternoon. That's when they get really squirrely. I need this swim!"

Chlorine stung Ann's nose as they entered the pool area. Their laughter echoed on the tiled walls as they joined others who were already lapping the pool.

Afterward, they talked while showering and dressing.

"This Christmas will be different for you. Ann, love, I'm so happy for you. It's been hard, I'll admit now, watching you all these years. What you needed was a new man under the tree."

Ann gasped, looking around frantically to see who might have overheard. "Fern!"

Fern giggled while shimmying her nylon knee-hi's up her calves. "What does Ritchie think?"

"Ritchie and Colleen aren't sure they're coming this year."

They both thrust feet into shoes at the same time. "So you can hold off your surprise for a while, then." Fern said. "How's your mom?"

Ann adjusted Fern's golden pin, making the little bells jingle. "Doing well, thanks. She came over to make fruitcake with me a couple of days ago."

"All right! I'm so glad you didn't have to put her in one of those homes."

"They're in assisted living now, Fern. It's not like the death sentence a nursing home used to be. Sure, there are crummy places, but you have to watch. And there's also special rehab places, like half-way stops to retrain before going home."

"You're probably right. That's one area of my education I have purposefully neglected. I'm not ready yet." Fern grabbed her coat. "I can't do coffee, sorry. I have to set up the movie." She kissed Ann's cheek. "I'll see you at the party, right?"

Ann felt her mouth pucker and twisted it into a lopsided grin. "Of course. Wouldn't miss the company Christmas do. 'Bye, and Merry Christmas."

"Same to you, sweetie." Fern quick-stepped out of the locker room. Ann followed slowly. She had nothing scheduled until the evening, when Mark invited her over to his apartment for dinner. This would be her first visit to his place. On empty days like this, she envied Fern and her classroom of company. Ann went home to read and dream until their date.

In the womb of early winter, Ann searched for the right number on the correct building, anxious about being late. Mark must have been watching, for he stood waiting to let her in through the windowed door of the ground floor entry.

"Hi. Did you find me okay?"

Ann kissed his cheek. "Of course." The heat of his fingers through her knit gloves radiated up her arm as he led her up the stairs.

Mark unlocked the door and ushered her in.

"Nice view," Ann said, going immediately toward the large window. His building faced a wooded area. "You don't have to look in your neighbor's windows."

"That part's nice." Mark took her coat and hung it in his closet. "Dinner will be ready pretty soon."

"It smells heavenly."

Mark grinned. "Never fail crock pot stew. It's about the only thing I make from scratch." The grin turned into a grimace. "That and lots of toasted cheese sandwiches."

"Can I help with anything?"

"Thanks, but I've got it. Make yourself at home. Can I bring you tea or something?"

"Yes, I'd like tea."

While Mark went into his kitchenette, which was separated from the rest of the room by a half-wall with a counter, Ann walked around. "You must like blue a lot."

"What? Oh, the furniture. I'm renting, you know. The place came furnished." He brought a mug to her. "But, yes, I do like blue." He ducked back behind the half wall.

"Who's Lucy?"

"I don't know," Mark called from his place at the stove. "What do you mean?"

"Someone named Lucy sent you a fax." Ann had stopped at his work station and stood looking at a cheerfully colored sleigh and Christmas greetings in large round handwriting. The "i" was dotted with a snowflake. "I'm sorry. I'm prying. Never mind."

"Oh! You must mean Lacy. Yeah, she sent me a card from her computer at school."

Ann bit the inside of her cheek, not daring to ask another question.

Mark came to her. "How can I be so fortunate as to have two beautiful women concerned about my welfare?"

Ann couldn't check the double beat of her heart. "Uh . . ."

Mark picked up a framed photograph. "This is Lacy, a couple of years ago when she helped save her home in the mining case."

Mark had his hands on the shoulders of a washed-out looking young girl. Ann's lips turned upward.

"She calls me regularly to check up on me, and emails constantly. This is the first time she faxed." Mark set the picture down with a frown. "I hope she doesn't get into trouble."

Ann laughed. "Me, too. Lacy, huh?"

"Yes." Mark wrapped Ann in a hug. "What did you do today?"

"Not much. I went swimming with Fern, then lazed."

"I bet." Mark kissed her nose. "Why don't we try and meet, work out together? I don't mind giving up my lunch, and it would give us a chance to be together."

"We swim at the Y in Clayton. The pool is usually booked for lessons later."

"Oh." Mark's mouth brushed hers. "Does it have an exercise room? I could meet you there sometimes."

"But we wouldn't really be together in that crowd." She kissed him back. "Besides, I might turn into a Mrs. Universe if I worked out so much."

Mark tipped his head and stood back to study her. "Right. You're perfect the way you are."

Ann shook her head. "Only you."

A timer chimed. "Saved! Come, let's eat."

After being served by Mark and remarking that she could probably get used to being waited upon, Ann helped rinse dishes. "Thank you. That was a wonderful meal."

"You're welcome."

"Colleen called this afternoon."

"Oh?" Mark poured them each a coffee

and led the way to his living room.

"She said she and Ritchie want to come for Christmas Eve, then go in the morning up to her mother's." Ann anticipated his response.

"I'll stay out of your way. We can get together any time."

"They're not coming until after supper, Colleen said. Their church was having some kind of early service and potluck."

"I didn't know they went to church."

"Colleen does."

"That's good. All the same, you'll want time alone with them."

Ann held her cup in both hands. "I want you with me, Mark." She stared at a glass-covered framed print of a mountain landscape.

"Do we hold the same strategy, then? You be you, and I'll be me? That worked pretty well for your family."

"Mark." Ann swirled a piece of coffee ground floating in her cup.

"Don't you think Rachel or someone told them about us?"

"He would have called me."

Mark removed his arm from behind her shoulders. "So, then, what do you want?"

"I don't want to upset Colleen."

"Of course not." Mark set his cup on the

coffee table and leaned forward, elbows on his thighs, to stare out of the black rectangle of the picture window. "I don't even know what I would say. If it were Tiffany, I guess I wouldn't be shocked. But for you —"

"What about me?"

"You're so normal. And Ritchie is . . . volatile, I guess."

"Thanks." Ann stood.

Mark followed suit. "Ann."

"I'm sorry, Mark. I'm trying, I really am. I just keep remembering that time when he hit you."

"When he was in high school? We've met since, and been civil."

"I know." Ann circled the room and stopped in front of a crammed bookcase. "I just wish I knew what he would do." She fingered bound years of the In-Fisherman and Cabin Life magazines, dating back a decade. Kipling, C.S. Lewis, and a fat several-volume set of Wisconsin history tomes all vied for space.

"We always had this Natural Wisconsin magazine at home, too. This issue? I loved it. There are photos of Black Earth Creek, after the restoration project."

"I saw them."

"Did you read about the way streams naturally move across the landscape? Meander, they call it?"

"What about it?"

Ann fanned the pages. "Oh, I just liked the idea, that's all. Water wants to flow straight, until it hits a hard place. I didn't know that. The whole course of a river can change, to move around the rock. But it always wants to return to a straight path, so it bends."

She showed him the picture she liked most, an aerial view of a valley flattened by eons of rushing water, woven and scarred with twists and joins. "It bends so much that it meets its original path."

Mark's eyes brightened with laughter. "You're really into this."

Ann laughed, too. "I guess so. It just seemed like an analogy of me at the time. Meandering, after Gene left, looking for the straight path."

"Have you found it?"

"I'm beginning to think so. You see, what happens is that once the river runs on, the waters that were in the old curve are cut off and make a lake. Eventually they dry up." She held up the picture again. "And make scars. Meander scars." She closed the magazine and slipped it back in place. "I just liked the idea. Even after you find the right way, the hard times you went through influences the map of your life."

Wanting to change the subject, she pulled out a worn and patched black fabric volume. "These are sermons. From a long time ago."

"Yes. You'd be surprised at how much we haven't changed in the last two centuries. Ann, I won't hide. But I want you to be comfortable with whatever decision you make. If you think this is the right way to go — if your straight path is with me, I trust you, too."

Ann paced to a spot in front of the window, where she stared into the reflection of the room, with a solid Mark behind her. He was putting a lot of faith in her. She hoped she was worthy. "I want you to be with me, with us for Christmas Eve. That is, if you want to." Ann crossed her arms. "And, I want to feel it out. If he knows already, we can talk to him together. If he doesn't, then, let's just wait. His father — um . . . It's peculiar, isn't it?"

"To say the least." Mark's reflection melded with hers. Ann shivered as his arms enfolded her. "I'll come. We can't make everyone happy, but we'll have forever to work out the rest."

CHAPTER ELEVEN

After the three o'clock family Christmas service at Hope Church, Mark stopped the car in Ann's drive. "You sure about me staying to see Ritchie and Colleen?"

"Yes." Ann unlocked the door and handed her coat to Mark to hang up. "Dinner should be ready soon."

"Wait." Mark encircled her. "Then I want to give you my gift."

"I have something for you, too."

Ann had made her own version of Mark's crockpot stew. It seemed the easiest thing to manage so that they'd have a little time together between dinner and Ritchie and Colleen's visit. Ann clasped her fingers tightly on her lap while she watched him unwrap her present. They sat facing each other on her long tapestry sofa, the multicolored lights of the tree they had decorated together glowing softly in the background.

She felt like part of a Norman Rockwell scene, and considered herself fortunate. She'd bought him an engraved pen and pencil set, but the other gift was one she cared about. Ann closed her eyes when he read the title of the book she'd chosen. Bronte. The handmade bookmark tucked inside told him, for the first time, that she loved him. He was silent so long. Ann felt sweat start at her hairline.

She opened her eyes to see him stroke the entire length of linen she'd embroidered, stitching every letter in the words "I love you" with a permanence that couldn't be misunderstood. Had she made a terrible mistake? Maybe he'd been so put off by her reluctance to tell her son about them that he wanted to break up with her.

She reached to cover his jerky hand motions, then touched the cheek of his bent head. She pulled away at the odd sensation of dampness, puzzled. All of Ann's senses heightened, threatening to overwhelm her. The lights became so brilliant they made her eyes sting. The sound of Stella's *Silent Night* combined with the scent of cinnamon and frankincense potpourri in a convulsive bubble.

"Mark?" He lifted his head so she could see his tears, the gap in his soul. She knew he needed to hear the words, not just see them. "I love you. I do."

Mark's struggle for control was all the answer that mattered. Ann folded his head to her breast and stroked the hair from his temple. She filled her lungs with the warmth and strength emanating from him. Holding him against her like this was not even a remotely parental act. She fit herself into the empty place in Mark as she committed to love him.

In time, he drew back and cleared his throat. "Thank you." He kissed her fingers. "I love you." Then he handed her a small package. "This is for you."

Ann's heart again spasmed at the feel of the jewelry box. She took in a deep breath and gingerly slit the tape to fold back the paper. She let out the breath — in relief? — at the sight of gorgeous black onyx roses set with sparkling diamond earrings. The name on the box made her cringe at the thought of the expense.

"They're beautiful, Mark."

He touched her lips before staring at her mouth. Closing his eyes, he rested his forehead against hers. They remained joined by touch and soul until stamping sounds from the front porch let them know Ritchie and Colleen had arrived.

"Ho, ho ho!" Ritchie clumped into the foyer, arms around a wrapped box. He leaned in to kiss his mother on the cheek. "Merry Christmas!" He set the box down. "What have we here? Mark. Still haunting the old neighborhood?"

"Merry Christmas, Ritchie. Colleen." Ann hung Ritchie's coat in the closet, while Mark took Colleen's from her.

"You look so pretty, dear," Ann told her daughter-in-law. Colleen wore a stretchy red sweater with a lacy collar. "Thank you for coming."

Colleen returned her hug. "Merry Christmas. Thank you for having us."

"Come in," Ann invited them into the living room. "I have some cider or hot chocolate."

"I see you got the tree out," Ritchie said. "You must have had help."

"Yes, Mark came over." Ann left to get their drinks. She returned to a silent group, all staring at the tree. "Here we go. How about some music?" Instrumental hymns, she thought. Violins filled in some of the vacuum. "How was church?"

Colleen stepped right up to the plate. "Oh, it was so much fun. All those little ones. I can't wait until we have our own child next year. Wasn't it fun, Ritchie?"

"Yeah." Ritchie lifted his arm around his wife. "Nice and quick."

"The children played the Christmas story. The little girls in tinsel halos were adorable. I can't wait to dress up our baby."

"So your church put on a children's program?" Ann sat in a straight-back chair near the fireplace and sipped her mug of fragrant cider.

"They even had a live lamb. Somebody's 4-H project." Colleen started ransacking her purse. "Here." She held out the folded bulletin toward Ann, who set her cup down to reach for it.

"You must have sung a lot," Ann said, after paging through the stapled bulletin.

"Yes. Some of the older children played their instruments." Colleen said.

Ritchie cleared his throat and removed his arm. "Let's give mom her gift." He got up and brought in the box he'd set down in the hall. "Here you go." He set the red foil wrapped package on the floor in front of her.

"Thank you both so much," Ann said before opening it. "You received my check and the certificates, I assume."

"Yes, we did," Colleen answered promptly. "I'll get a note out to you right away."

"Oh, that's not what I meant," Ann told

her daughter-in-law.

"And we love the restaurant you chose," Colleen said. "I don't know if we'll have time to go before the baby comes, though."

"Oh." Ann tore the paper from the box of fruit. "Well, thank you both. This will keep me well supplied for a long time. How nice."

"Yeah, it was a fund raiser thing at school," Ritchie said.

"We thought you'd like it," Colleen told her.

"Oh, I do. Thank you again."

"Sorry, man," Ritchie said to Mark. "We didn't know you'd be here, still hanging around my mother, or we would've got you something. Why aren't you in Florida, or somewhere, with your dad and stepmom?"

"Ritchie —" Ann's remonstration was automatic.

Mark sent her a warning glance. "I just started a new job, remember? I don't have that much time off yet. I brought you something, though." He got up and reached under the tree for a small flat box, which he handed to Colleen. With a round-eyed look at her husband, Colleen slit the tape. "Boudin Sourdough Bakery? Bread of the month club?"

Colleen's sincere thank you made Ann get up to collect used mugs in a hurry. She barely made it to the kitchen to smother her giggles. When she returned, another small box was on her seat.

"From me," Mark said.

"Oh." Ann sat and opened it, conscious of being the center of attention. "Gourmet coffees. How thoughtful." She smiled at him, feeling the heat on her neck and hoping desperately this wasn't the start of another hot flash that seemed to plague her over the past week. Her headaches didn't usually start this way. "Thank you all. I have some cookies and more hot drinks in the kitchen."

Ritchie took their bags upstairs when Colleen declared she and the baby were tired, just after ten o'clock. She waved and said good night.

Ritchie lingered, helping himself to more cookies. "So, what are you up to tomorrow, old man? You should come here. Mom's probably got plenty of food for lunch. Right, Mom?"

Ann still couldn't tell what her usually transparent son knew about her and Mark. She decided to play ignorant. "Certainly, if Mark would care to join us. I have a ham and scalloped potatoes." She laughed. "And fruit salad."

"I don't want to intrude," Mark said.

"We have to stop over to see Grandma

and Grandpa in the morning," Ann warned.

Ritchie swallowed the remainder of his cider. "He can come after that, can't he? What, we'll be back by noon. I can invite my friends over, can't I? Especially if he's all alone. It's the Christian thing to do, isn't it?"

"Of course," Ann said.

"Well, I think I'll follow my wife to bed."

"I'd better get going, too," Mark said, proving he took the hint. Ritchie climbed the stairs, while Ann got his coat from the closet.

"There's one more thing I want to check," Ann said, her voice meant to carry. "Could you come in here, Mark, see if I have enough." She let her voice trail as she led him back to the darkened burrow of the kitchen.

By the light of the dials on the stove, Ann pushed him against the counter. "Just one more kiss." Mark let her pepper him with kisses before he held her away.

"What if someone comes? I don't think they know."

"No, they don't." Ann pulled his face close to hers, not sorry at all to have aroused this bout of late-night passion.

Mark groaned against her lips. "I think I'd better go."

"I just managed to get you alone, and now you want to leave."

Mark laughed softly, cradling her close with one large hand at the small of her back, threading his other hand through her hair and nuzzling her ear. This was what she loved most, his gentleness, his self-control. That had a familiar ring to it, something she'd heard sometime . . . but where? She brushed her lips against the skin under his ear, breathing in his familiar scent. If she became blind, she'd be able to pick him out of a crowded room. Ann lost all sense of the present while their mouths ground together.

"Mom? What's going on? I thought I heard something."

Ann dropped her arms in a flash and straightened, glancing at Mark briefly before twisting her bruised lips into a smile. "Mark's still here."

"Obviously." Ritchie snapped on the overhead light. His eyes smoldered, while his jaw clenched so tightly she worried he'd crack a tooth. He folded his arms and inhaled deeply. "What is this? Were you two . . . ? That's disgusting. How could you do something like that? What about Dad?" And before Ann could open her mouth, Ritchie rounded on Mark, fist pulled back. Mark stood his ground, head cocked, but with arms ready to brace a blow. "And you!" Ritchie's face matched the color of her magenta table runner. "What's the matter with you? Can't find anyone your own age? Or are you after her money?"

"Ritchie!" Ann's cry was echoed by another female voice.

Colleen appeared in the door of the kitchen, wrapped in a robe. "Ritchie, what's going on?"

"Go back to bed," Ritchie told his wife, still facing his mother.

Colleen came into the room. "I don't think so," she said. Ann had never heard that rounded full tone from her daughter-in-law. Colleen's politeness normally flattened and measured every nuance. "What's happening?"

"You don't want to know. It's disgusting," Ritchie danced up and down, like a little boy who couldn't keep a secret.

"What's disgusting?" Colleen advanced into the room, her blond curls tousled. Her look volleyed between her husband and her mother-in-law.

Ritchie turned his back on Ann and folded his arms. "Those two — It's just sick. I can't believe it. Get dressed. We're leaving."

Colleen didn't move. "Ritchie, wait. I'm sure your mother has an explanation. Let's just sit down and talk, okay? It's Christmas."

Ann said, "I'll make some coffee."

Ritchie remained on the far side of the kitchen island with his back turned while Mark held up the counter next to the sink, hands braced on either side of him as if an earthquake had been predicted in the next thirty seconds.

Colleen planted herself at the round breakfast table and folded her hands on top of it. Ann cautiously joined her. Someone needed to speak. Take charge. Ann suspected they were the only ones who could exchange appropriate words at the moment. "Um, Colleen, I appreciate your willingness to listen." Ann grimaced. Coffee trickled into the carafe. "Well, the fact is, Mark and I —"

"Are in love," Colleen said. "I could tell. Even last fall."

Ann clasped her ringless fingers in a white-knuckled grip. She cast a glance at Mark, but lost sight of him behind the hanging light fixture anchored above the table. He'd crossed his legs and leaned against the stove. She focused on her daughter-in-law. "Yes."

With a snort, Ritchie poured a mug of coffee. He unlocked and slammed open the patio door to the deck, the violence of his motion making the light sway. The chilled air swirled around their feet. The coffee maker sighed and burbled a last drop. After a few moments, Mark helped himself to a cup and followed her son, without looking at Ann.

"What are you going to do?" Colleen asked.

Ann blinked and shook her head. "What?"

Colleen reached a hand to set on hers. "I asked you what you were going to do."

Chapter Twelve

"You can't touch her money, you know."

Mark turned to face his former friend, to really look at Ritchie and try to see past his anger, his act of revulsion. Mark kept his peace. He raised his cup to his lips, waiting for Ritchie's next outburst.

Ritchie stared back. "What are you, some kind of pervert? I suppose you've already slept with her."

Mark's hands clamped around the cup. "You can insult me all you like, but you really shouldn't talk about your mother like that. She wouldn't do anything to hurt you."

"What? Now you want to be my daddy?" Ritchie slammed his mug on the rail. "You've got to be kidding! That's all Mommy ever did for the family. Hurt us. All the time."

"When, Ritchie? Explain it to me, because I never saw it. Not when you were nearly expelled for giving Emmy Thorson a black eye in fifth grade and she stood up for you, not when she begged your grandmother to pay your college tuition. Not even when Trey died."

"That's not fair!"

"You bet it's not fair. We were devastated. Trey was a good kid."

"It wasn't my fault."

"Yeah."

"It's over. You can't bring it up again, and you can't get anything out of it anymore. Case closed. You can't touch my mother's money."

"Ritchie, wake up. Your mother has no money."

"Get real."

"That's why she drives a ten-year-old Ford and hasn't had a vacation in eight years? Ritchie, get a grip. Her only luxury is going to the Y."

"My father's business does very well."

Mark stared at Ritchie, wondering how to get through to someone so insulated from his own family. "You don't have any concept of how the Ballard Trust works, do you? Even when your father was here, your grandmother controlled all the money. All of your dad's profits went into the Trust."

"So what? It's still our money. And I have my own trust fund. How do you know all this, anyway?" Ritchie faced the black hollow of the yard, elbows on the rail. "It just proves my point. Your interest in this family is all about the money."

Mark leaned against the small deck railing, breathing hard. "Why do you think your mom stays here, in this huge empty house all by herself?"

"She likes it. And it's our home. Always has been. Planning to move in?"

Mark ignored that. "And you and Colleen like coming back here, staying here, sponging off your mom."

"You leave me and my wife out of this. You're the one with the problem, not me, man. I wouldn't be hitting on someone else's wife."

"Hitting on? Is that what you think? Or don't you think at all?" Mark started to turn away, disgusted. He closed his eyes against the thought of Ann's hurt that he hadn't made more of an effort to reach out to Ritchie. "Let me ask you something. What do you love about Colleen?"

"She's my wife. You want her, too?"

Mark swallowed the bile rising in his throat and took an experimental punch at one of the supports holding the fence around the deck. "Really. I want to know. Humor the pervert. What do you love about your wife?"

Ritchie laughed an ugly squawk. "Okay. Here's my chance to teach you something, since you obviously don't have a clue. I love the way she looks at me, how she talks, the way she knows I'll take care of her. She loves me back. And she's giving me a child. That's something you'll never know, pervert."

"So, what if you found those same qualities in a different package? One that didn't look like Colleen? Would you still recognize it and be able to call it love?"

"This is rich! You trying to convince me that you could love my mother. You could never make her happy."

Where did that last dig come from? Mark grasped it like a lifeline and tugged. He put on his jury voice and squinted at Ritchie. "Did you ever stop to think what makes your mom happy? Do you think she was happy when your dad didn't come back? All those times she had to go to New York to identify some mangled body, hoping it wasn't him, yet praying to put an end to all this waiting? Did you?"

"I went to look for him. At least I tried. She never bothered."

"Why can't you let her have some peace? It's time to let him go."

Ritchie poked him in the chest. "You let

go, man. You'll never see a penny of Ballard money. Stay out of my business."

Mark saw Ritchie's blood-shot eyes, heard the spiteful words and kept himself from slamming the boy's nose deep into his skull. *Back away, man, back away. Pity the poor fool who knows not.* Mark willed himself a step away. "I don't need your money. I don't want it. Ann deserves more than the crumbs of affection you tease her with." Mark pressed his lips tight against wasting any more of his soul on this hapless man. He turned back to seek the light and warmth surrounding Ann.

Ann's son dove through the patio door a minute later, stumbling into the kitchen. "We're going home," he hissed. "Now, Colleen."

Ann trembled but accepted Colleen's defiant hug before she obeyed her husband. She followed him up the stairs more sedately than Ritchie, who could be heard leaping over every other tread.

Mark slid the patio door shut behind him and stood in front of it. Ann was melted to her seat and could only stare back at his pale cheeks. He shrugged. Ann looked away and hugged herself, already feeling prickles of the dim light reach behind her eyeballs and start to squeeze. This migraine was going to be ugly.

A clomp back down the stairs and the slam of the front door was the only goodbye Ritchie offered. Ann shivered after her son squealed his tires on her driveway. She followed Mark out to the hallway. His face remained impassive while he put on his coat. She closed her eyes when he touched her hair, and felt his lips rest on her temple, the warmth of his breath when he spoke. "I'll call you tomorrow." He let himself out with a chill rush of night air and a quiet click.

Ann was so cold, so very cold. She couldn't stop trembling and wrapped herself in an afghan. She took her pills mechanically, then settled on the sofa, after deciding to leave the tree plugged in. Mark had left his gifts. Ann cradled the book of poems while she stared at the prisms of Christmas lights with the pain of self-pity. Tears welled and dammed. She blinked once, molten lava burning a course down her cheeks. Everything was gone. Her life was over. She blinked again and slid down a dark tunnel into oblivion.

A jangle sliced through Ann's brain. She thrashed her head to dislodge it. An icy hand shook her shoulder and tugged her hair. "Wake up! What's the matter with you, anyway?"

Ann's eyes were so heavy, pain throbbed behind them. "What?"

"What is the matter with you?"

"Rachel?"

Ann dragged herself from the tangle of the afghan. "What?"

"I didn't mind that much when you were messing up your own life, but when you involve my daughter, that's the end!" Ann watched her sister pace in front of the jauntily-lit Christmas tree. She'd left the blinds open. Weak sunlight competed with the glow from the strings of tiny bulbs tucked in the pine branches. "How could you do that?"

Ann blinked and put a hand over her eyes. "Do what? What are you screaming about? What time is it?"

Rachel halted in front of her, arms on her hips. "Oh, no, you don't. I don't care if you're hung over or having one of your migraines. We're talking about Maeve! About you letting her go off to live in some sort of commune. I can't believe you allowed her to do that."

Ann scrubbed at her face and smoothed her hair to give her fury a chance to even out. Taking a deep breath, she re-ordered her scrambled thoughts. "She's not a child anymore, Rach." Ann thrust the blanket aside and got shakily to her feet. Caffeine. Definitely caffeine would offset the throb. The book of poems fell on the floor, opened to the stitched bookmark. Ann watched Rachel stare at the letters spelling "I love you."

"You're crazy, you know that?" Rachel bit out.

Ann stumbled to the kitchen. Coffee was burned against the sides of the carafe. No one had thought to turn off the machine last night. She poured herself a viscous mugful and waved the pot at her sister. Rachel pursed her lips. "No? Merry Christmas." Ann gulped a burning swallow. The flame of the drink overrode the pickhammering elves behind her eyeballs.

"She needs direction, support. Ann, she was this close to getting her degree."

Through a squint, Ann judged Rachel's thumb and forefinger to be about two inches apart. "So why didn't you direct her when you were raising her? All I agreed to was to allow her to live here."

Rachel's hands remained anchored on either elbow. "Which you obviously failed to do, since she informed me that she's no longer living here."

The phone rang. Ann swayed and put her hands over her ears. The sisters glared at each other until the answering machine magnified Mark's voice. Ann let her hands fall.

"Ann? Are you all right? Pick up, please. Talk to me. Come on, Ann. I'm coming over." Mark's click echoed through the speakers.

Rachel tapped a booted toe on the wood floor. "Yeah, and then there's that. Honestly, Ann, Ritchie came in to visit the folks this morning, all tied up in knots over finding you with your boyfriend late last night after the lights were out. Mom started wheezing while Dad started thumping that cane of his. Then my daughter breezed in and dropped her little bombshell. You could have sent Mom back to the hospital. I should have you committed."

Ann snorted and went to work, cleaning the coffee maker and brewing a new batch.

"Well?"

"Well, what, Rachel? What do you want? I can't tie your daughter to the bed, I can't follow her around from class to class, or back to your house and work."

"You could have told me you suspected she was having problems."

"Problems? When would I suspect that?

When she started piercing her nipples? Whenever she changed her hair color? You're her mother. You're the one who's supposed to notice when she comes home on weekends."

"What do you know about this Chandra person?"

"Absolutely nothing." Ann turned away to breathe shallowly. The nausea was back. "I'm going to take a shower and get dressed. Goodbye."

Rachel put her hand out. "Not so fast, sister. Maeve said you met her."

Ann spoke over her shoulder. "Only once, when Maeve moved her things out. I didn't talk to her, Mark did."

"Are you telling me that I have to talk to him?"

"You are welcome to do as you wish. Oh, and your daughter left a couple of notebooks and some laundry. I'll send them to you."

The shower cleared her head. When Ann returned to her kitchen, Mark had taken Rachel's place.

"Are you all right?" he asked.

"Yes." Ann prepared to say more, but nothing sounded right. She accepted a mug of fresh coffee from Mark, who made no other move to touch her. "Headache?"

"On its way out. Would you like breakfast?" she asked. "I can fix something."

"We can go out."

"On Christmas morning?"

"Places are open."

"I'd rather not. I'm getting out the waffle maker."

Mark took out her mixer. "I met Rachel on my way in. She was leaving." He plugged in the cord and waited while Ann brought eggs and milk from the refrigerator. "She said you told her to talk to me about that girl Maeve brought here a couple of weeks ago."

"Chandra. And I didn't tell her that. Only that I didn't know anything about her, but that she'd talked to you while I was upstairs with her daughter."

Mark jerked the beaters into the waffle batter.

"I'm tired of being treated like I'm the irresponsible one, here," Ann shrilled over the whine of the mixer.

Mark turned off the beaters. "Is the griddle hot?"

"I think so." She handed him a measuring cup to scoop the batter. "She also accused me of not telling her that Maeve might have problems, and that I nearly killed my parents when Ritchie told them about you and me."

"I think they already knew." His shoulders relaxed. "I'm on your side, you know. I just need to be prepared."

"It all happened so fast."

He pointed to the blinking answering machine. "You didn't answer my call."

"We were in the middle of an argument. Then she left and I went to get ready for you. I had no idea she would accost you in the driveway."

"Fair enough. Hey, those are burning!"

They lost the first batch of Belgian waffles. Mark forked the charred mess into the garbage and faced her. "What's so funny?"

"Merry Christmas, Mark."

He set the fork down. "Come here."

CHAPTER THIRTEEN

In early January, Ann had caught up enough at work that she could stay home for a couple of days. She put away her decorations as Stella crooned carols one last time in the background. Ann sorted through her basket of cards, reflecting on the messages.

Gene's mother, Donna, sent a card that included a photograph of the family the year Ritchie started high school. Donna had always insisted on hosting the family Christmas at their home on Lake Monona. Donna and Genevra rarely visited their Madison estate these days, preferring to live in Florida. Donna hadn't sent a gift since the second year of Gene's absence. Ann continued every year to send something unique from Wisconsin, such as a basket of cranberry-themed goods, or cheeses and the like.

When the doorbell rang, Ann sprang to answer.

"Colleen! Hello. Is everything all right?"

Ann looked past her daughter-in-law, expecting to see her son.

"I came alone."

"Please, come in, Colleen. You came all by yourself? Are you feeling okay? How's the baby?" Ann hung Colleen's coat away and poured them some tea from the pot she'd started. "Why don't we sit in here? I was just going through the cards. Cleaning up."

"Thank you. I hate putting Christmas away. It's so sad."

"Yes." Ann folded herself into a chair, legs crossed, hands crossed, smile plastered on, and waited.

"You're probably wondering why I'm here."

"Colleen, I'm delighted to have you visit whenever you want."

"I started maternity leave, you know. I told them last fall already that I planned to take off after Christmas." She tapped her rings against the cup. "Ritchie and I spent a few days with my mother. In Green Bay. Then my mother went to New York."

Ann felt her smile fading and hurriedly twisted her lips and nodded again to show Colleen that she was still listening. "And how is she? It's been, what, maybe two years

223

since we last saw each other?"

"Right. That first Christmas after Ritchie and I got married."

Ann bobbed her foot. When the silence stretched, she asked, "Can I get you anything? Or did you want to eat lunch with me?"

"Well, yes, thank you."

"Come, talk some more in the kitchen won't you?"

Colleen perched on a tall stool while Ann fixed tea. "I have some paella left. I'll heat that up after awhile, how's that?"

"Thank you."

Ann snapped her mouth shut to avoid blurting out, "Stop saying thank you!"

Colleen reached in the pocket of her maternity sweatshirt and held out a folded envelope. Ann didn't recognize the handwriting, although it was addressed to her. "Ritchie talked to my mother. At Christmas."

Ann took the note from her.

"That's from her. My mother. It was her idea."

Ann opened the envelope.

Dear Ann,
Thank you for your note at Christmas. I would love to have you stay with me in

224

New York for a week, at your earliest convenience. Call me when you know your flight number and I'll pick you up. We'll see a couple of shows, visit some museums, and I'll give you the nickel tour of the neighborhood. Please say yes!

Katherine

"Ann, since Ritchie's not here, I wanted you to know that I don't agree with him."

Ann watched the letter shake like willow leaves in her hands.

"What, is he hoping that your mother can talk some sense into me?"

"Mother simply asked if I thought you'd like to visit her. Ritchie wanted her to talk to you, but I don't know what Mother will say."

Ann dropped the letter to the counter and turned away. "There's nothing wrong with me."

"No one says there is. Well, I guess maybe Ritchie thinks so, but I don't. And I don't think my mother does. And you know what they say, that if it's really meant to be, he'll wait for you."

Ann turned back to see Colleen sip at the tea. "I don't know what to say. Mark and I should have been honest with you and Ritchie from the beginning."

"How long have you been . . . um, going out, or whatever, anyway?"

"Since Thanksgiving."

"You're kidding! The way he looks at you . . . Wow. I would have guessed years."

"Aren't you . . . I mean, doesn't it bother you?"

Colleen shook her head. "No. It's a little unusual, I guess. If Ritchie's dad were totally out of the picture, then maybe Ritchie . . . well, then again, maybe not. I mean, I suppose if Ritchie didn't know Mark from when he was a kid. Wow, this is complicated."

Ann heated up her chicken and rice dish while she and Colleen talked about preparations for the baby. By the time Colleen was ready to drive back to Portage, Ann felt as though she'd reached a welcome intimacy with her daughter-in-law. "Forgive me, Colleen, but I just wondered. Well, I was never certain exactly how you felt about me. I enjoyed this time together so much."

"Oh, I love you, Ann. Of course I do."

"You seem . . . distant sometimes. I thought you were close to your own mother."

"Actually, my mother and I took a long time to learn to love each other."

"Your father died when you were young,

is that right?"

"Yes, I was eleven. Mom had some trouble after that. With alcohol. I couldn't leave her alone, or trust her. I felt more like I was raising her, than the other way around. She's better now. She enjoys New York and has friends there who understand her. I think she'll be okay with the baby. Maybe you can tell me what you think, after your visit. Sort of like a scouting report."

Ann pulled Colleen's coat from the closet. "I don't know what kind of judge of character I'd make."

Colleen smiled. "You seem to have done all right. Ritchie likes to complain, but from what I gathered between the lines, his father wasn't around very much."

"He doesn't always remember it like that." Ann helped Colleen tuck the coat around herself and reached down for the girl's handbag.

"He'll figure it out," Colleen said. "Once the baby is here. We're excited."

"Me, too." Ann hugged her.

"I hope you'll go to visit my mother. She enjoys staying half the year in New York. She inherited that apartment, you know. We all take turns staying there."

"I'll call her."

Colleen pulled her hair from her collar.

"And talk to Mark."

Ann cocked her head. "Yes."

"You'll be back before the baby comes. Ritchie will come around, you'll see."

"I hope so." Ann followed her out to her car. "But it might take awhile. I think he still feels bad about the accident."

"When Mark's brother was killed? He told me about it."

"I'm glad. I had him in therapy for a few months. I don't think it did much for him."

"Were the Roths terribly angry? After all, Ritchie said Trey was driving."

Ann sighed. "I don't know. More stunned. And Mark was long gone, already graduated and working then. He came back for the funeral. He even went to Ritchie's graduation that year."

"Wow. That's support. Well, I guess I need to leave. Thank you for having me. Goodbye."

"Goodbye. Be safe."

Ann wandered back to the kitchen to stare at the invitation as if she expected it to reach up and sink fangs into her. She'd refrained from asking what exactly her son had said about Mark.

Ann went to her address book to look up Katherine's phone number. The least she could do was thank the woman. Platitudes scrolled through her brain: *It never hurts to take a step back, take a look at the big picture. If your feelings are real, they won't change. If he doesn't have ulterior motives, he'll wait forever.*

What ulterior motives?

The judge wanted to continue hearing testimony in Mark's current case, even as the lunch hour passed. When he finally called a recess, Mark walked down the block to Shepherd's Jewelers to pick up the re-sized ring. He'd used up a lifetime searching for the right style. When he gave Ann the earrings at Christmas, he didn't tell her that they were part of a larger set that included engagement and wedding rings. A matching necklace and bracelet would be her wedding gift. Mark fingered the velvet box in his side pocket. If he could judge by the raised eyebrows and questioning eyes of Ann as she opened his gift on Christmas Eve, she might not reject the idea of an engagement.

The two of them might have forever, but it was closing in faster than he cared to think. He could always care for Ann, but he had to consider both their wellbeing. This trial wrapping up today showcased the worst of humanity. Not only had relatives begun a fight over an estate, they had started the proceedings while their relative still lived.

Mark shook his head to clear away the hatred he'd lived in for the past week. He patted his pocket again. The ring was mounted with three glowing diamonds nestled in onyx roses. He had no plan other than to ask her to marry him. Forever, always, to stay with him, love him, let him love her in all the ways he needed to show her.

He delighted in Ann's developing playfulness. She'd seemed stifled when he first sought her out, but now she didn't hesitate to touch him, tell him what she thought or even satisfy her curiosity by looking at his books or papers. Work would stay private, but Mark wanted her to have no questions, no doubts, about anything in his personal life.

She loves me. Mark savored the sensations that the words made on his ears, tingling along nerves and blood vessels until his being was permeated with her. He stopped by a bench in front of the courthouse, ignoring passersby. In twenty years would he learn her every mood? Would he unlock the secret to counteract her fears and anticipate her joys? Know when to anticipate the pain that

sent her world reeling? He would do anything to keep the sparkle in her hazel eyes.
Her creamy skin would show subtle crepe
paper softness. Laugh lines would crinkle
into her temples. Silver strands would
spread from those temples, creating a fine
web of lacy frost through her dark hair.

In twenty-five years he would be near
sixty. Mark planned to guide them toward a
community where they could live without
fear in their later years. If they planned well,
they would be able to use their assets to
help others. How many couples did he know
who stayed together that long? A lifetime.

Until then, he could do everything he
could to make sure both he and Ann stayed
in the best health possible. Time to go back
to work.

Nine o'clock. Dark. Mark ran down the
steps to the courthouse and along the slushy
sidewalk to the parking lot. The only surprise in the verdict had been the length of
the judge's deliberation that afternoon.
He'd spent the rest of the time with the
clients and paperwork.

Once in his car, he pressed the button of
the cell phone. "Ann? Is it too late to stop
by? I have something important to talk to
you about. You have something to tell me,

too? Okay. No, I don't need food. I just want to see you. Good. I'll be up there in about fifteen or twenty minutes. I love you."

Mark caught a newscast while driving. Since he did not have a television set, or the time to watch it, he relied on hearing about the outside world from newspapers and the radio. The now-familiar drive to Ann's house took only part of his concentration. He'd worked up the perfect scenario for popping the question by the time he parked in her driveway.

She opened the door to him as he arrived. "Ann." She led him in before her welcome kiss and the story of the strange invitation.

A half-hour later, he paced the boards of her kitchen, in and out of the light shed by the swags over the center island. Mark rolled up the sleeves of his shirt and loosened his tie as he listened to Ann tell about her encounter with her daughter-in-law. He draped the jacket with the jeweler's box still in his pocket on the back of a kitchen chair.

"Here's the note from Katherine."

Mark took it like he would a suspicious clue in a case. He read it twice. "Ann, you know what they're trying to do."

She nodded. Lines he'd never seen before appeared on either side of her mouth. He dropped the letter on the table and covered those lines with his thumbs. Drawing her face against his heart, he filled himself with the fragrance of her soft hair. "If anyone can come between us, this relationship is not meant to be."

He felt her shiver. "I don't know what Katherine means by this invitation. She's never asked me before. She lost her husband when Colleen was even younger than Ritchie was when Gene left." Ann hung her arms around Mark's shoulders. "But it doesn't matter."

"Why not?"

Ann shifted and sighed, then pulled away. "This is not a good time to leave town. I don't want to risk being gone when the baby comes."

"You said it was only for a week. Colleen's baby isn't due until next month."

"What if something happens? She won't have either her mother or me close by."

"What did Colleen say?"

Ann bit her lip and folded her arms.

"Ann?"

Ann wouldn't meet his eyes. "She said she wanted me to check on her mother. See if she's, um, fit . . . or something, I don't know. It doesn't seem right." She let her arms fall.

She made it to the other side of the island,

where he could pick out her form in the dim light. "Okay, go to New York," he told her. "I have another case going to trial soon anyway. But we'll talk when you get back."

Ann turned her profile. "I told you. I can't go."

"I don't think you have to worry about the baby. I'm sure Moseby would understand and let you off work for a few days."

She shrugged. "It's not that. I won't go into debt for something like this, Mark. I wrote a hefty check to Ritchie for Christmas. My club savings. If I'm to pay the second half of the property tax, I need the rest of —"

"Stop. I'll have Jennifer book you a flight. I'll take care of it."

"You're paying to send me away?"

Mark went to Ann and reached for her elbow. "Ann! Don't you dare read anything into this. Maybe it will be good for you to back off a little, make sure this relationship is really what you want."

She allowed him to hold her arm. "You mean, what you really want?"

His head snapped back as though she'd hit him. Breathing hard, he asked, "What else do you want from me? I came back here for you. I'm still here despite grief from your son. How much more evidence do you need?"

Ann pulled her arm from his grip to hug herself. "I'm sorry. I didn't mean that. Please . . . you're right." She faced him. "You must be made of patience. How can you put up with me?"

Mark let himself count to five and relax his facial muscles before answering. "I didn't expect everything to be easy."

"Don't you ever have doubts about how you feel?"

"Not after the first second I saw you again." He watched her eyes brim and overflow before tucking her head against his shoulder. "Shh. Things will work out. I'll miss you every minute you're gone. I'll be here when you get back. We'll prove them wrong."

He felt her shoulders shake and hugged tighter. She put a knuckle to her mouth and cried.

Mark was not far behind and took deep, regular breaths while he held her.

Mark's shirt was still damp when he got back to his apartment. He hung his coat in the miniature hall closet before realizing that he'd left his suit coat at Ann's. With the ring inside. He felt for his car keys and reached for the door in one motion before he reconsidered. Ann knew how he felt. Even if she looked in the box and found the ring, she would only come to one conclusion. Maybe she would be more comfortable if she kept those things until she returned. He would never change his heart about her.

Should he tell her about the ring? Or wait to see if she found it on her own? Undecided, Mark locked the front door. He took a shower before bed then set his alarm for five. He planned to meet with Jim Parsons at five-thirty at the Y for a little racquetball and talk about getting Gene Ballard properly buried.

The phone rang a couple of minutes after he turned out the light. "Hello."

"Mark?"

"Hi, Ann. Are you okay? You feeling all right?"

"Yes," her voice whispered in his ear. "You left your suit coat here."

Mark turned onto his back. "Is it in your way?"

"No."

He waited in the dark, listening to her breathe, longing, aching, for her presence. "Ann?"

"There was something in the pocket. I

don't know what it is. Do you need me to bring it to you right away in the morning?"

"No. I need you to hold on to it until you get back."

"That's it? You're sure?"

"Yes, I'm sure."

"Mark?"

"What, Annie."

"I hung it in the closet in my room."

Mark curled around the second pillow, cradling the phone. "I'm glad you did that. No headache?"

"No. Not now. Good night."

"Sweet dreams, Ann. I love you."

CHAPTER FOURTEEN

Ann answered her doorbell on the morning she was scheduled to fly to New York City. Expecting Mark, the sight of her lawyer made her fingers nerveless. "Oh! Excuse me, Jim."

Jim Parsons picked up Ann's gloves and handed them to her. "Here you go, Mrs. Ballard."

"I'm just, ah, getting ready. Come in, please. I didn't realize when Mark said he had a ride for me, I thought . . . Well, never mind."

"Mark's with a client this morning. I have some paperwork for you to look at, so I was glad to be able to drive you to the airport."

Ann pulled her coat around her shoulders while she watched him pick up her suitcase. Should she tell him to call her Ann? No, after all these years, he would only wonder why and any answer she gave would be awkward. Better to keep a professional distance.

"Oh? Has something changed?"

"Maybe." Ann indicated that she was ready to leave and followed him out to his car after locking the front door.

"There are some new rules pertaining to widowed heads of household I think you should consider, put in place for women in your position."

Ann allowed him to open and close the car door for her. "My position?" she asked when he'd buckled himself in. "And what would that be?"

Parsons cleared his throat and signaled left onto the main road into Madison. "I've been looking again into your situation, and I feel that if we tried for a finding of death in Mr. Ballard's case, we could be successful this time."

"Oh." Ann folded her hands on her lap and stared at her knees clenched together. What had Mark told him? "May I ask what brought this on? I don't remember asking you to look into this matter again."

"I realize that, Mrs. Ballard. As your attorney, I'm just looking out for your best interest. If you were legally widowed, we'd be able to make a claim of inheritance on the Ballard Trust. Since you and Mr. Ballard signed a marital property agreement, you have a claim on his property." He maneuvered his SUV around her drive. "I just think it would be in your best interest," he repeated.

Ann gripped her hands tightly on her lap and stared out of the window at the blustery flat clouds that hung in leaden skies. "I don't know, Jim. Do you think it's enough to work? Donna made everything so difficult last time."

"It's been five years since the last attempt at a finding. Surely Donna Ballard would do nothing to stop you now. Unless, of course, there's been new evidence."

"Nothing that I'm aware of."

She couldn't think of anything else to say during the twenty-minute drive to the Madison airport. Jim parked in the lot and took her bag across the ramp into the terminal. "Will you think about it? Here's a copy of the paperwork for you to look at while you're away."

Ann took the brown clasp envelope, managing to hide the worst of her shaking under the leather gloves. "I don't know. I'll think about it."

"Well, I'll be in touch when you return. I wish you a pleasant journey, Mrs. Ballard."

Ann checked her bag and went to get coffee while she waited. The smells of warm caramel rolls and berry muffins made her stomach roil. She hadn't flown in six years. So far, smiles from the airport personnel and well-marked signs eased her tension but did not enhance her appetite.

When her flight was announced, she went through all the motions in the right order: handing her pass over, taking a seat and closing her eyes. The engines revved and they left the ground. If only Mark were here. If only she could get a do-over for Christmas. If only . . .

Entering LaGuardia Airport after the flight from Madison was a different world. A muddle of every language and shade of skin imaginable greeted her. Katherine had promised to meet her near the baggage claim.

Katherine Hallen, Colleen's mother, wore a maroon all-weather coat. She stood about Ann's height, but was heftier. Definitely not fat, but solid. Her thick blonde hair showed the paler signs of age. Ann recalled her as being a no-nonsense woman who managed her daughter's wedding with good humor.

"There you are!" Katherine took her arm. "How was the flight? I'm so glad you came. You checked a suitcase? Let's look for it."

While they stood near the carousel, Ann

asked about Katherine's holiday and how she felt about the new baby.

"Oh, I'm happy for them," Katherine replied. "They're so young, though, don't you think? I'll head back next month. Colleen asked. I would have stayed in Green Bay but January in Wisconsin is just torture." She turned her shrewd, faded blue eyes on Ann. "You'll want to spend some quality Grandma time with them, no doubt."

"I'll come whenever Colleen and Ritchie want me," Ann told her. "Ah, there's my bag."

"Let's get out of here, shall we?"

Katherine lived in the quintessential second-floor brownstone. Ann listened again to the story of the inheritance and the fund that paid taxes and utilities. "I love being able to invite the family here. Ann, you must consider yourself family, too. You're welcome whenever you can come."

Ann waited for the questions about Mark. During Katherine's English muffin and chicory coffee breakfast the next morning, during the deli run or the afternoon museum tour, Ann kept up her guard, rehearsing what she planned to say about Mark when the subject came up.

"I'm not much for going out," Katherine

told her the second morning. "In fact, my favorite hobby is an evening at the library."

On the fourth morning in the apartment, Katherine brought the newspaper to the sofa where Ann sat, paging through a magazine. "I promised you a show, didn't I? Here's a list of what's playing. We can stand in line at the TKTS window if we go early enough to get tickets for something today if you would like. We have to go to Times Square, though, which is a show in itself. What are you interested in?" Together, they picked out a new musical that was getting mixed reviews. "That shouldn't be too tough. We'll go get in line, then window shop or something afterward."

Katherine seemed to know just how to maneuver against the human flow of traffic on slushy 91st Street. Ann trailed in her wake, wanting to grab onto the woman's jacket or hand so they couldn't be separated in the twilight. The matinee show had been pleasant, but not outstanding.

"We'll stop at Tom's," Katherine called.

Ann could barely hear her in the wind. Icy drizzle stung her cheeks.

"You'll like it. It's just three more blocks."

Ann marveled at Katherine's natural

tendency to walk everywhere. They had already come seven blocks from the subway stop. That would make their jaunt, what, almost a mile? Ann shuddered. A mile back home would rate an automatic car trip. Yet she did not feel tired. Katherine was pulling ahead. Ann hurried after her.

The door to Tom's Coffee Bistro jingled the first measure from "Yellow Submarine." At least, that's what Ann thought she heard. The dozen customers ignored them. Following Katherine's lead, she removed her coat and hung it on a wooden tree near a metal shelf and rod that bore no hangers. Yeast and roast coffee bean scent made her salivate.

"You don't order here," Katherine said under her breath.

"Wha— ?"

"Just follow me."

"Okay."

"Hi, Tom," Katherine called as they crossed the diamond-patterned linoleum floor and approached a battered wooden counter. "I brought a friend today. She's from —"

"Midwest."

Under the lanky proprietor's long stare Ann couldn't stop the earthquake shudder that began in her knees. After he moved his head to address Katherine, Ann felt rubbery. "I'll bring it to you," he said.

Katherine led the way to a two-person table under a wall covered in scotch-taped posters advertising concerts or demonstrations or peace marches from the 1990s.

"You could have warned me," Ann hissed when she felt sufficiently calmed.

"About what?"

"That he has only one eye."

Katherine sat back in her chrome chair. "I forgot." She leaned in and put her elbows on the table. "Tom's all right. Don't stare."

"But he's not even wearing a patch, or anything."

"He says he can see your soul, and you know, I believe he can. Really, Ann. You're as bad as the kids. Anyway, he's got a gift. He looks at you and through some sense, knows just what you want to drink, even if you never thought of it yourself."

"What if I don't like it?"

"I've never heard anyone complain." Ann felt Katherine's stare almost as deeply as Tom's earlier study. "This used to be a bar. Tom's wife was killed by a drunk driver. After that, he changed over to serving coffee. Said he wanted a different clientele. Except the regulars kept coming back. Just in the morning."

Ann felt the confession in her friend's soul. "You were one of the evening regulars, too, weren't you?"

"Yes. Tom and I go way back. We helped each other through AA."

Katherine's forthrightness was beginning to wear on Ann's Midwestern sense of privacy. Ann would never have shared such personal information with a virtual stranger. But wasn't this the kind of information Colleen wanted her to know? Ann would trust her with a baby and she would say that to Colleen when she got back.

A shadow crossed the table. Ann couldn't bring herself to look into Tom's empty eye socket. The aroma from the chunky brown mug caused her to squirm with a physical sense of pleasure. Cocoa, definitely, and maybe cardamom?

"Thanks, Tom." Ann echoed her companion, braving a look at her host.

"Someone else from your part of the country comes in regular." The one-eyed man slowly rotated his head in the direction of a dark corner table across the room. Ann watched a stocky man awkwardly help a young boy into a coat, while nearby a beige-haired woman buttoned her own. The man gave the child a coin to leave on the table and then took the child's hand. For a moment they faced her.

Gene Ballard?

CHAPTER FIFTEEN

Mark walked a few blocks from the office to visit Markell's Natural Foods Co-op. He was on a mission to find a new free-trade coffee his assistant, Jennifer, raved about and brought in to the office so they could all try. Ann would return from New York in two days. He wanted to treat her to something special.

Ann would probably like some fresh food, too, to restock her fridge. Rounding the corner at the back of the store near the coolers, he halted at the sight of two women in colorful peacock blue and green headscarves, pondering over items on a shelf. One of them noticed him.

"Aren't you Mark?" Mark recalled her unusual name: Chandra, Ann's niece's friend.

"Yes. Hello. Hi, Maeve." Mark shifted his heavy basket to his other hand.

"I see you picked up some of that new

free-trade coffee. I hear it's good," Maeve said.

"Maeve, you know caffeine is not the way to enlightenment," Maeve's companion scolded.

"That doesn't stop me from appreciating the smell. How's my aunt?"

"She's been visiting Colleen's mother in New York, be back on Saturday," Mark said.

"Ah, so you've been on your own." Maeve sighed and looked around the shop, her glance settling on the small juice bar.

"Can I get you ladies something to drink? I'd like to hear how you're getting along." Mark smiled. "I know Ann would like to know that you're all right."

Maeve studied Chandra. "Sounds good to me, thanks."

Chandra nodded. They made their way to a table, set their baskets down and went to order at the counter.

Chandra set her tall glass on the table. "Oh! I see Paolo. I've got to talk to him."

Mark waited for Maeve to take her place before sitting next to her. "You look like you could use a taste of this coffee."

"Boy, and how." Maeve did not hesitate to reach for the cup Mark brought from the counter. She offered her own peach nectar to him, which he declined. While keeping watch on Chandra, Maeve took hurried sips of coffee.

"How are you?"

Maeve set the cup back in front of Mark. "Thanks. Um, could be better. I guess."

"The path to enlightenment not as peaceful as you thought?"

Maeve looked at Chandra before leaning in close to Mark. "The fact of the matter is, I want to go back and finish school."

Mark studied her dull eyes and lined mouth. "How can I help?"

"Is there something legal — some way I can get reinstated? I registered, but I didn't pay. Classes started but I don't know my standing."

"This is your third year, right?"

"Technically seventh semester, with credits from high school. I have to do an internship at some point, too."

"Does it matter what order you do the coursework and the internship?"

"I don't know. I don't know if I can even get the courses I need if I lose my place."

Mark nodded, but remained silent, thinking. One of the firms in his caseload had a marketing department. He could check about an internship for Maeve. The company was located south of Madison in Cottage Grove. Not that far away, but enough of a distance to separate her from her current situation. "Call me tomorrow," he told her, before he checked out.

Before he drove home, Mark ran back up to his office to look up the information he needed and made an appointment at the university to discuss Maeve's academic career. Should he talk to Rachel? Mark stared at the phone in his hand. Maeve was an adult and had asked for his help. She'd indicated perhaps her mother wouldn't welcome her home.

Home and fed for once before eight o'clock at night, Mark took a chance and telephoned his contact at Hellstrom and Company, the small printing firm in Cottage Grove he'd represented in a recent acquisitions case. If Maeve could fax her résumé and course list, and set up an interview, they'd be happy to look into taking her on. There was no pay involved, of course, and one of the new graphic artists was looking for a roommate. Perfect.

Mark's final hope was Maeve would understand about the need to look professional. The coal black spiked hair would probably pass, but most of the piercings would have to go. At least during office hours. Rachel and Ann might appreciate that part of the deal as much as the rest.

Friday passed, filled with research and meetings. Maeve called in the afternoon. Mark was able to tell her that things were fixed up with the bursar and about Hellstrom if she was interested. The card game was that evening. Saturday evening meant Ann's return.

Ann stored the address of the coffee bistro and the few turns needed to get back there in her memory. Katherine might have guessed her intention, but mercifully demanded no information. How could that possibly have been Gene? The waitress hugged the little boy. She must know something. Ann had to talk to her, to rule out the absurdity that the balding hefty man with a vacant stare was what Gene might have become over the past seven years.

When they reached Katherine's apartment, Ann claimed that she'd forgotten her gloves and said she would just go back and get them.

"I'm all right, Katherine. I remember how to get back."

Katherine hesitated while staring squinty-eyed at Ann. "Here, take the cell phone, please."

Grateful not to have to come up with more excuses or even try to figure out how to talk about what she saw, Ann hurried through the twilight back to the bistro. Only one customer sat at the counter.

Ann beckoned the waitress to a private distance from the counter. "Excuse me, but you seemed friendly with that couple who was seated at this table at lunch time. The man seemed familiar to me somehow."

"Oh, now, that could be you saw his picture in the paper years ago, poor man. That's a real love story, let me tell you."

"Can you tell me anything about it?"

With a glance at her other customer, the skinny brunette said, "I guess so. It was in the newspapers at the time. You're not from around here, are you?"

"No. Tom indicated that they were from the Midwest."

"I don't know about that. Let me get you something." The woman gestured for Ann to sit. The man at the counter paid and left. The waitress turned the sign on the door to the "Closed" side and pulled the net from her hair. She brought two white ceramic mugs of coffee to the table. "Well, let's see. Been about six, seven years I guess, since the story broke. He was in a coma for months after a hideous beating and robbery. She was a nurse on duty when they brought him in. Took care of him. When he regained consciousness, he didn't remember anything. Not much about anything in his past. Brain injury, they say. Anyway, Linda nursed him back to health and they fell in love, got married and had a baby."

"He was in a coma, you said?"

"That's what they told me. Poor guy didn't recover all his marbles, you probably noticed. His wife has to remind him that he's not the same age as the little fellow. So, what are you? Just curious, or what?"

Ann thought for a moment. "I think their story would make a great feature article. Do you know their names or how I can reach them?"

"Who do you work for?"

"Oh, I'm not the writer, but I want to tell my friend about this. You know readers go gaga over stories like that."

"Yeah. I love reading about stuff like that, too. Well, all I know is that they come in here all the time, walking, so I don't think they live far from here. Alan and Linda Smart. That's really their name. Smart. She told me. Little guy's named Richard Michael. Maybe they're in the phone book, or something. Say, I'd better start cleaning up. You want me to call a cab for you?"

"No, thanks. It's just a few blocks. How much for the coffee?"

"It's the end of the pot, hon.' No charge."

"Thank you." As Ann left, motion in the shadowy storeroom doorway caught her attention. Tom stood silent, watching.

Katherine let Ann into the building. "Midge called from Tom's to tell me you left. She also said you had lots of questions about a customer."

Ann took her coat off and hung it in the closet.

"You could have just said you had questions. I would have helped you."

"I'm sorry, Katherine. That was rude of me."

Katherine patted her hand. "Did you find what you were looking for?"

"I beg your pardon?"

"At Tom's. Your gloves."

"Oh, right. Yes. Yes, I did."

"I was going to tell you earlier that I didn't have any particular reason to invite you here, other than you're family. You may have wondered whether or not I was going to lecture you or even offer some kind of east coast wisdom about making choices." She laughed and helped herself to Kung Pao chicken she'd had delivered while Ann was out. "I'm the last person who ought to tell anyone how to live. I just wondered if maybe you needed a break from the family commotion. I'm not a bad listener. And I'm not a gossip, despite telling you about the phone call from Tom's."

Ann pushed the rice around her plate, hoping she wouldn't be sick. Her earlier dread of talking about Mark was nothing to this new despair. Mark — what could she possibly tell him about her suspicion? "Do you think I could find a newspaper story from a few years back?" she asked Katherine. "About a — an accident victim? That man at Tom's, for instance?"

"I think so. Did you want to go to the library tonight? They're open until eight."

Katherine offered to help Ann search. Forty-five minutes later, they sat at matching microfiche machines, scanning back issues of the Times. If the story had made the New York papers, why hadn't she heard anything in Wisconsin? Surely the police would have been involved in her missing person case.

Seven-thirty. Hurry.

"Here," Katherine said, at seven-fifty. "This must be it. But it's only from five years back. I thought your husband went missing earlier than that."

Ann glanced at the picture. "Yes, he did. Can we make a copy of this?" They paid

256

and left as the place closed down for the evening. Katherine's questions erupted even before the door to her apartment closed. "Can I ask why you're interested in that man's story? Do you think he might be your missing husband? What will you tell your boyfriend?"

"My husband is dead. Excuse me a minute, won't you." Ann closed the door on the tiny bathroom and leaned over the sink. It couldn't be. It couldn't be.

"Man Once Given up for Dead Fathers Child." The story told of a nurse named Linda Smart who cared for a gravely injured man brought into the emergency room one night. The man had been severely beaten. Once he regained consciousness and slowly began to recover, it was obvious he couldn't recall anything of his former life. He and the nurse fell in love. Linda's terminally ill mother's last wish was to see her daughter married.

Ann stared into the mirror over the sink. Talk about tension with a capital T. This should be enough to bring on the mother of all migraines. She closed her eyes again and tried to feel the start of the pain. Nothing yet. She took some pills anyway. Her eyes were bloodshot, no doubt from staring into the microfiche machine. That man couldn't have been Gene. The hazy picture showed a round-faced man. Gene's face had intelligent eyes set on either side of a thin nose. This man's nose was squashed on the end, bulbous. This man couldn't have been Gene. Couldn't.

"Ann? Are you okay?" Katherine knocked and called through the bathroom door.

Ann flushed the toilet. "Oh, sorry. Be right out." She brushed her teeth and washed her hands before returning to the kitchen. She gave her hostess a bright smile. "Must have fallen asleep in there for a minute. All those articles. I should warn you, I get migraines sometimes. Bad ones. I took some medicine." She fluffed her hair and poured herself a glass of water. She paced from the table to the sink and back.

"I hope you'll be all right. You must tell me if I can do anything."

"So far, so good." She sat across from her hostess.

"That man doesn't resemble Gene." Ann stared at Katherine.

Katherine watched over the rim of jeweled reading glasses. "Well, you would know."

"You can show the article to Ritchie and Colleen. Even Ritchie will say that's not his father."

"I believe you," Katherine said.

The next morning, Katherine arranged for a taxi to the airport and hugged her when she left. "You must come back some time."

"Thank you." She changed the directions en route. She scribbled on a piece of paper and handed the memorized address to the driver. "I need you to take me here, first, please."

"You sure this is it, Mrs. Ballard?" The driver halted in front of a high chain link fence surrounding an abandoned construction site.

"Yes. Could you wait just a minute, please? I just have to see something."

"Sure, sure. Take your time."

Ann hesitated at the fence. A spot inside the rusty padlocked gate marked the place where Gene's wallet had been found, next to the corpse of a man who hadn't been her husband. Six years ago, she stood here with a detective and uniformed officers, then visited the morgue. What had happened to Gene Ballard? Had he tired of his life and run? Had he been killed? Or had he somehow lost his memory and lived as a stranger?

Ann threaded her fingers through the links and rested her forehead against their icy smoothness. What should she tell Mark? Anything?

A powdering of fresh snow in Madison was enhanced by the sparkling strand of diamonds that made up Madison's city lights. Mark drove to the airport, following road signs with automated efficiency. He paced in the terminal, oblivious to the few people around him who chatted or sipped lattes. Initially elated at his success at helping Annie's niece find an internship and get back to school, and even after Rachel's call to thank him, Mark now wondered if he'd gone too far. How would Ann feel about his interference in her family's lives, without asking her first?

Mark leaned against a pillar, crossed his legs and arms, and closed his eyes. When he opened them at the commotion of a new string of chatter and people emerging from the terminal entrance, he watched for her. Against the backdrop of anonymity, Mark studied Ann, trying to find an objective middle place in his heart and mind to really look at her. She hadn't begun to search for him, but stood waiting quietly, bent over her carry-on bag and coat, much the same way he stood hunched around his own coat. She looked tired. If he had to use another word, he would say she seemed sad. What had happened in New York City? Had Colleen's mother convinced her she was making a mistake by continuing to see him?

When Ann was free of the line snaking down the walkway, still he hesitated, hoping for some sign how she would greet him. What if this woman, whom he wanted to marry, rejected him? If he still had this much doubt, how could he think he was ready to share her life?

There, she sees me. Terror mingling with ecstasy rooted his feet. She came closer, smiling. "Mark."

Her hand settled on his forearm. Slowly, he unclenched his fists under his coat, dropped it and took her in his arms and pressed his mouth to hers. "I missed you."

"Good." She returned his kiss. "I have to wait for my bag."

He picked up his coat then reached for her carry-on. "How was the trip?" They had spoken just twice while she was gone, the last time from LaGuardia to let him know that her flight was leaving on time.

"Katherine has a wonderful apartment. It's so different there. We saw a couple of museums and a show, but mostly, we hung out at the library."

"You mentioned that when I called."

"That's right. There's my suitcase."

On the way out to the car, he asked if she wanted to stop for dinner.

"I think I'd rather just go home. After being alone so long, I'm not used to spending nearly every waking moment surrounded by people. I think I'd just like to relax and sleep in my own bed."

"How many other people were staying with you?"

"Oh, at the apartment, it was just Katherine and me."

"I thought two was company. Did she harass you?" Mark stopped at a light and turned to study her expression in the artificial light. Her eyes were closed.

"No, Katherine didn't harass me about us. In fact, your name only came up once."

"Oh. I don't know if I'm hurt or not." He brought her bags into the house and stood, coated, in the foyer. Ann disappeared into the kitchen.

"Mark?" Ann appeared again in the hall, shoeless. "What's the matter?"

"I'll leave you alone."

"What? You want to go? I hoped you could stay a little, talk."

"You said you wanted to relax."

She padded close, took his hand. "With you. I want to know what you did while I was away, and to hear again about how much you missed me. Which reminds me — your suit coat. You must have missed that all week. Here, let me run up and get it."

"No — wait, Ann. It can wait until I go."

Mark sat at the counter and watched her sort through her mail, loving the way her hands seemed to dance in the mundane task.

"What's the matter?" she asked.

"Nothing. I just love having you back."

"I love having you to come back to."

"Even though you're used to being alone?"

"Being used to something and liking it are two different things. Come, let's go sit by the fire."

They settled in their customary position on the sofa, Mark lounged in a corner, Ann huddled in his arms. "So," he said. "You talked about me once?"

Ann shifted slightly to rub her nose against his collarbone through his shirt. "Um, well, sort of. She called you my boyfriend. I guess that counts for tacit approval."

"What were you talking about?"

"Oh, just some old papers we were looking at in the library. She wanted to know if I was planning to tell you about it. That library was amazing, Mark. You would love it. It's got these high, high ceilings and huge old wooden shelves. And it's only one of dozens just like it. They put on lots of different kinds of programs. We walked all over. I used different muscles. It will take me a while to adjust to swimming again. Maybe I'll use the treadmill for a while instead. What do you think?"

"I think you enjoyed your trip."

"Thank you, Mark, for buying my ticket."

"You're welcome. Next time, though, I get to go along."

Ann jumped up and rubbed her arms. She crossed to the window and pulled the drapes tight.

Mark watched her stare into the flames, seeing things he couldn't. "Ann? You don't think we're making a mistake, do you?"

She turned to him abruptly, startled like a fawn. "Of course not. I just . . . I have some thinking to do. About those papers Jim sent with me. What do you know about that?"

"I asked him to look into the case again."

"Why?"

"Ann. We talked about this — isn't it time to put the past to rest?"

"Of course. I've been waiting so long to do that." She returned to pull at his hand, to bring him to his feet. "I may need to go back to New York before that, though. To talk to the detectives and make sure they think it's all right."

Mark followed her to the entry, puzzling out why detectives needed to approve a judgment. "Plan it for a time I can go along," he said. "We'll do it together."

"Maybe."

"Maybe?"

Ann walked around him, helping him into his coat. "Some things a woman has to do on her own, to prove to herself that she's capable."

"Capable of what?"

"Handling the hard things."

Mark caught her hands and kissed her knuckles. "You've done that already."

"Somewhat. My trip has led me to one conclusion, however."

"What's that?" He opened the edges of his coat and pulled her inside, holding her against him.

She nuzzled his jaw. "I decided that I'll stay with you as long as you want me, until you get tired and want someone else."

That wasn't what Mark expected to hear. He pulled back to look into her eyes. "You'd better make sure that's what you want, because I will never tire of you."

"That's what I can offer right now."

Mark needed a moment to catch up with

his thoughts. "I seem to be missing a suit jacket."

"Now you remember. Let me get that for you."

He tried to sort his whirling thoughts while listening to her walk around upstairs, open and close her closet door. When he heard her start down the treads, he made up his mind. It was not yet the right time to give her the ring. He could wait.

"Here you go."

Mark accepted the jacket with the box still in the pocket. Careful not to let it fall out, he draped the garment over his arm and kissed her good night.

Mark and Ann sat with the Mosebys during worship the next Sunday. Mark felt Ann's restlessness must have matched his own. He hadn't slept well, wrestling with his conscience over trying to make peace with Ritchie before asking Ann to marry him. The desire to simply grab her and fly to Las Vegas just to get it over with was strong. Was that any way to think about marriage? He'd been back in Clayton four months. How could he expect Ann to make a decision like marriage in such a short time? He'd loved her all of his adult life. Allison had been the exception — an attempt to try a conventional life with a nice woman. Their relationship had been more a matter of pleasant companionship. Mark lost fifteen pounds by the time he told Allison he couldn't marry her.

After the service, the four of them reclaimed their coats and agreed to have brunch.

"John said you've been in New York, with your daughter-in-law's mother," Paula said after they'd been through the buffet at a nearby restaurant. "How was it? We've never been there."

Moseby grimaced. "We've been lots of other places."

Ann set her fork down. She sat back from the table of the large corner booth the couples shared. "I hadn't been back, for fun, you know, for a long time. Katherine had an apartment, of course, but there was a school nearby, as well as plenty of old houses. Corner markets instead of the supermarket."

Paula asked, "How about shows? Did you see anything new?"

"No, not too new. You can get these standby tickets if you go wait in line on the day of the performance."

"It must have been nice to get away," Paula said.

Ann shivered. "It was different."

Mark took her hand and rubbed her knuckles. He remembered she said she and Katherine had been looking at old papers. Could she have meant newspapers? When they were all ready to go Mark went to pick up their coats.

"Strange how people meet, isn't it?" Ann said in the car.

"What do you mean?" Mark adjusted his seat belt and hesitated before turning the key in the ignition.

"I've always liked John and Paula. But Gene and I . . . Well, we never mixed socially with them. And since John's technically my boss, I didn't think about getting together outside of work. Certainly not as a couple. Oh!" She laughed. "I haven't thought of myself as part of a couple since, well, forever."

Mark strained against the seat belt to give her a hearty kiss. "You just keep thinking that way." Her smile faded a touch. Mark ignored it. They would stay happy.

At the first stoplight he broached the subject of the judgment in Gene's case. "We can set it up any time you're ready, Ann. Jim Parsons will take care of it."

"Can't we wait until after the baby comes? I don't want my son to feel as if I'm trying to get rid of his father. Having a child is stressful enough for Ritchie without being distracted by having a lunatic mother trying to kill off his father."

"You're not trying to kill anyone, Ann. The man's been gone a long time already. You just want to find peace with the situation."

"Yes, perhaps," Ann said. "But let's just wait. It's only a few more weeks."

"I know you said you wanted to talk to the detectives again. Would you like me to arrange a conference call, with Jim there, too?"

"I'm not sure that's the best way to handle it." Ann squirmed and tugged on her belt. "I'll try and arrange a meeting with Jim, okay? And thanks for thinking about this."

Mark signaled and waited to drive into the cul de sac to Ann's house. "Are you all right?" he asked. "Did something happen in New York that bothered you? You mentioned looking at old papers. Did you find some other information from the past about Gene's disappearance?"

CHAPTER SIXTEEN

"Aunt Elle? Did you ever keep secrets from Uncle Art?"

Ann watched her tip her nose down so she could look over the reading glasses. They sat in Elle's miniscule kitchen, over coffee and doughnuts on Saturday morning. "Who wants to know?"

"Elle!"

"Sometimes you don't tell 'em about their birthday gift or how much you spent on Christmas, or that you lost his new screwdriver."

"But what about something bigger than that?"

"Girl, if you have something to tell that young man of yours, you'd better do it."

"It's big, Elle. I don't know exactly what to say. I need advice."

"Ask your mother." Elle slid her chair back from the table with a scrape and went to dump the remainder of her cold coffee in the sink. She turned on the tap to fill a watering can.

Ann watched her finger a philodendron that curled around the window and add some water from the can. "I need you, Aunt Elle."

Elle stared at something outside of the window. "You're acting like a new bride. You were married near as long as I was."

"I'm not a new bride."

"You surely are not."

"Mark is pushing to have Gene declared dead legally."

"About time."

"You know what happened the last time I tried that."

Elle, looking over her shoulder at Ann, let her chained glasses settle against her sweater. "How old are you?"

Ann smacked her hand against the table. "Will everyone please stop asking me that?"

"When I visited New York City some years back with Aunt Adaline and Aunt Isabelle," Elle said, with her back turned on Ann, "I thought I saw your Gene. This was not long after he vanished, you know, so I was sure it had to be him. I wanted to protect you if that husband of yours had simply decided to walk out on you and the boy." Elle faced Ann and leaned against the counter, fiddling with the sugar spoon. "But it wasn't him."

"How do you know?"

"I asked him."

"I can't stand this, not knowing."

"What you should ask yourself, Ann, is what are you afraid of?"

"Afraid?" Ann hunched at the table. "I don't know."

"Maybe Gene's been waiting for you to put him to rest."

"Maybe. I wasn't ready, before. I'm not sure I am, yet."

"Are you convincing yourself, me, or that lovely man who has already waited long enough?"

"I need to tell Mark about something that happened in New York. I'm just not sure how."

"Oh, honey, you've always known what's right and what's wrong."

Ann went over to hug her aunt. "Keeping big secrets is wrong, I guess."

Elle patted Ann's shoulder. "Then you best not do that."

"What if he gets angry?"

"That's been one of your problems all along. Not enough anger, not enough passion or emotion let out. Shouldn't you be angry, too?"

"Maybe I should." She put her coat on. "Thanks, Aunt Elle."

At the door she asked, "Don't you want to know what I have to tell him?"

Elle snorted. "Of course I do. Somebody in the family will blister the phone lines soon enough. I'm more excited to find out who'll tell me first."

Back at home, Ann groaned at the ringing phone when the caller ID Mark installed for her showed Rachel's name. Ann worried about Maeve. Of course she did, but seeing the man who might be Gene had driven those troubles out of Ann's thoughts. She picked up the handset on the fifth jingle. "Rachel?"

"You're home. I wondered. Um, hi, how was your trip?"

"It had its moments. What's up? I talked to Mom earlier, and she seems to be good."

"Oh, right. Mom's made a great recovery, hasn't she?"

Ann held the phone away from her ear and banged it in frustration. Rachel had called her. She put the phone back against the side of her head and waited, trying not to breathe too heavily.

"Ann, I just wanted to say thank you. Mark really stepped in there. I guess, well, I don't know how things would have turned out if he hadn't done what he did."

Ann raised both her eyebrows. "What are you talking about?"

"Well, I know it might seem like nothing."

"Rachel —"

"But it meant the world to me. Maeve is so happy, and scared, too, like I am, and I —"

"Rachel! Wait. I don't understand."

"What Mark did for Maeve, of course. I take back everything"

"What did he do?"

"The job —"

"What job? Where —"

"In Cottage Grove. The internship. Didn't he say where it was? I should have Maeve —"

"He hasn't said anything. No one told me anything. Rachel, start from the beginning."

Ann pulled a fleece throw around her shoulders while she listened to her sister tell of Maeve's return to school and her move from the retreat center to an apartment in Cottage Grove.

"I've been back a week," Ann said. "Why am I just hearing about this now? Mom didn't even tell me."

"I don't know, Ann. Maybe you should ask Mark."

"Maybe I should. Rachel, I'm glad you called."

"I'm sorry, Ann, about the things I said. I really do love you, you know."

"I know."

"And I want you to be happy."

"Thanks."

"Are you?"

Ann bit her lip to keep from crying. Rachel would know something was wrong. "Yes."

"I can hear you, all teary over there," Rachel's voice buzzed over the line. "So I'll let you go. Just know you have one good man there. Don't let him forget it, okay?"

Only when his cool fingers grazed the top of her brassiere did Ann realize the buttons of her blouse were open. Her gasp was automatic. She wrenched away, scrambling to pull herself together, embarrassed to meet Mark's eyes. When his hands gently turned her face to his, the vulnerability of his expression made her wilt. Ann settled her hands on his shoulders. Her fingers dug into his muscles. What answer could she give to his silent question? She'd caused this passion in a man and didn't know how to handle it.

Ann unclamped her fingers and began to

re-button her shirt, still mesmerized by the firelight reflecting off his skin. Her fingers shook so hard she couldn't match the button with the hole. Mark helped her. When she reached to cover his hands with hers, another outpouring of desire gripped her. Her gaze dropped to his mouth and she squeezed her eyes shut.

When had love so inflamed her before? Menopause was supposed to decrease her desire. She was filled with remorse at the memory of Mark at Thanksgiving gently telling her no. What had changed? Why had he let things get away like this?

Be fair, I've been leading him on. Is this how I want to treat him? Force him to do something I know we'll both regret? What kind of love is that?

As if reading her mind, Mark immediately pulled away, but not too far. Her passion muffled his voice. "I'm sorry. I thought for a moment . . . I thought when you took my shirt off we —"

Ann looked down, now, mortified to see his bare chest, lightly haired where Gene's had sprouted an impressive pelt. Gene's skin also had an array of dark splotches. Mark's skin glowed, his muscles subtly rippling along his rib cage as he leaned forward to pluck his shirt from the floor. She watched, eyelids at half-mast, while he tucked his arms inside and buttoned two middle buttons.

Ann took a deep breath after their eyes met. She fell against him, unresisting as his arms wrapped around her again. She felt his mouth against her temple, the warm rush of air as he spoke. She struggled to concentrate on his words while burning saltwater gathered behind her eyelids.

When Mark had arrived that evening, while they sat together in the living room, instead of blurting out the fact that she thought her husband was still alive, Ann had chickened out and acted like some kind of sleaze. "I'm sorry, Mark. You need to go. I can't hurt you."

Mark turned and gently finished re-buttoning first her blouse, then his own shirt. He pulled her back tightly against him to shield her — from what? God's eyes?

"This act would have made us husband and wife in the eyes of God," he whispered.

Ann forced herself away from him. "Marriage?" She jumped to her feet, back pedaling. "What are you talking about? I can't marry you."

"Why not? We love each other. I'm ready to redefine our relationship."

"I told you, I don't want to change who

we are."

"Why is it so hard for you accept that I want more for us?"

"Maybe I don't think anyone should be with me."

"Marriage isn't only about love, you know." Mark got to his feet and walked toward her.

Ann backed up, almost frantic. "I'm already married. M-married. To Gene Fi-fitzgerald B-ballard." She closed her eyes. "Please."

She could feel him. He stood that close, but did not touch her.

His voice whispered harshly. "Please what? Don't hurt you? Wonder how you're going to pay your bills? Think about you doing normal things like cooking and washing clothes and raking leaves without me?" He bridged the gap and leaned his forehead against hers. "Please what? Wither if I can't be with you any more?"

"Help me." Ann felt her knees buckle and Mark grab her elbows. "It's going so fast. I think I, I need . . . I can't let anything happen to you." She let him lead her back to the sofa where he spread an afghan over her, then settled her head on a pillow on his lap.

"What could happen to me?" he asked. When she opened her eyes, he told her, "We have to talk about Gene."

Ann's stomach convulsed and this time she couldn't stop the sick rush. With both hands over her mouth, she barely made it to the powder room in the hallway. Mark followed to support her head over the toilet, then gently wiped her mouth with his handkerchief. "Over?" He took her back to the living room. "I'll be right back."

She heard him rummage in the kitchen, then the tap running. He returned to crouch in front of her with her pills and water. "You probably want to go to bed," he said. He brushed her cheek with the back of his hand. "We can talk later."

Ann leaned on Mark as he helped her up the stairs to her room. This time she did not protest when he unbuttoned her blouse and helped her slip into a flannel nightshirt she left on the bed. He sat with her in the shadowy dark, holding her hand, until she relaxed into the rhythm of the pulsating pain.

He leaned over her to kiss her forehead before he left. "I'll call you tomorrow. I love you."

After he was gone, Ann let the tears roll across her cheeks.

Mark reached for his phone a half a dozen

times the next morning. Was she awake yet? How did she feel? But, mostly, what could he say? He skipped church in favor of a long walk followed by newspaper and coffee in a local donut shop. Back at home, the silence of the too-blue apartment drove him outside.

He drove aimlessly around town. Something had happened to Ann in New York. Outwardly, she seemed fine, but in the past two weeks, instead of welcoming his calls, she seemed to cut short their conversation and visits. He wanted to call Colleen, ask how to get in touch with her mother, Katherine. He could probably figure out how to track the woman down himself, but what kind of excuse would he give to pry information out of them? He would never want to hurt Colleen, especially when she was so close to giving birth.

When the restlessness got the better of him, Mark drove to Ann's. There were no lights in her house, no evidence she'd ventured outside that day. He picked up her Sunday paper, then punched in the code at the garage door and let himself in.

Mark started calling as soon as he set foot in the kitchen. "Ann! Annie, where are you? Are you okay?"

When she did not answer, he called again

into the silence of her house. "Annie! Answer me!" Alarmed, he ran up the stairs to her room, where he'd left her last night.

Her eyes were puffy, her hair a tangle. He knew she was awake by the way her chest rose and fell. "Ann, have you been here all day? Look at me. Are you okay? Do you need a doctor?"

He sat next to her still form on the bed and took her hand. He leaned close to hear her whisper. "You should leave now."

For an answer, he tossed his jacket on the floor and kicked off his shoes. He slipped beneath the comforter, lying quiet for a time before moving close to her, separated by sheet and blanket. "Of course I'm not leaving. Ann. I'm here. Tell me what to do, how to make it better."

"It can't get better. You should stay away from me."

"I'm not leaving you, Annie. It's not just a migraine, is it? Whatever's wrong, I want to help."

"That's what you're good at, aren't you? Helping."

Mark smoothed her rumpled hair. "Among other things." He put his lips on her temple and wrapped an arm around her. He stayed silent, waiting for her until he couldn't take it. "Whatever you're feeling, you can tell me."

"I'm tired," she mumbled. "And scared."

"If you're afraid I'll leave you, I've told you over and over that I'm here for the duration. I'm not going anywhere." He stroked her cheek.

"What if I did something really terrible?"

"You? Like, what?"

"Just — I don't know." She turned a little, facing him for the first time. Her eyes were dark, ringed with red. "What if it was something you couldn't forgive."

"Ann, I can't imagine anything I couldn't forgive. And I've seen a lot of unforgivable activities in my line of work. Do you have something you need to tell me?"

Her eyes closed. "Yes."

Mark waited again. He could feel his heart try to thump sideways, painfully, as he lay against her cocooned figure. When he saw the tears squeeze from behind her lids, he willed his lungs to keep inflating. "Do you want to pray about it?"

He watched her lips tightened around the "no."

"Annie, if you can't tell me now, that's okay. I'll wait. But whatever it is, I'll always love you."

She nodded, her whole face scrunched as

if in pain. "I need to go back to New York. Alone."

He swallowed the acid that rose to his throat and bit his lips to keep from screaming, "You met someone else, didn't you?"

"When?" he asked instead.

"Tomorrow. Just for . . . just for a couple days."

He did not offer to buy her ticket this time.

CHAPTER SEVENTEEN

Ann winced as the uniformed woman behind the counter at the airport handed her the credit receipt to sign. Two months' future salary was going toward this trip. She calculated quickly in her head. It would take four months to pay it off. She paced and fidgeted while she waited in the lounge area. The rows of uncomfortable chairs were arranged so that she couldn't walk more than a few paces without running into something or someone.

Her flight left on time.

Katherine had already gone to Green Bay to wait for Ritchie and Colleen's baby. She'd left instructions with the neighbor to let Ann into the New York apartment where Ann planned to sleep for two nights. Hopefully only two. If her plan worked, Ann would go to the Smarts' apartment, introduce herself, talk to them, and assure herself Alan Smart and Gene Ballard were very different people. Afterward, she would turn around and come home to tell Mark everything, and beg him to forgive her for being afraid. He would understand.

Now, she prayed that baby wouldn't decide to come while she was gone. Ann didn't want to give Ritchie any more fuel for his continued resentment. She and Colleen talked regularly on the telephone these past weeks. Colleen constantly mentioned her mother and mother-in-law's upcoming visits when the baby arrived. Ritchie hadn't actually banned her from their lives. Ann hoped he would soften with the arrival of his son.

She raced through LaGuardia upon her arrival that evening, overnight bag in hand, getting into a waiting taxi like a seasoned big-city dweller. Ann tried to set her nerves aside and carry out her plan with automated efficiency, stoked on adrenaline. Once in Katherine's apartment, she turned up the heat and popped two over-the-counter painkillers purported to help her sleep. She made up a bed and dropped into a deep, dreamless slumber.

Ann woke late to leaden skies and cold rain. A perfect day to cuddle up by the fireplace with a book and be thankful she didn't have to go out. Except that she was already out. Ann peeled the blankets back. *Out of my element. Out of my mind.*

She stood in the shower until it ran cold. Shivering, Ann toweled and dressed in wool slacks and matching green jacket. Beige silk blouse, the cloisonné pin Gene had given her on her thirty-sixth birthday. Brush hair. Makeup. Her hand shook so hard she decided against mascara. No breakfast. Definitely no food. Maybe toast. Half a piece. Coat. Umbrella. Open the door, Ann.

She didn't need a taxi, right? For six blocks. Ann reviewed the streets in her head, the address of her destination burned into her brain. She could walk. Nice neighborhood, middle of the morning, only a few blocks. Criminals were out when it was dark. And never in the rain. Had Gene disappeared at night? Had it been raining? Or had he simply vanished into the black?

It's morning, now. Walk, walk, walk, Ann.

Take a right. Yes, this way. Two blocks. Then turn the corner. Cross the street. Keep going. Oh, God. Oh, God. No prayers came to mind. Raindrops pattered on the umbrella. Ann gripped the handle and held it like a shield against the sky. Someone's coming this way. Am I supposed to talk to her? She looks okay.

A woman in a trench coat and scarf

greeted Ann. "Hello." Ann's knuckles tightened on the umbrella's handle and nodded back, her throat too dry to make words come out. Two more blocks. Don't step on the cracks. Keep going.

There it was. The building corresponding to the street and number listed under Alan and Linda Smart in the phone book. Ann took out a piece of paper from her pocket and checked it. Her hands were trembling with cold, making the paper jump so she couldn't read the numbers. She put it away again.

Maybe they're not home. I should have called, introduced myself first. "Hello, this is Ann Ballard. You're holding my husband hostage, aren't you?"

Oh, God. Oh, God.

Ann walked past the front entrance to the brick and white clapboard-sided building, just to see how it felt. Nothing said she had to go inside. Nothing. The end of the block is right there. She could turn around, go back to Katherine's, call a taxi to take her to the airport and go home. Take another step, Ann. One foot forward.

Ann blinked. She stood in front of a door painted brown and stenciled with B-3 in faux gold. Ann stared at the glittery color of the letters and numbers. There was a peep hole in the middle of the door. She swallowed. *Did I walk up here? I thought they weren't home. I've never been so rude, calling unannounced.*

Her knuckles stung briefly. Ann looked at her hand in surprise. *Knocked? I knocked?*

The man she'd seen in the restaurant opened the door. He stood still, head cocked to the left. Ann hadn't noticed earlier that one of his eyes was cloudy. Ann counted to ten. He said, "I'm supposed to know you, aren't I? I'm brain injured." He laughed. "I forget a lot of things. Lin-Lin! Lady at the door!"

The beige-haired woman peered around the man. She put her hand on his arm. "Thank you, Alan." Alan turned away.

Ann cleared her throat twice before she could get her frozen lips to bend around the words. "I'm sorry to intrude. My name —"

"I know who you are," the woman said. She had an unnatural calm. Her smile would have been called mocking on anyone else but, on her, indicated expectation met. At least, that's how Ann read it. "Come in." She gestured for Ann to follow her inside.

They walked into an open area that seemed to serve as living room and dining area combined. Ann could see a dark open entry that may have led to a kitchen. A hall was at the back right. The woman did not offer to take her coat.

Ann hung onto the umbrella. "You must be Linda Smart," she said, for propriety's sake.

"Yes. Would you like to sit down?"

Ann perched on the end of a worn sofa. A television set was on, the volume very low. Several toys and books littered the brown shag carpet. A few framed photographs were displayed on the wall above the television. A picture of Alan and Linda in what could have been wedding clothes, an infant, a toddler, a boy in front of a birthday cake, a child with dark hair and a fine aquiline nose. Like his father's.

"What do you want?"

Ann jumped at the sound of Linda's voice. She studied her hostess, whose expression hadn't changed. "My husband disappeared several years ago, Mrs. Smart."

"Call me Linda."

"Linda. His name was Gene Ballard. Almost everyone thinks he's dead."

"But you don't."

"After the first few years," Ann cleared her throat, "when he didn't come back, I thought he had to be dead."

"I remember the story. You're not from

New York, are you?"

"No. And neither was my husband. He was here on business."

A young boy came barreling from the hall. "Mom, Mom!" He looked at Ann, then put a finger in his mouth and plopped his head on his mother's lap.

Linda laughed. "Richard Michael, say hello to the lady."

The child raised his head. His eyes gleamed. He grinned, pulled the finger from his mouth, said hello and quickly hid his head again. Alan lumbered into the room. Linda patted the space beside her on the rocking love seat. "Alan, come sit by me."

Alan sat. He stared at Ann. "I'm supposed to know you," he repeated.

"What makes you say that, Alan?" Linda asked.

"I forget everything."

"No, you don't," Linda soothed. "You know me. You know Richard Michael."

Alan nodded his head. "Yes, yes that's right. I'm a father."

"I'm sorry you were hurt, Alan," Ann said. "When was your accident?"

Alan turned to Linda, a puzzled frown on his face. "I had an accident?"

"A long time ago, dear," Linda told him. "Before you were a father."

"How long?" Ann asked.

Linda looked at her. "Richard Michael is five years old."

The child climbed onto Alan's lap, and held up a hand, fingers spread out. "Five," he said.

Ann tried another tack. "May I ask when you two met?"

Alan and Richard Michael began a game of thumb wrestling with their left hands, giggling. Alan's right hand looked puffy, the fingers crooked. He let it sit, like a wooden thing, on Richard Michael's knee.

"Richard is a good name for a boy," Alan said.

Richard Michael giggled. "That's my name."

"Michaelzzzz. I know Michaelzz," Alan said, still thumb wrestling with his son.

"Why don't you go play, now?" Linda suggested.

"I want to watch TV," Richard Michael said. He slid from Alan's lap and plopped in front of the set, but didn't adjust the volume.

"Why did you come?" Linda asked Ann quietly.

"I have to go," Alan said.

"Okay. Go ahead," Linda told him. Both of them watched him shuffle in an uneven gait to eventually disappear down the hall. "Why are you here now?"

"A couple of weeks ago," Ann whispered, with a glance at the child, "I was visiting a friend, here in town. We had coffee at Tom's, and when I saw you and your hu-husband and son, for a moment, I thought it looked like —"

"Even if what you thought was true, what could you do about it?"

Ann's heart began to pound so hard it hurt to take a breath. "Do? What could I do about it? Linda, I've lived every moment of the past seven and a half years in torment, not knowing whether my husband was alive or dead."

"If he were alive, wouldn't his absence mean he didn't want to be with you any more?"

Ann wanted to pull the other woman's hair, scream, throw a spit ball, anything to make her change expression from that eerie half-smile. "If Gene didn't want to be married to me anymore, he could have simply divorced me. He would have at least had the courtesy to do that."

"If you think he's dead, why are you here?"

"What if he's not? I want to see your marriage certificate."

She and Linda stared at each other. "It won't give you any more information than you already know." Ann heard the toilet flush. Richard Michael reached a hand toward the television set's volume control and turned up the music to the children's program. "What do you get when you put one and one together?" asked a puppet's sickly gooey TV voice.

"Three?" Linda suggested. "There isn't anything to gain here. The three of us are happy. Nothing ever stays the same. That's what my mother always said, and I believe it. You can never go backward and hope to recapture the same moment of joy. You have to keep moving forward."

"Keep moving forward," Alan echoed, as he came back into the room. "I'm supposed to know you, aren't I?" he said to Ann, his eyes on her front, where her coat opened. "Pretty. Pretty pin."

"Say goodbye to Mrs. Ballard, boys," Linda said. She rose to her feet. "It was nice meeting you, but we don't want to keep you from whatever you were doing."

"Ballard, Ballard, Ballard," Alan said.

Richard Michael stood and stared at Ann with wide eyes. "She's not Mrs. Ballard."

Ann's cell phone buzzed. In a dream, she pulled it out of her pocket and looked at the screen. *Boy David Ritchard 7 lb. 1 oz. 20 in. 7:27 AM.*

Ann couldn't have gotten to her feet even if Linda Smart pulled out a gun and ordered her.

"Help me out, here," she said to Linda. "Why did your son say I'm not Mrs. Ballard?"

"There are a lot of Mrs. Ballards. Richard Michael, will you please go get your shoes on in your room? We're going to go to the park."

"It's raining." Alan looked out of the window, his forehead scrunched. He shifted his feet.

Ann listened to the boy plod down the hall, clearly reluctant to leave the scene. "What other Ballards do you know?"

"In Florida," Alan said, eager to join the conversation. "We go to the beach all of the time." He contemplated Linda. "We should go there, instead of the park. It's not raining on the beach."

"Do you mean, you visit Donna, Ge— Alan?" Ann asked.

"I'm sorry to seem so rude, ma'am, but I need to ask you to leave now," Linda said. She put her hand on the doorknob.

"Donna?" Alan shook his head. "No. The beach."

"Why don't you get your jacket, Alan? We'll go out for lunch," Linda said.

When Ann was alone with Linda, she forced her rubbery knees to hold her weight. Every ounce of will went to direct one foot in front of the other. When she reached the door, Ann held out the phone to show Linda the screen. "Gene is a grandfather. Just this morning. Our son had a baby boy named David. David Ritchard. He should know that."

Linda Smart's enigmatic smile was back in place. She opened the door. "I hope someday you get to tell him that. You'll understand that I don't ask you to come again. Goodbye."

Ann stood her ground, anger rising over nauseous fear. "That man deserves to know the truth."

Linda's smile cracked. "The truth of what? You've seen him. In a couple of years, maybe even sooner, Richard Michael will surpass his father's mental capability. If I do it right, maybe, just maybe I can teach the boy not to despise his father for his limitations. Alan is comfortable with us. He's happy here. We've given him familiar surroundings. He knows me and he trusts me. Only a cruel and vicious person would even think of taking that away from him."

Linda looked her up and down. "I don't know you, but you don't seem the cruel and vicious type. I hope I'm not wrong."

"Even if I agree with you, where does Donna Ballard come into this?"

Alan and Richard Michael came into the living room, jacketed and holding hands.

Linda waved at them and inclined her head at Ann. "Goodbye."

Ann walked in the rain, her open coat flapping around her. She clutched the closed umbrella and the open cell phone with its message in numb, lifeless hands. Ann circled the blocks, hardly paying attention to her course until the street lights came on. She forced herself to look at the numbered street signs and found the one that corresponded to Katherine's.

Ann did not know how wet she'd gotten until she saw the puddle she left near Katherine's front door. She set the umbrella in the stand and hung the coat in the bathroom. When Ann saw that the cheery light display of the cell phone was dark, she rummaged in her bag until she found the charger. When she plugged the instrument in, she jumped at the spark and crackle and quickly yanked the cord. That was probably not a good sign. Well, everyone knew where she was. Katherine did not have local service to the apartment. Ann briefly contemplated finding a pay phone to call Ritchie and Colleen. She shivered and decided to take a shower first.

Under the hot water, Ann felt a tremble of reaction start. The shock of what she'd seen and heard, the fact that she'd missed being there for her son at one of the most important times of his life, caused her to sink to the bottom of the tub where she wept long after the hot water ran out. This time, the pain was from her swollen eyes and stuffed nose. Not a migraine, thank heavens. Even though she expected it, she knew she couldn't deal with that, too, right now.

After dragging herself from the bathroom and fixing hot tea to take with aspirin, Ann sat on the sofa, her only light coming in from the street. She cradled the cup to her cheek so that the steam rose against her puffy eyes. What's the right thing to do, Lord? Had there ever been such a situation on the face of the planet? Was she vicious and cruel? For a few minutes back there at the Smarts' she would have to say yes, definitely, vicious and cruel described Ann Ballard to perfection.

How could the detectives have missed such a huge clue? For that matter, what about the hospital? Didn't they have some sort of obligation to report patients brought in with no ID and no memory? Then the police could check against missing persons cases. It was supposed to work that way.

The Smarts' apartment had been filled with the signs of their faith: portraits of saints with halos covered the walls, along with a huge crucifix including the bloody figure of Jesus in living color. Middle-aged nurse Linda Smart wanted a husband. A man was brought in to the emergency room. Had Linda guessed the injured man's identity and deliberately hid it?

What's the right thing to do? For her sake, for Ritchie's, for the man himself? Ann could see that Alan had probably reached the limit of rehabilitation. The scary, hurtful question she asked herself was, what would she have done if Gene had been brought home to her in this condition? Ann felt the tears drip from her chin. *I don't know . . . I don't know that I would have loved him still, that I could have cared for him like Linda has. What kind of a monster am I?*

Did Ritchie deserve to know about Gene/Alan? Linda admitted nothing. Ann replayed the conversation. No names had ever been mentioned. No undocumented circumstances had been brought up. Linda would deny everything if Ann tried to force her hand to the authorities. What would Ritchie want to do? Especially in light of his own fatherhood. "If I do this right," Linda had said, "I can teach the boy not to despise his father."

Teach the boy. Ann jerked her head back with a snap as she realized she was falling asleep. She set the half-filled mug of cold tea on the end table and stumbled to bed. The one person she couldn't absolve in this whole mess was Donna Ballard.

CHAPTER EIGHTEEN

Mark hurried down the long corridor to Judge Wilbert's court, threading his way through groups of people who seemed to be moving in all directions at once. Jennifer normally took care of the paperwork that had to be filed at the county courthouse. She hadn't protested when he offered to take it, saying he needed to visit the State Law Library, anyway.

Ann must have decided to go ahead with the hearing. For the past three days, since she returned from New York, she'd been holed up in Portage with the new baby. They had spoken daily. Ann had talked of nothing but her grandson and how Colleen and Ritchie were handling the parenting chores; even something about Ritchie and his first diapering, caught on camera. Mark took a harsh breath, tamping down a stab of envy. A baby named David claimed Ann now. When Tiffany and Dad brought Trey home, Mark had been nine years old. The baby had fascinated him. He stood at Trey's crib for hours, watching the tiny chest heave and the little mouth pucker. If Tiffany caught Mark in there when Trey started crying, she usually blamed him for waking the baby.

Mark had arrived at the office at his usual six-thirty in the morning to get some of the fussiest chores out of the way. The note had been left on his desk sometime overnight. Parsons had left word that at one p.m., the judge would hear Ann's request for a finding of death in the matter of her long-missing husband. Ann said nothing about it last night when they talked. Of course she would be there. So would he, whether he'd been invited, or not.

Mark caught up to her just before she and Parsons entered the courtroom.

Parsons eyed him. "Excuse me a minute, won't you? Dry throat." He stepped away.

"Ann!" Mark took her hands and kissed her on the cheek. He did not let go when she stepped back. She wore one of her severely cut dark suits. She was pale, her eyes huge, he supposed, from staying up with the baby so Colleen could get some rest. "I'm sorry I missed you yesterday. Are you okay?"

"Of course. I-I'm glad you're here." She pulled out of his grasp as Parsons returned. They walked into the empty room together.

Mark only half-listened to Wilbert's usual opening comments, the question of whether the required notices had been sent to all interested parties, and, for the record, who was all present today. If Mark had thought Ann pale before she entered the room, now she looked translucent. He studied her, wondering if he needed to say anything. Parsons looked straight ahead while they waited through the formalities, oblivious to her shudder. Parsons wouldn't understand the way Mark did that Ann's hunch meant she wished she were somewhere else. The look he was beginning to recognize as one of pain.

Wilbert looked over his half-glasses from the bench, papers in hand. "If there are no objections, the court finds —"

Ann stood. "Excuse me." She turned, gray-faced, to Mark. "Can I talk to you? Alone?"

Mark sat on the bench outside of the court-room. Ann crouched in front of him with her head bowed after spinning the most fascinating tale. Fairy tale. Had to be.

"Help me," she said. "I don't know what

the right thing is. I don't even think there is any right thing to do. Mark, you should have seen him. He's a child playing with his son one moment, the next, a confused and broken old man."

Mark's diaphragm stuck in place. He couldn't make it expand. Pinpricks of light circled in front of his eyes. "Look at the stars, Ann," he would have said, if he could have gotten the words out. "Aren't they pretty?" Mark tried to direct his heart to beat, but it wouldn't obey him, either. His brain synapses kept firing, though. He would rather stop thinking than breathing or circulating blood. How could he make his brain stop thinking?

From a distance, Parson's voice filtered down to him. "How's it going out here? Everything all right?"

"No," he said.

Parson's shoes came within range of his bent head. Polished, nice. Black. Little holes in a pattern. Mark started counting the holes. Parson's voice intruded. "What?" Mark asked.

He raised his head with an effort. He'd only gotten to seven and there were more fascinating holes to count. Two rows of them. "Your client has something to tell you," Mark said. Someone laughed. That wasn't right. Nothing funny about this whole thing. Nothing at all.

"Mrs. Ballard?"

Then again, Mark decided as he pushed himself to his feet, actually, it was pretty funny when you thought about it. "Dead man walking," Mark said, as he made his way down the hall.

"Mark, wait!" Whose voice called? Didn't know, didn't care.

Mark got in the elevator and pressed buttons. By the time the crazy thing deposited him near his car, Mark regained control of himself. To a point. Not enough to speak to anyone, but enough so that he could drive. Crazy stupid one-way streets around the capitol building, around campus. What idiot designed downtown Madison? Honk, honk. I know. I know. Two lakes, isthmus. Stupid. When Mark saw the sign that said, "To Interstate 39," he switched lanes to another round of angry horns and raced north.

In Wausau, he exited the freeway, numb with tiredness. There were still more one-way streets that confused him in the dusk, and when he saw the blue and red lights flashing in his rearview mirror, he was almost glad. A few minutes later he rolled down his window.

A bright light flared briefly in Mark's face.

"License and registration, sir."

"Yes, of course. I guess I'm just tired, and I don't know the area well. It was a one-way, wasn't it? I'm sorry." Mark fished in his glove compartment and handed the registration along with his driver's license to the officer.

"Have you been drinking, sir?"

"No. I'm just tired. In fact, if you could direct me to a hotel —"

"I'm going to ask you to step out of the vehicle, sir."

Mark wondered if he should protest. The officer would see soon enough that he wasn't drunk. He really wanted to find somewhere to crash, though, and if being compliant would get him to a hotel sooner, then so be it.

"Touch your nose with your forefinger."

Mark was glad no one knew him in Wausau. If this were Madison, he would be worried a client would see him and call the office. He did as he was told. "See, I'm fine. I'm sorry I was confused in the dark."

The light flashed in his eyes once again. His papers were returned to him. "You may return to your vehicle." Once Mark had gotten behind the wheel, the officer told him he was being forgiven. The man pointed in the direction of the yellow Best Western sign. "I'll watch until you get there," he told Mark.

"Thank you. I appreciate it." Mark rolled up his window and carefully waited for a break in the line of cars before he pulled into traffic, going along with them this time. The hotel was only a quarter mile down the road. By the time Mark had checked in, sans luggage, and sat on the bed, he felt ridiculous. He'd never run away from home even when his mother's boyfriend had done something stupid.

He kicked off his shoes and stretched out on the bed so that his head was near the telephone. The longing for Ann was visceral. "What if I did something you couldn't forgive?" she'd asked.

Mark put a hand on the telephone, as if just touching it would bring him comfort. What had she done, exactly? The first time she'd gone to New York, she thought she saw someone who looked like her dead husband, whose body had never been found. Annie had just come to terms with moving on, with being in love with someone else, and maybe she'd been stressed. She returned to New York, actually talked to the guy and his wife, who didn't admit anything about stealing the dead husband's identity. Why would they? Smart, Annie said the name was. Ann said she didn't know what to do. The man acted brain damaged. She did not think he would ever be wholly functional. A child was involved somehow.

But why didn't Ann tell me any of this? Doesn't she trust me? Mark raised his arm over his eyes. Why? What have I done to make her not want to tell me something like this?

Mark sat up. Nothing. He hadn't given her a chance. He pulled his phone from his pocket and dialed.

"Hello?"

"Ann." He couldn't get any more out.

"Oh, Mark, thank God. Where are you?"

He cleared his throat. "I just drove for a while. I'm so sorry. So sorry. Please, don't be mad."

"Mad? Mad? Mad at you?! Are you kidding? I'm the one who's sorry. Mark, please, believe me. I just wasn't sure, I didn't know what to say. And then the baby. And what if it had been me? I kept thinking that —"

"Ann, it's all right."

"Are you coming home? Please, Mark, let me explain —"

"Yes," Mark whispered.

"When? Where are you?"

"In Wausau. At the Best Western. Room — I don't know. Wait, it's one-seventeen."

"I'm coming right up."

"Ann, wait. Don't drive by yourself."

"I'll be right there. Well, in a couple of hours. Wait for me . . . promise? Please?"

She hung up before Mark could reply.

Two hours later, Mark bolted upright. A clattering knock at the door sounded. "Coming. Just a sec." Mark had fallen asleep despite the jumble of his emotions. Ann practically fell into his arms when he pulled the door open. She pressed herself against him, teary and trembling, apologizing over and over.

The only way he could think of to get her to stop babbling was to press his mouth firmly against hers. It worked pretty well until she started crying and choked. With that, he drew her to the bed, where they sat lounged arm in arm until she calmed enough to speak. "So, you understand? You understand how hard this is? I love you so much and I was so afraid you would think I lied. So that's why I didn't tell you everything."

"Didn't you even consider not telling me was just as much a lie?"

"Of course not. If you can't say anything good, don't say —"

"Ann! That's what parents teach their children."

"But isn't it true?"

"Only to a certain extent. Allowing me to believe something that's not true is fraud."

"Oh. I didn't know. I'm sorry. And now I have to go." Ann scrambled away from him.

Mark barely managed to catch her elbow. "What are you doing?" Her eyes were wide with relief and trust. He couldn't understand the gist of what she was telling him at first.

"Don't you see? That's the whole point. What if this kind of accident happened to you? I don't know what I'd do. I don't trust myself to know that I would take care of you, like Linda. I don't think I could have done it with Gene. In fact, I know I wouldn't. I would have put him away somewhere safe where I wouldn't have to look at him all the time and feel guilty that I just couldn't . . . Oh, Lord, I'm vicious and cruel. Just like she said I was." She pulled from his grasp. "I have to go."

Mark lunged and missed her arm. He managed to grab her before she pushed her feet into her shoes. "Stop that. What if this was you? Don't you want to know I'll still be there for you, no matter what?"

Ann looked at him again with that innocent expression that made his heart throb. "I hope not."

Mark shook his head with unbelief. "What?"

"You have to promise me you'd never do that. If something happened to me where I was never going to get better, you have to say that you'd move on, continue to live without me."

"That's not what love is about."

"Real love means everyone gets what's good for them, right?"

"Don't start that crazy version of your theology on me."

"If the best thing for me is to be left in some kind of institution, then you have to do it. Especially if I needed special care, or was a danger to others."

"You sound like a brochure for an Alzheimer's unit."

"It happens." Ann pushed her feet into the shoes and began to look for her coat.

"What about me? You said you didn't know what you would do."

Her back was turned to him. She went still. "I think, maybe I would die if something like that happened, something that would take you away from me."

He approached silently in his stocking feet. She jumped when his hands settled on her shoulders, before he turned her and gathered her close. "Ann. Stop. Let's think what to do now. Together, okay? We can work together on this now, right?"

"What about when it's over? When it's fixed?"

"Then I have a question to ask you. When it's fixed."

"No, I mean, once there aren't any more problems, once I don't need your help anymore? You'll get bored."

"Now what are you talking about?" Mark stepped away from her. "I don't understand you!"

"I figured it out, Mark," Ann nodded her head for emphasis. She even put her hand on his arm. "You have to be where you can help people. But what happens if you don't have someone to help?"

"Ann! I can't help everyone! I don't know where you get these crazy ideas. You know what I thought you were doing in New York, when you told me you had to go back, without me?"

She ducked her head and winced. Maybe because he was shouting. He forced himself to voice his accusation with dignity. "I thought you'd met someone else."

"Oh, Mark." This time she breached the gap to wrap her arms around his waist.

Gradually Mark felt the tension ebbing from them both. He urged Ann to join him once again on the bed, where they could sit together. It might not be entirely the most appropriate setting, but the hard chairs around a small table in a corner of the room were the only unappealing alternative, besides the floor.

"Are you ready to talk about this?" he said.

"Yes."

"I have to ask you," Mark said, gritting his teeth. "How do you feel about Gene?"

"Feel? You mean about my husband, or Alan?"

"Your husband, no matter what's happened to him. Do you still want to do what's best for him."

"Oh, yes. That's why everything's been so hard. I can't believe otherwise, but the first thing to do is prove Alan and Gene are the same person. Donna is involved in this," Ann said. "I don't understand why she wouldn't say anything all these years. It just doesn't make any sense."

Mark closed his eyes in concentration. "Wait. Tell me the names of everyone again."

"Linda Smart — that's the name of the woman nurse. We checked her records. She's got a birth certificate with that name, and her tax records indicate she's had the same employer for over thirty years. Pretty hard to fake that." Ann snorted.

"We?"

"Um, once I told Jim Parsons about all this, he jumped right in and started a search."

Jim. Not him. Well, Parsons was her attorney. He was just the boyfriend. "Okay. Next."

"Then there's Alan. The man's name is Alan. We couldn't find a marriage license record anywhere in New York state. But she gave him her own last name. Alan Smart. No birth certificate, either, so we don't know what year he was born. Well, I do, of course but that's a problem. Jim says he'll start a state by state search."

Mark had a feeling he knew which state they should start with. "And you said there was a child?"

"Yes. A son. Five years old. Spitting image of the blueblood Ballards. Even more than Ritchie. His name is Richard Michael."

"Smart?"

"Yes, of course."

"Ann." Mark sat away from her. "There's a file in the Ballard Trust records. I think I can find a way to prove that Donna's been involved."

"How?"

"One of the names of the beneficiaries in the Ballard Trust is Richard Michael Smart.

I remember it because it was so close to Ritchie's. And your maiden name, Michels. Let me make some calls. You don't happen to have your attorney's home phone number handy, do you?"

Ann smiled and slid off the bed. "You can fit a lot of stuff in a purse."

Mark was afraid to start kissing her again. He wouldn't be able to stop. He and Ann talked until they began to compete for the longest yawn. Mark moved away from her warmth reluctantly. "I'll take the other bed. You want the bathroom first?"

After thinking he'd never sleep with her so near, he remembered little but the sound of her breathing until he woke. The clock shone five o'clock. A plan on the edge of his consciousness gelled while he slept. An airport nearby would be handy. He took the phone book and his cell into the bathroom. Mark needed to call Jennifer, too. When he returned to the room, Ann was awake, her eyes on him.

"Good morning, love. Feel like a trip to Florida?"

CHAPTER NINETEEN

After picking up the rental car at Panama City's Bay County International airport, Ann directed Mark to the Ballards' gated estate on the Florida panhandle. The closer they got to her mother-in-law, the angrier Ann felt. Not just for herself, but for Ritchie and the new baby who would never know his grandfather, no matter how this turned out. She and Mark had debated whether to announce their visit or drop in on Donna. Ann planned to telephone when they were close to the gate.

Jim Parsons had offered to join them, as well as call the authorities. After searching through the LMS Enterprises file Mark told him about, the one with Ritchie's and Richard Michael's incriminating names, it was obvious Donna knew her son's current situation. Seeing Donna shackled would improve her mood. But then what about Alan? Mark had asked for time, to see if they could determine exactly what happened. Jim had faxed over several pages from the file to the hotel in Wausau, where she and Mark waited to snatch them up before heading to the airport.

Ann summoned some pity for Donna. The woman had raised two children alone. As adults, neither was independent, nor able to direct the family business. Gene would have taken over the administration duties of the Ballard Trust by now. Donna planned to sign authority to him on a certain date that had come and gone. Gene would have seen the investments spread into carefully diversified stocks and bonds, making sure everyone in the family would be well-cared for. Donna must have been afraid Ritchie did not have the same business sense of his father, and the family legacy would be siphoned off to an indirect branch of Ballards.

Ann asked Mark if he would let her talk to Donna first. She wanted Mark there, but please, let her say her piece. Nerves made her fingers fumble as she pressed the buttons on Mark's cell phone.

"Hi, Donna, this is your daughter-in-law, Ann," she said, once Donna had been summoned to the phone by the maid. "I'm down here on business. In fact, I'm nearly

316

at the gate and would like to say hello to you and Genevra, please."

Ann wondered if Donna would agree.

"Perhaps, for a little while," Donna said, her voice thin and forced. "I have not enjoyed the best health this year, but you are welcome."

"Thank you."

Ann and Mark exchanged glances. "She didn't sound like her usual self," Ann said.

"How long has it been you've spoken with her?"

"At least four years. She didn't come to Ritchie's wedding, although she sent a check. I wrote to her about the baby. Funny she didn't ask."

"Maybe Ritchie already told her."

"He's never liked her much, and I believe the feeling was mutual. Here, stop and push the button at the gate."

He touched her knee. "You feeling all right? It's been a rough couple of days. No headache?"

"No." Ann grimaced. "Or at least, not yet."

Mark drove through after the double-mesh panels slid aside. Ann had always been impressed at the sight of the huge red brick Georgian house and the surrounding gardens. She and Gene had come down at least once a year during the earlier years of their marriage. Donna and Gene's sister, Genevra, opened their Madison house in the summers, although they hadn't been up during Gene's absence.

A uniformed maid Ann didn't recognize greeted her and Mark at the door and ushered them into the parlor on the left of the central hall. Ann stopped up short at the sight of Donna Ballard, seated in a high-backed wing chair. She didn't have to work hard at summoning pity this time. The woman Ann had once feared and begged from was clearly not enjoying any kind of good health at all. Her blanketed frame was topped by a shock of white hair, where only a few years ago she'd sported black hair only lightly threaded with gray. Her thin hands and cheeks attested to emaciation of the once robust golfer.

"He-hello, Donna, Genevra. Thank you for seeing us."

"Come in. You've brought a guest."

Donna's voice quivered slightly, but otherwise held no inflection. She cleared her throat and started coughing. Genevra, seated next to her mother, pushed her big glasses higher on her nose then held a glass of some liquid for her mother.

Ann continued to walk into the dim, high-ceilinged room. "This is Mark Roth, an attorney at Jung and Royce."

Donna recovered. "Todd Royce is a good man."

"We've also been seeing each other for several months."

Donna's expression did not change.

Ann and Mark sat on a hard sofa angled away from the chairs occupied by the women. The maid rolled in a cart with what looked like a pitcher of lemonade and a tray of cookies.

Ann jumped when Mark spoke. "The fact is, Mrs. Ballard, I want to marry Ann. We've recently uncovered your secret. You've been deceiving her for years."

"I kept her all these years. I've allowed her to live the kind of lifestyle she'd never known in her modest upbringing, but to which my . . . son accustomed her." Donna's chest rose with effort. "I gave her more than she deserved, far more than she earned through her work with my son's company." Donna coughed harshly again.

Mark waited until the gasping cough ceased, then spoke before Ann could stop him. "You deprived her of her freedom, Mrs. Ballard, and you committed fraud. Ann could have moved on, gotten past the anguish and grief of not knowing her husband's fate. You knew what really happened all along. Ann and Gene's lawyers know the whole story. It's only because of Ann that you haven't been arrested yet."

Donna waved Genevra away. "Thank you. I'm all right, child." Without turning her head in Ann and Mark's direction, she said, "You want me to play the 'I'm dying' card? I was protecting my son. The same thing any mother would do."

Ann jumped up, unable to contain her outrage any longer. "Protecting him from what? Me?"

"Perhaps."

Ann thought again about the apartment where the man named Alan laughed and played with his son. She reminded herself that she would probably not have done what Linda did by taking care of him. She went to stand by the tall window with a view of the rose garden.

"What you've done is criminal, Mrs. Ballard," Mark said.

"Mark, wait," Ann said. "We have to make this clear, first. I believe Alan Smart and Gene Ballard are the same person. If we ask for a DNA test, Donna, will my belief be confirmed?"

Donna scratched out a barely audible "Already . . . done."

"How long have you known about Gene's

condition?"

"After the first year."

"Then what did you do?" Mark asked.

"Went to see him." She cleared her throat and accepted a sip of water from Genevra. Her voice sounded stronger. "At the nursing home in New York City. Vile place. He had bedsores . . . so deep. That nurse was there, visiting. She said she took care of him when he was first . . . injured. She gave him the name Alan. His rehabilitation was just beginning. Naturally I had him . . . moved."

"Why didn't you tell me?" Ann asked.

"Many patients with severe trauma such as Gene's undergo terrible bouts of . . . anger," she gasped for air, but kept going, "as they begin to heal." Genevra held the glass against her mother's lips again. After a moment, Donna continued. "I was afraid. Gene was so violent during that period. When that nurse was there, he was calmer." Ann hurt with Donna's desperate breathing. "If I was afraid of my own son, I couldn't take the chance that . . . you would reject him."

"What you really mean is a divorce would give Ann a huge claim on the Ballard Trust," Mark said. "You had no right to make a judgment call like that without talking to her."

Ann turned to face her mother-in-law. "Mark, stop!" Afraid the truth would show, but too deep into accusations to stop now, she repeated the thing she'd told Donna several times since the first attempt to have Gene declared dead. "Donna, I never wanted to take anything away from you."

Donna's silence unnerved her.

"Is that really what you thought?" Ann's voice squeaked. A band of pressure began to tighten around her eyeballs, squeezing. "That I would abandon my husband? Gene and I had a marital property agreement, but I wouldn't have —"

"Taken your half of Gene's accounts, of his business? Wisconsin is a community property state," Mark cut in.

"What about Ritchie?" Ann asked Donna.

"Eugene Ritchard was provided for by his . . . father." Donna struggled for breath.

"He and Colleen have a son. David Ritchard. I brought pictures."

Donna continued to hold her head unnaturally straight. She blinked. "What is wrong with you?" Ann meant it as an insult.

She approached her mother-in-law. The sight of a cleverly concealed neck brace sticking out from the high collar of Donna's blouse took her aback. A squat machine of some kind whirred discretely on the floor just out of sight. "Donna?"

"I've already . . . lasted much longer than I should have. Soon now. ALS." She coughed. "I've taken care of . . . Genevra, don't worry."

"When were you diagnosed?"

"Eight years ago."

The "I'm dying card" had been laid on the table at last. What a gruesome, but somehow fitting, end. Ann mentally berated herself. Her own pain snapped like a rubber band and faded. No one deserved that type of torture, not even Donna. Had she truly done what she thought best?

Ann looked at Genevra. She was two years younger than Gene. Retarded was the label from her generation. Cognitively delayed would have been politically correct now. She was how old? Middle fifties. Did she understand that she would wake up some morning in the not-distant future without her mother to care for her?

Genevra ducked her head and combed a hand through her straight hair. She peeped at Ann through the cloudy plastic lenses of her glasses. "I would like to see pictures," she said.

To give herself room to concentrate before saying anything else, Ann returned to where she'd left her purse on the sofa next to

Mark. His deep blue eyes looked dull in his pale face. Lines around his mouth and nose attested to exhaustion. Everything that had been happening was so unfair. He worked hard, then stepped in to deal with this mess on the side. She touched his knee. He twisted his lips. She recognized his thinking hard mode and left him alone while she showed Genevra pictures of the week-old baby.

Genevra handled each print carefully, giggling at the sight of her nephew holding an infant and trying to smile at the camera at the same time. After she handed the last photograph back to Ann, Genevra whispered, "They come here, too. Gene-Alan and little boy Richard Michael with Nurse Linda."

Donna began to wheeze. Genevra called the maid who ran into the room accompanied by a uniformed nurse who must have been hiding in the kitchen all this time. Genevra calmed down at the sight of the nurse. The maid cast a look at Ann that pleaded with her to take Mark away. With a last sigh at the sight of her mother-in-law, Ann led Mark to the hall. Genevra walked Ann and Mark to the front door and out to their car.

"Thank you. Goodbye, Genevra. You can

call me, you know, too, whenever you need to."

"It was nice to see you. I liked the pictures."

Genevra accepted a kiss from Ann, then waved shyly as they passed her in the driveway.

The first five miles back to the airport in Panama City were silent. Ann couldn't find the words to describe how she felt about the whole surreal scene.

"Tell me about the Ballards," Mark said, eventually breaking the quiet. "Not just the public stuff, but anything you know."

"Well, you probably knew that Gene's father was Senator Fitz Ballard."

"Yeah, I did. Distantly related to the Kennedys. Everyone out east breathes politics. You have to know someone or be related to someone to make a ripple. Once I heard the name, I checked into it. How did the family end up in Wisconsin?"

"That's kind of strange, because they were old money planted in New England. Fitz was a lawyer, too. I know he was in the Navy during World War II, and injured, but I don't remember how. Then he sold out his partnership and became a senator. That's when the Trust was set up, according to Gene. Fitz was killed in a boating accident not much later, or he might have been president. At least, that's what some of the press was circulating at the time. Donna has a scrapbook of articles. Gene told me he didn't want to be in his mother's shadow and went to school in Wisconsin — instead of Harvard — much to her horror, and stayed. Gene said she eventually brought all the Trust business in Wisconsin. To make it easier for Gene to deal with and take over."

"What about Donna?"

"Usual. Old Southern tobacco family, I think. Seems like the older the family, the fewer the kids. Both she and Fitz were only children. She was pregnant with Genevra when Fitz died."

"That must have been a horrible time."

"Probably. Fitz is buried in Arlington. We've visited the grave."

"How far do you think Donna went to keep you from finding out about Gene, and why?"

"What do you mean? What could she have done?"

They arrived at the airport. After turning in the car to the rental agency, they went to wait in the lounge for their flight.

"I have never traveled this much in such a short time period in my entire life," Ann declared. "I don't even want to think about the bills."

Mark grabbed her hand. "I'm not worried. Hungry?"

"No. Tell me more. You think Donna helped Linda somehow? Maybe sent them to Mexico for a divorce?"

"You said Linda Smart seemed to be very religious. But she wouldn't show you their marriage certificate."

"I can't believe I even asked that. Of course she wouldn't."

"But she says she's married. A conservative religious person would make sure she could marry someone legally so her child would be legitimate."

Ann shrugged. "I don't know. She had this creepy smile the whole time. I'm not sure what she's capable of. She had a lot of pictures and stuff all around. Rosaries, too. A couple of those Mary statues. They were kind of pretty, actually."

"And she called Alan her husband. If Linda is a devout Catholic, she would have a previous marriage annulled so she could have the blessing of the church."

"As if it never happened? Can just anybody do that? Don't I have to sign something? What about Ritchie? It's pretty obvious my marriage was real since we produced a child."

"It's not phony marriages that can be annulled. Usually there has to be a pretty good reason, like the person was in jest, or there's incest, abandonment, or illegal age issues. But I think they might have used a mental incompetence plea."

"Plea? Like in court?"

"Well, if you can prove someone was mentally incompetent, or even temporarily or permanently insane when they made a legally binding decision, you can usually get that decision, like marriage, reversed."

"But Gene wasn't incompetent when we were married."

"In a busy circuit court, if a mother brings in a son who's in as bad of shape as you said Gene appears to be, and has a daughter like Genevra besides, and asks for the son's first marriage to be annulled on the grounds of mental incapacity, there's no protest from the spouse, especially if faked, saying you were served the papers. It can happen. It shouldn't, but it could. It's still fraud. She would have had to pull a fast one for Gene to marry again after being declared incompetent. But if the dissolution was in one court and the marriage in another . . . things happen."

Ann wondered if this was what a boxer felt, receiving blow after blow, right before he went down for the last time. She shook her hands to get the blood circulating again. "He was Alan then, I suppose. Linda had him take her name later. I keep wondering why Donna would do this. We weren't close, but I never thought she hated me. The only thing I can think of is that she knew Ritchie wasn't interested in business and waited to see if Gene's other son would be able to take over at some point. You think Linda and Donna arranged this?"

"Think about it, Ann. Linda was a middle-aged woman, wanting a husband and child. One is presented to her, in her mind, but he already has a wife. What does she do?"

"Not ask his mother for help."

"Unless the mother likes you, was recently diagnosed with a terminal illness and has the means to grant your wish in exchange for the promise to make sure her son is cared for after she's gone. Linda was there. You heard Donna say that. She seemed to be concerned about her children."

"I would have been there. They didn't give me the chance." Ann excused herself for a rest room visit before their flight was due to board. She splashed water on her face and pinched some color into her cheeks. She took her migraine meds just in case. Lord, could Donna and Linda have believed they were doing the right thing?

Ann went back to Mark. "Is there a way to find out for sure if that's what they did? Annulled my marriage?"

CHAPTER TWENTY

The day after the impromptu flight to Florida, Ann went back to work at Ballard, Gorman and Wicht as if nothing at all out of the ordinary had happened in her life. No more secrets in the family, she'd told Mark. She had to tell Ritchie what happened. When they had the facts straight, she would tell him herself. Jim Parsons had been asked to look into the possibility of a Florida ruling in the annulment of her marriage. Health information privacy laws wouldn't allow her to confirm that Donna Ballard suffered from the horrible disease she claimed to have. If she did have ALS, perhaps that was punishment enough.

On Friday, Parsons rapped on the top of the cubicle divider just before lunch. Ann stared at the clasp folder in his hands, trying not to let the sympathy in his face reach her. She stood. "Jim. You could have called. I would have stopped in."

"No trouble. I had some other business in the building. I hope this answers your questions."

Ann took the envelope. "Thank you. I think."

"If you need to discuss anything, please call. I'll make sure my assistant makes time for you whenever you need it. And, I'm sorry about all of this. I wish we could have put the situation to rest a lot sooner. If you want to press charges, we can talk."

"I'll look it over," Ann told him. She picked up a framed photograph of Gene and Ritchie posing in the driveway, with Ritchie's new driver's license in hand. She set it down and picked up one of Ritchie and his new son. "Who would have thought to look for a missing person by checking the Florida circuit courts for marriage annulment decrees? That's pretty drastic, don't you agree?"

"Yes, pretty drastic. I'm sure Mark can help you, too, with any of the terminology. This has been a hard time for you. I don't know many people who would remain as dignified about everything as you have. I would press charges on the grounds of fraud, at least."

"Please. Call me Ann. Pressing charges won't help anyone. In fact, I believe such an action will only hurt the people involved, even more than we already have been."

"You may be right, but that doesn't always mean we can do what we want."

Ann tapped the envelope. "Thanks again for doing all this."

"You're welcome."

Ann watched him walk down the aisle separating the tan cubicle dividers before she tucked the envelope into the pocket of her coat. She would take it home to read. She wanted to look at everything first and then decide what to tell Ritchie and the rest of her family.

At five o'clock Ann saved her current project and closed down all of her computer programs. She hadn't forgotten the envelope and pulled it out of her coat pocket before jamming her hand inside. She left a message on Mark's cell phone to tell him that she'd received information from Jim. Colleen had repeatedly urged Ann to bring Mark soon to visit, and he'd finally agreed to this Saturday. He should call her tomorrow when he was ready to go to Portage to see the baby.

Ann let herself into her house. She hung up her coat and wondered what to make for supper. She was surprised at the enormous bouquet of long-stemmed variegated pink roses in a crystal vase on her kitchen desk. The little card read "We missed Valentine's Day, M."

"Good thing I only have one boyfriend whose name starts with M." Ann kicked off her shoes. She would have to get a new cell phone sometime this weekend, too. The old one had never lit up again, despite her attempts to either ignore it and hope it would work in the morning, or keep trying to recharge it. When she'd called the store to ask about whether or not it could be fixed, she'd sheepishly admitted to allowing it to get wet and then trying to charge it. "That's a hundred-dollar phone," the teenager on the other end of the line scolded her.

After changing clothes and eating, Ann had nothing left to do but open the tan envelope.

The first document was the paperwork attesting to the annulment of the marriage of Eugene Fitzgerald Ballard and Ann Jordyn Michels Ballard, dated six years and three months earlier.

Nice Christmas present for all involved. She set it aside for copies of hospital reports. Her heart fluttered at the horrifying photographs of Gene's facial and bodily injuries from the night he was brought into the emergency room. She would never have recognized Gene if she'd been asked to identify him at that time. Her eyes welled at the catalog of injuries. She translated them in her mind from the medical terms that she knew enough to figure out, to make it easier to explain to the others tomorrow. Eight ribs cracked or broken, left kidney and spleen damaged so severely they had to be removed. Both legs broken, right hand stomped to jelly, head hit so hard that one eyeball popped out. The doctor had replaced it, but noted his doubts that vision could be restored. Orbital cracks, nose mashed. Severe trauma to the head was the worst, swelling on the brain that needed surgery and drainage tubes.

Ann shuddered, recalling Alan's cloudy eye and his useless hand.

Linda Smart had signed several reports under the various interns. If she'd suspected this unidentified person had once been somebody with a family who needed him, it apparently hadn't occurred to her to make it easy for the police to match him to any open missing persons cases.

Finders, keepers. How about once the story of Gene's disappearance hit the media? Hadn't Linda thought about coming forward then? The woman had to have purposefully kept him and his story out of the news. Or were there so many anonymous people in New York City that no one really cared? Maybe Ritchie had been right. She could have moved there, planted herself in every morgue, demanded to look in every hospital room until she found him. She could have. Why hadn't she?

"Patient repeats 'Alan' in his sleep," Linda wrote. "His name is Alan."

"Maybe in your sleep, Linda Smart," Ann said. "I'm sorry," she said immediately after. "I'm sorry I even thought that. You're a much better person than I am, deep down. I'm grateful, really, that you've taken such good care of Gene. And you're right. He's happy. He loves that little boy. He'll never be more than a little boy, himself, and if you can teach Richard Michael to respect the man his father will always be, that's more than I was able to accomplish with my own son, who hates me."

Ann stuffed the rest of the papers back into the envelope. Should she bring it to Portage tomorrow? Maybe she should call a family gathering. Tell everyone at once, instead of treating it like a legend, like a fish story that grew more fantastic with each rendition.

She got up and started her evening routine, checking all the doors and locks. She stood in the foyer a long time, staring out the side window, longing for headlights to appear. Ritchie should know about his father first. Tomorrow she would ask him if the two of them could go for a walk after they admired the baby. Maybe it wouldn't be so cold, yet, and they could walk by the river. Maybe watching the ice melt on the Wisconsin would somehow soften the blow.

How would Ritchie take the news? Now he had a half-brother, like Mark had once had Trey. Maybe now that he had something in common with Mark, he could accept the fact that Mark was going to be part of their lives.

Feeling foolish, Ann continued maybeing. Maybe she and Mark would get married. Maybe she wouldn't have to tell Rachel about Gene.

What will her parents think about all of this?

Maybe she should go to bed.

In Portage on Saturday afternoon, Ann hadn't been prepared for the look on Mark's face when Colleen asked if he would like to hold David. To her surprise, he'd eagerly agreed.

"Where's Ritchie?" Ann asked as the four

of them settled in her son's living room.

"He went to get diapers," Colleen said. "He should be back pretty soon."

Mark's smile looked poignant. Ann hoped he would look at her, so she could tell what he was feeling, or whether he was comfortable holding the sleeping baby. Mark remained glued to the baby's face. David had a blue crocheted cap on his tiny head and held his tiny, tiny fingers near his ears. When he yawned, she and Colleen moved closer.

"Colleen, I need to tell Ritchie something," Ann said. "Would it be all right if the two of us went for a walk later on?"

"Sure. Of course. I have dinner planned for six, if that's okay."

"We didn't expect you to go to any trouble, dear," Ann told her. "We could take you out."

Colleen flashed a smile at Mark, still apparently enraptured with her son. "It's a little hard, with that bundle of joy. I don't think I'm ready. Don't fret about food, though. I'm just heating a lasagna Mom left in the freezer. Ritchie's supposed to bring home salad and bread, if he remembers."

David squealed and stretched his arms. His little legs tried to bend against the swaddling. His toothless mouth opened in protest. Colleen waited a moment longer. When it appeared the baby was serious about distress, she reached for him. Mark surrendered David with a lingering touch to the cheek.

"I guess it's feeding time. I was hoping he'd wait a bit, yet. If you'll excuse me. Ritchie should be back any minute." Colleen headed for a back bedroom.

Ann took Mark's hand. "You looked like you enjoyed holding David."

"I did."

Ritchie came in through the front door. He silently set the case of diapers on the floor. "I'm home, Colleen," he called.

"Hi, Ritchie," Ann said.

Mark echoed the greeting and asked if there were more bags to carry in from the car.

"Just one," Ritchie said. "I'll get it."

"Colleen's feeding the baby," Ann told him. "And I have to talk to you. Maybe you and I can go for a walk."

Ritchie eyed Mark as if he expected to hear something distasteful. Mark didn't blink, or take his hand from Ann's.

"I'll be right back. Then you can tell me your news, Mom," Ritchie said.

Colleen returned to the living room. "David's asleep for the moment. Did I hear Ritchie?"

"Yes," Ann said.

Ritchie brought a bag of groceries in and handed it to Colleen.

"Your mom wants to talk to you," Colleen said over her shoulder as she walked into the kitchen of their cozy house.

"Whenever you're ready, Ritchie," Ann said, picking up her coat.

Ritchie removed his own jacket and hung it up. "Whatever you have to say, I'm sure you can say in front of all of us."

"I can," Ann said. "It's just that I wanted you to hear it first."

Ritchie's smile was mocking. "Before Mark?" He sat on the other side of Ann on the sofa.

Ann looked at Mark, who shrugged. She glanced at Colleen, who stared at her husband. "Ritchie," Colleen said, "maybe you want some privacy. Mark and I can go out back, or something."

Ritchie sat down. "Mom, just tell us."

Ann bent and picked up the clasp envelope from under her purse. She turned the envelope over and over in her hands. Colleen gestured to Mark, who followed her into the kitchen.

"It's about your father," Ann said.

Ritchie's mocking smile stayed plastered, long after the shock dawned in his eyes.

"That's probably not what you were expecting to hear."

"Ah, no. What about Dad?"

Ann turned the envelope over again, staring at it. "I found out what happened to him."

"Was Mark there, too?"

"Why does that matter?"

"I should have been the first one to know, not him." Ritchie folded his arms across his chest. Hugging himself, or in a defensive posture, Ann couldn't tell.

"Ritchie —"

"So, is he dead, or what?"

"Not exactly." Ann handed over the envelope. "He was hurt, Ritchie. Terribly, terribly hurt."

CHAPTER
TWENTY-ONE

Mark watched Colleen. It wasn't hard to hear what was being said only a few short feet away in the living room. She tipped the coffee pot to pour, eyes on the living room. He lunged to stop her from overfilling the cup. "Oh, sorry. Thanks."

Mark filled the other cup for himself.

Colleen's mouth thinned with tension. "Is that true?" she whispered. "Did you find out what happened to Ritchie's father?"

Mark nodded, uncertain if he should be the one to say anything to Ann's daughter-in-law. Colleen put a hand to her mouth.

They both heard Ritchie's reaction. "I want to go see him. This is in New York City? You saw him, didn't you? Where is he?"

Mark followed Colleen to the living room.

"He won't know you," Ann was telling her son. "He didn't even know me. He kept saying, 'I should know you, shouldn't I?' But I could tell that he didn't recognize me."

"What happened? Why didn't anyone tell us about this?" Ritchie surged to his feet, fury and grief almost sparking off his frenetic motions.

The frightening photographs spilled from the sofa to the blue-gray carpeting.

Colleen bent to gather them. Tears spilled down her cheeks as she scanned them. "Oh, Ritchie. How horrible. Ann, I'm so sorry. Is he alive?"

Ann's face paled with worry. Mark went to her.

"Did he talk to you, too?" Ritchie asked Mark.

"I didn't see him, Ritchie," Mark said.

"So he's alive? Even after —" Colleen shook her head at the pile of pictures. "He must have been hurt so badly."

"He was severely beaten and robbed," Ann said softly. "Taken to a hospital emergency room. He suffered traumatic brain injury."

"Then what, Mom? Why didn't the police figure out who he was?"

Ann cleared her throat. Mark watched her, almost feeling her pain, her struggle to talk. He perched on the arm of the sofa and squeezed her shoulder before he spoke for her. He tried to tell what he knew without emotion. "What we understand is that the nurse who cared for your father in the hospital continued to care for him after the accident. He apparently had amnesia, besides all the other injuries. We don't know how it happened, but no one connected him with your father's missing persons case."

Colleen stood next to Ritchie, who had planted himself in front of the door. "But, now?" she asked. "Can we go get him? Where's he been all this time?"

Mark looked at Ann to see if she was ready to talk more. Her mouth trembled. "He's being cared for," she said.

"What, in some institution?" Ritchie demanded.

Ann pleaded with her eyes for Mark to say the awful truth. "In fact," he said, "the nurse, Linda Smart, is still involved with him. He lives in her home. She gave him a new name because he didn't know his own. Ritchie, she married him. They have a son."

"But he's already married. To Mom."

"Your mom and dad's marriage was annulled. In some cases, it can be done. The decree is in there," Mark nodded at the pile of pages.

"And you didn't know anything about this?" Ritchie asked his mother.

"No."

"How did you find out?" Colleen asked. "Were you with my mother? Is that when you found out? And they've been in New York City all this time?"

"Sort of," Ann said. "When I was there, with your mother, I saw someone . . . He looked vaguely like Gene. But, you can tell by the pictures, he was so badly injured. I don't know how I could have thought it was the same person as your father."

"Didn't that nurse try to find out if he had a family, or who he was?" Colleen asked.

Mark did not feel that he should be the one to reveal Donna's involvement. Ann would say it her own way.

"No, I guess not," Ann said.

Colleen had more questions than Ritchie, who seemed to have lost some of his bluster. "But he's got a little boy? A brother to Ritchie?"

Ritchie sat down abruptly. "How could one person have pulled all this off? I don't get it. If Dad — this man was so hurt and doesn't know who he is, how can he get married, have a baby. How is that possible?"

"I don't know," Ann whispered.

"I want to see him," Ritchie said again.

"They may not want to see you," she said.

"They have to! He's my father."

"Linda never admitted anything to me,

that her husband was Gene and she knew it."

"We can have her arrested," Ritchie said. "She took his identity away from him. That's wrong, isn't it? Fraud, I don't know what all. Kidnapping! You know what to do, Mark, don't you? That's what we should do, right? Arrest her?"

Mark thought Ann looked near the end of her endurance, sitting there in stunned silence. She'd probably be sick later. Had she simply thought her son would accept the strange story and go to bed that night, satisfied that the most horrible mystery in their lives was closed? "That could happen, yes," Mark said. "But there are other people involved, as well as circumstances that would adversely affect more than just your father's new family."

"What do you mean?" Ritchie looked greenish.

Mark could smell the warmed lasagna he guessed would go uneaten. "From what Ann has told me, your father has the mental capacity of a child. He'll probably never get better. For all intents and purposes, the only life he's ever known is the one he has now as Alan Smart. If we interfered with that, took him away from his wife and child and forced him into a strange environment, what will that prove? He'll never be the father you remember. Where is he going to live? With your mother? With you? He needs professional rehabilitation and expensive medical care with all the problems he has, as well as constant supervision."

The baby let them all know he was awake. Colleen hurried to comfort him. Mark stared at the pattern of the Berber carpet until Colleen reappeared with David in her arms. Ritchie took him from her, the wonder of this new life replacing some of the despair that formerly molded his features. "I wouldn't let anyone take David away from me," he said.

"You said that Ritchie's dad needs expensive care," Colleen said. "This woman, Linda, is a nurse? How are they paying for that? It's expensive enough just living in New York."

Ann shuddered. Mark rubbed her shoulder.

"Before I tell you anything else," she said, "you need to know that your Grandmother Ballard is dying."

Mark accompanied Ann to Donna Hawthorne Ballard's funeral on the first weekend of May. Oddly enough, the Hawthorne family's church and cemetery were only an hour from Mark's former home in Lynchburg. About a dozen somber, dark-clad people attended the simple graveside ceremony. The day was absurdly bright and hot. Mark felt sweat trickle down his back while he stood in the sunshine, dressed in a suit coat and slacks. Ann wore black. The earrings he'd given her last Christmas winked with sparks of light when she turned her head. At the final amen, the gathering broke up. Genevra had sobbed the whole time. Ann stood next to her sister-in-law, an arm around her shoulders.

In the end, Donna had done the right thing. Before her death, she signed a statement admitting sole responsibility for any criminal wrong-doing. She declared that she acted alone in filing for the annulment on behalf of her son. Gene's mother also asked that her son be spared further trauma and be allowed to remain in a safe and familiar environment. Royce and Jung would handle the Trust, much of which would go for the care of Gene and Genevra. The Florida house was sold. Genevra and staff were installed in Madison where Ann could spend time with her.

Parsons was riding high.

Mark fingered the ring box in his pocket. He hadn't wanted to leave it in his hotel room or even in the car where Ann might find it. He'd spoken to Ann's father and son at Easter, to ask their blessing on his marriage proposal to Ann. Mark supposed it was somewhat cowardly, talking to them together so that perhaps Ritchie might not air his objection in front of his grandfather. Ritchie had said little at the prospect of Mark joining the family, but neither did he protest.

Tomorrow, he and Ann would take Genevra and her new home living companion to the airport in the morning. Ann agreed to spend the rest of the day with him, visiting his favorite haunts. He knew the place where he would stop and ask her. This early in the season, there would still be plenty of people around the GW, but maybe the crowds wouldn't be overwhelming. The trail to the Apple Orchard Falls bridge wasn't too hard of a hike. He would ask her there, with the sound of the water in the background and blossoms in the air. Perfect.

Contrasting tourism between the east coast and Midwest, Mark preferred Wisconsin. He still had trouble adjusting to the fact that he could visit Blue Mounds Park west of Madison, even in the summer, and sometimes not see another person for hours. It was never that way in Virginia. People from all over the world came, saw, and went any time of the year. National parks and forests, like the George Washington, were open all year round.

Mark had slept soundly last night, much to his surprise. He'd been certain he would be too keyed up. He checked them out of the hotel in the morning, for they would fly home that evening. Home. Mark smiled to himself. For breakfast, he'd arranged for her to meet Lacy. Allison brought the girl, making excuses for her fiancé, who couldn't get away from work. The women took their time warming up to conversation, but Mark had a good feeling about their encounter by the time it was over.

Ann wore a visored cap for their hike. He had a picnic lunch from the hotel on ice. But first, the falls. They dodged a few couples on the trail, a family with toddlers, several college students, one dedicated sandaled backpacker who was probably detouring from the Appalachian Trail. When they reached the falls, Ann stopped to admire the sight.

Mark took her hand. "Let's walk on the bridge."

"Looks misty."

"You'll love it, I promise."

And, now. He watched her lean over the rail, visor in hand as she gazed at the splashing water. A tiny tendril of hair near her ear waved in the breeze. Mark reached to touch it. He slid his fingers down to her chin and turned her face toward him. He ignored the Japanese couple behind her, snapping photos.

For this moment they were alone in the universe. Under God. "Ann?" Her shining gaze locked with his. "Will you marry me?"

Her hand rested on his, which he held against her cheek. "Mark. Are you sure?"

Gently in mock exasperation he touched his forehead to hers. "Oh, yes. This is all I've wanted."

He heard clicks and excited chatter, and guessed the moment was being recorded by someone who would undoubtedly replay the scene for the family in Japan. "Americans in love," or something.

"Ann?"

She pulled back to look at him. "I'm going to say yes. Soon. I know I will, but I want to be careful about this. I love you so much. I need to be careful."

He let her hands go to fish the ring from his jeans pocket. Mark tugged her left hand toward him so he could slide the diamonds onto her finger. "I understand. I want you to have this now and forever. And I love you, too."

This time, the Japanese couple made no secret of the fact they had watched the whole thing. Flashes went off, and they clapped. Ann laughed. She took his hand, and waving at the tourists, pulled him willingly back along the trail to the parking lot.

That evening after they returned the car and boarded the plane on the first leg that would take them to Madison, Ann held out her hand to admire his ring. He watched her turn it this way and that, to catch fire in the dim overhead light of the cabin. She cocked her head and touched her empty earlobe.

"Mark?"

"Hmm?"

"This matches my earrings, doesn't it?"

Mark took her hand in his and kissed her fingertips. "You think so?"

"How long have you had this?"

He smiled. "A while."

"Wow."

"Mm hmm."

"What's Ritchie going to say?"

"He didn't protest when I . . . ah, asked him. And your dad."

Ann pulled her hand away and sat up straight. "You did? When? I can't believe you kept a secret like this from me."

Mark recaptured her hand. "We probably shouldn't go there, should we? And it was only after Easter dinner, when you women were otherwise occupied."

Ann tugged his hand until his arm wrapped around her. Across the armrests, she leaned her ear awkwardly against his chest. He saw her eyes close. She yawned. "Okay." Then she turned a sleepy smiling face up to kiss his jaw. "Thanks."

Mark didn't feel right, putting off his announcement any longer. On the Saturday before Mother's Day, he called the folks. Tiffany must have been out, for his father answered the telephone.

"Hi, Dad, it's Mark. How are you?"

"Oh. Good morning, Mark. Getting quite hot for this time of year in Arizona. Have to get a round in early in the morning. We're thinking of heading east."

"Good. How's your health? No more angina?"

"No, no. Tiff should never have even said anything."

"She's worried about you."

"Could be."

Mark let the silence settle, a precursor to his news. "Dad? I wanted to let you and

Tiffany know I'm getting married."

"What? Married? To . . . who, again? Andrea?"

"No. It's not Allison, Dad. We broke up, about a year ago."

"Oh, who, then? Who did you say?"

"It's Ann, Dad. Remember the Ballards? In Clayton?"

"Ballard . . . that boy. You're marrying who? They didn't have a girl, as I recall. Just the one boy."

"It's Ritchie's mother, Ann."

"Ann Ballard? Why, she's —"

"A little older than me, I know. It's all right."

The silence stretched.

"Well," Edward Roth said. "I guess I'd better let you go. Thanks for calling."

Mark did not expect a word of congratulations from his father. Edward Roth had always done much better with customers than family. With customers he could talk shipping, orders, colors, quantity. No messy feelings. Three minutes later Mark's phone rang again.

"You can't honestly expect me to believe you're marrying that murderer's mother."

"Tiffany! How kind of you to call."

"Besides the fact that she's older than I am, how can you sleep with a woman knowing her son caused the death of my son?"

"Tiffany, you know that's not true." Mark forced himself to relax the death grip on the phone. He switched hands and examined the red skin of his palm. "Trey was my brother, too. I'll always miss him, but Ann had nothing to do with how he died."

"You can never know what it's like to lose someone you love. I will never forgive them. I will never, ever get over losing Trey like that. He was my only son."

Mark felt the exhaustion in the muscles of his neck. He twisted his head to the left and right, trying to get the kinks out. Tiffany's grief had solidified into hatred over the years. But now he was tired of it. "That's right," he heard himself say. "Your only son. I surely never counted."

"You had your own mother."

"For a few years, yes, that's true. Then I had you."

"I had a new baby of my own to care for."

"The fact is, you never treated me the same. Even the name Trey. Third. What was I? Fourth? You meant to exclude me, didn't you? He was third and I was . . . nothing. Tiffany, I gotta go."

"Don't expect anything else from us. That woman will never be —"

Mark hung up. "Well, I guess we won't

have to argue about which side of the family to visit on holidays." He sighed and forced himself to yank out the vacuum cleaner and pick up a few things. Ann had volunteered to make supper here tonight. He thought about what she'd said about how the hard things that happened in your life always left a kind of scar. Where had the idea come from? A winding course . . . of a stream. Meandering.

But they'd found each other and planned to travel straight on, together. He hoped she would agree to set a wedding date. He was awfully tired of blue drapes, blue carpet, blue sofa and blue fixtures in the bathroom.

CHAPTER
TWENTY-TWO

Ann stood in Mark's blue tiled kitchen. She debated whether or not to remove the ring before she washed chicken. If Mark saw she'd taken it off, what would he think? And what was she afraid of? That she'd get it dirty? She'd worn her other rings all the time and never thought about it. Ann held her hand out again.

"No wonder dinner's taking so long," Mark complained when he caught her. They laughed. "If I'd known giving you an engagement ring was going to cost me dinner, I might have opted for something else."

"Never! I love it," Ann declared. "I was just contemplating whether such a lovely thing should experience chicken innards up close and personal, or whether I should take it off."

Mark's eyes twinkled.

"What?" Ann asked. "You have no advice?"

"You didn't ask me."

"Are you going to be one of those husbands?" Ann pushed him against the counter.

He held up his hands in surrender. "What are those husbands?"

"The ones who like to say after a disaster, 'Well, if you'd asked me.' "

"Hey, I already asked you a question, to which, by the way, I am still waiting for a definitive answer." He slid his arms around Ann slowly, menacingly, and pulled her tightly against him. "I can only handle one dilemma at a time." He kissed her.

Ann pulled back. "I don't believe it."

"Oh, yes. It's true. When I'm working on something, I give it all of my best attention. Like this —"

Ann managed to pull away from his mouth. "Do you want dinner or not?"

"She's asking me another question. What am I supposed to say?"

"I'm hungry."

He nuzzled the side of her neck. "Me, too."

"Mark!"

"Annie." He stopped and stared at her. "Let's get married soon. As soon as we can."

"I'm not getting any younger, am I?"

Mark's grip tightened painfully around

her waist. "We've both seen what time can do. Waiting too long can hurt just as much as jumping in too quickly."

Ann agreed with him. She knew she wanted to be married to him, too. She settled her ear against his chest to let the steady beat of his heart calm her jangled senses. "Do you have a date in mind?" The rhythm jumped. Ann smiled. His voice thrummed through her ear. She could melt right into him.

"If we have a church wedding, I'd like it to be at Hope," he said.

"Yes. Do you want a big wedding, reception, dinner for a thousand and all that? Five groomsmen in matching tuxes?"

"Is that what you want?"

Ann shook her head and reluctantly lifted herself away from him. "Do you want to help me with supper while we talk?"

By the time the chicken was cleaned and cut, dredged in flour and lemon pepper and baking along with potatoes, they had decided on a simple ceremony with family and mostly local friends.

"You know, Mark, it's pretty hard to get a church and music and reception hall reserved at this late date. If you don't care about a sit-down dinner, can we just have hors d'oeuvres and cake and stuff in the

Hope Church gathering area after? It's big enough."

"I like that idea," Mark said. He tore more lettuce into bite-size pieces for their salad.

Ann started scraping a carrot. "And, you know, who says we have to get married on a Saturday, right?"

"That's true. What are you thinking?"

"Why not on Sunday, like after the last service? A lot of our friends are already around. Do you think your folks will want to come?"

Ann waited for him to answer while she chopped the carrots into tiny pieces. "Mark?"

"No. They won't come."

"Oh. Do you want me to call them? It's been a long time, but surely —"

"Ann, it's pretty far for them."

"But if they know in advance —"

"Just leave it for now, okay?"

Ann stopped slicing radishes to look at his taut back. "Mark? Did you tell them?"

"Yes."

"This is going to be a problem isn't it? Because of Ritchie and Trey."

Mark turned around and set the bowl of lettuce near her so she could add the other vegetables. "We're past that, aren't we? Nothing will bring Trey back. Ritchie was only there that night. He didn't make Trey roll the Jeep."

"No, he didn't. Do you believe that?"

"I've always believed that. It's the truth. I'll always miss Trey. He was my kid brother, but he's gone. And I accept that."

"But your dad and Tiffany don't."

"Tiffany has a lot of issues."

"What do you want to do about it?"

"Nothing, Ann. There's nothing we can do to make people stop saying stupid things, believing something happened the way they want to remember. We have to live our own lives."

"Can we do that?"

"Of course."

Ann set the knife down and wiped her hands on a towel. "Mark, I'm sorry."

Mark's eyes turned thunderous, his mouth tight with anger. "Stop it. It's not your fault that Tiffany blames us for taking her only son."

Ann's consternation turned to incredulity. "Her only son? What about you?"

"Yeah." Mark grabbed the salad bowls and took them to the table. "What about me?"

After supper Ann sat next to Mark on his blue sofa, tossing out more ideas for the wedding. She could settle for simple, but she wanted him to be happy about the celebration. "I've done this once, already, so Mark, you should be the one who gets to decide what you want to do."

"Well, thank you."

Ann was glad he'd regained his gentle humor after the disappointing discussion about his stepmother's reaction to their news. She wouldn't let Tiffany Roth ruin their wedding. "When can we call the church, to ask about a date?"

Mark grinned at her. "So now you're eager to marry me?"

"You know it, buster. You've convinced me." She gave a huge sigh. "But, the biggest question is, can you get time off for a honeymoon? Where shall we go?"

"Honeymoon? What's that?" Mark shook his head in sorrow. "And I've been taking off so much time lately, chasing around the country with you. I may lose my job. They won't let me take any more days this year. You're right. We should wait."

Ann rose to her knees during his speech and whacked him with one of the blue pillows until they were both laughing.

In the quiet moments after their laughter she said, "You're a good man, Mark Roth."

"Well, it's a whole lot easier knowing what to do when you're firmly grounded in faith." Mark held up Ann's hand so they could both see the ring. "You do know what that means, don't you, Ann? To have faith, to really, truly know what's going to happen when our lives here on earth are over?"

Ann stared at Mark. The intensity of the question made her frown with concentration.

"Because we can't get married yet if you have any doubts," he said.

"I don't, Mark. Maybe I haven't always been as sure of things as you, but in these past few months of listening to the pastor's messages and reading the Bible with you, understanding some of those difficult concepts, like salvation, has finally made sense. I think I just needed someone to help me get it straight in my mind as well as my heart."

"Good." Mark leaned in to kiss her lightly.

Ann saw the clock. "I should go." Mark helped her gather her things and walked her to her car. "As soon as we find out when we can have the ceremony, I guess you'll want to give notice here," Ann said, before she got into her car.

Mark stood hunched slightly against the night breeze, with his hands in his pockets. He nodded.

"You want to move into my house, don't you?"

"Yes, of course," Mark replied.

"I meant, our house."

"Right." Mark unbent long enough to open and close the car door for her. Ann watched him in the rearview mirror, looking after her. He'd been hesitant about the house. She wondered how she would feel if she was the one moving in with him and his memories. Should she suggest they sell her house? Well, they could talk about it later.

Gary St. Clare agreed to perform her and Mark's wedding ceremony after the last service on the second Sunday in June. Ann put off the problem of finding a dress almost too long. Fern and Paula announced they would kidnap her if she didn't agree to let them take her shopping today. It was Fern's first day off from school for the summer break, but the upcoming excursion was all Fern could talk about during their morning swim. Ann was glad they wanted to help, even though Fern and Paula squabbled over styles and colors they thought Ann should wear. She told them from the start that she wouldn't wear white, or a long dress.

Just as Ann was ready to call a break for lunch, she spied a pale pink sleeve peeping around a white woven fence that hung from the ceiling of the West Towne Mall boutique. Once she saw the dress, she knew she wanted it. Made of shot silk, the pale pink dress itself was a simple fitted A-line. It came with a long-sleeved loose jacket that matched the length of the dress. The jacket was decorated with satin cuffs and binding with clear beads and seed pearls sewn on in an abstract pattern.

"Oh, Ann, it's perfect," Paula said.

"I'll ask it if comes in your size and has shoes," Fern said, and went off to find a clerk.

After lunch, Ann went to the courthouse, where Mark was defending a client over a contested probate account.

Sitting at the back of the courtroom, Ann did not so much pay attention to the arguments as she did the judge and the attorneys when it was time for each of them to speak. Ann watched Mark question his own client. Apparently the client had offered his cousin something that had been declined. Ann watched while Mark checked his notes, then brought up another point. In his gray suit and dark tie, he exuded self-confidence and professionalism.

When he first suggested that she visit the courthouse so she could watch a trial, she'd balked. A trial was such a personal, intense issue, wasn't it? Why would she intrude on someone else's private business? Mark reminded her that most courtrooms were public venues that citizens had a right to attend. And she could see him at work. Being able to watch Mark had been the attractive part. Ann smiled to herself. Her job had nothing enticing about it. Building spreadsheets and compiling reports was not an audience draw, that's for sure.

Ann daydreamed through the trial, until she noticed people filing past her seat. She got up and went outside the courtroom to wait for Mark. She soon saw him emerge with the client. She realized she did not know if the case was over. Mark held his briefcase easily in his left hand so he could shake hands with the client. He waved to the others ranged around the client and walked to her.

"Hi." He kissed her cheek. "How long were you there?"

"Long enough." Ann wrinkled her nose. "But I'm sorry I lost track of what exactly happened."

Mark laughed and took her arm. "That's okay. Nothing's settled yet."

He led her out of the building. "You want to get some dinner?" He asked. "Where are you parked?"

"Sure. I'm that-away. You want me to drive?"

In front of the fire at her house that evening, Ann worked up the courage to ask him.

"Mark?"

He looked into her eyes. She closed her own as he leaned close and mouthed "What?" against her lips.

"Was there a time, I mean, when did you . . . Mark!"

"Okay." He moved away, but kept hold of her hand.

Ann took a deep breath, feeling like a high school girl in a first crush. She decided to just ask him. "How did you ever decide you loved me?"

In the dappled yard light streaking through the drapes, Mark's expression took on his stoic trial face. Ann wondered if she'd gone too far with her question. She touched his elbow. "I'm sorry."

"Annie!" He grabbed her hand again in an almost painful grasp. He brought it to his lips, touching the pad of each tip with his lips. "Truthfully? Probably at the memorial service for Gene. Maybe I knew before, but then . . . Ritchie. He was so angry. He wouldn't shut up. He should have been sad, should have been supportive of you, knowing he was supposed to be the man of the family, the one who needed to be strong. Instead he kept blaming you, saying it was your fault, that you drove your husband away because —"

She started it. She had to know. "It was a long time ago, Mark. But, he said . . . What?"

"That you were cold, unfeeling. That's being polite."

Ann stroked his bristly cheek and bit his jaw gently. "Hmm, really?" After a moment, Ann asked, "What if I'd changed? You were gone a long time. What would you have done if I wasn't anything like the person you remembered?"

"Everyone changes, Ann. I didn't know what you would be like. Standing on your doorstep that first day was hard."

"What if I'd divorced Gene and had someone else in my life?"

"Do you want me to admit this?"

"Admit what?"

"I kept watch on all court proceedings."

"Oh. But that would only tell you after the fact."

"I would know about the matters being filed."

"That would have been a little late, though, don't you think? What if I'd gotten involved —"

"Enough. I love you. Do you believe it?"

"Yes."

Mark stilled while his breathing changed rhythm. Ann waited.

"Well?" Mark asked.

"What?"

"You're supposed to tell me back how much you love me."

Ann swallowed. "I didn't realize there was a formula. You'll have to lend me the book."

"Ann, it's not a game." Mark clutched her elbows to force her away.

"Of course I love you. Mark, what's the matter?"

He let her go. "I can't help it, comparing."

"What?" she asked him. "I want to learn how to be married to you. We can't do that by comparing what we knew to what we feel and experience now. But I think wanting to know how we acted and felt with other people is natural, too. You were engaged to Allison for three years. The thought of you kissing . . ." She pressed her lips together before saying, "Let's try this again. I love you."

"I know."

Ann choked in a gasp. "Hey! I thought —"

His kiss made her ageless. "We'll make up our own rules."

In the quiet before Mark would return to his apartment, Ann wanted to finish the discussion she'd begun earlier. "So, once you discovered that I hadn't turned into a different person, when you came back, you know, and stood on my doorstep that first time, quivering like a bunny, shaking in your boots, hands all sweaty and smiling like a —"

"Ann."

"After you came back, all grown up, and hot-looking, having spent years slaking girls off, disappointing women all over the country, strutting your stuff in court —"

"Ann."

"When you saw me again, you must have had to decide all over that you loved me. When did you?"

Mark shifted on the sofa before answering. "When you lost count."

"What?"

"That night, after we went to that . . . horrible place for dinner. You invited me in for coffee when we got back. I could see you were unsure about the whole thing, about me, about how you felt about me."

"What was I supposed to think?"

He didn't acknowledge her attempt to interrupt. "You were already losing it, I could tell. You were trying to make coffee, and you couldn't even do that. You found me so irresistible, you couldn't even count."

Ann took a deep breath, ready to spout in self-defense. She realized she didn't want to and let the breath out. She took a sip of tea, smiling a little secret smile of her own.

Mark's smirk slipped. "All right. It's your turn. When did you realize you were in love with me?"

She didn't need to think at all. "When I took Gene's rings off. I hadn't felt like I needed to do that until you made me realize that I had been in a holding pattern long enough, that I didn't want to wait any more. I was missing the best part of everything. And I was flattered."

Mark sputtered. "Flattered?"

"And very confused. It was hard for me to move past seeing you in that high school basketball uniform at first. I felt like some kind of pedophile."

"I turned nineteen that September."

"Yeah, thanks." Ann bit her lip. "That makes me feel a lot better."

Shortly after the news of her impending marriage circulated around the company,

Tim Wicht and Howie Gorman took Ann out for lunch.

"So, Ann, how're ya doing?" Howie Gorman asked her, after they had given their orders to the waitress.

"You don't have to ask," Tim Wicht said, a leer on his face. "Just look at the almost honest woman! Anyone can tell she doesn't have a care in the world."

Ann raised a brow at the taut-lipped look Howie passed to Tim. "I'm fine," she said. "Thanks for asking."

Howie adjusted the fork next to his plate.

Tim reached for a breadstick.

The waitress returned with their drinks.

Howie gulped his. "So, Ann, we want you to hear it from us, first."

"Yeah, that's why we thought, you know, we'd treat you to lunch and all," Tim said, earning another narrow-eyed look from his partner.

"The fact is, Ann," Howie said, "since the Trust is being reorganized, we're buying out the Ballard share of the company."

"We're not changing the name, or anything," Tim said.

"We will always have the utmost respect for everything Gene did," Howie told her. "He was the brains behind BGW, the front man, the start-up power, and we'll never let anyone forget that."

"I'm a little stunned," Ann said. "I guess that makes sense, of course." She shook out the linen napkin. "Thank you for keeping the name."

"And, ah, since we're buying out," Tim said, "we thought it would be awkward for you."

"Awkward?" Ann asked, feeling the frown creasing her forehead. She struggled to relax. "In what way?"

"For you to stay on," Howie said.

"Oh, no, I don't think so," Ann told them. "Why would it?"

Their food arrived. Howie took the few moments of reprieve to keep Ann in suspense while they made inroads on the meal.

"So, what should I have to feel awkward about?" Ann asked after she'd picked her way through her fish.

Howie used his favorite phrase. "The fact of the matter is, Ann, that we thought perhaps you'd rather not stay on with us. You know, afterward."

"After the buyout?" Ann felt the coldness of reality begin to slide down her arms.

"The wedding, too. It has nothing to do with the quality of your work, naturally," Tim said.

"Mostly it's a department matter," Howie

said. "We're always looking for ways to be more efficient."

"Right," Tim supplied. "Do the best for the company."

"The company," Ann repeated. "Of course. So, am I fired?"

"Oh no, of course not," Howie said in a wounded tone.

"But you understand," Tim said. "We need some kind of paperwork for HR."

"Like my resignation."

"It's not like you need to work anymore, right?" Tim said. "All those years when Gene was gone, we understood you wanted to stay close to the company, and needed some cash since the Trust held everything. But now, with the changes, getting married — you don't need us, do you?"

Need you? What's that supposed to mean? Ann picked silently at the grilled zucchini surrounding the fish. *Would it make a difference if I pointed out that most of the other Neanderthals had the decency to die out a long time ago somewhere in France?* "I'm glad you're not changing the name of the company. Thank you for letting me know. And you'll have my resignation right away this afternoon."

"Thanks for understanding, Ann." Howie said.

"You don't need to give notice, or anything," Tim said. "We trust you. Maybe now Gene can finally have some peace."

"I'm sure he'd be happy to know his company will continue," Ann told them. She forced herself to remain calm and pleasant through the next half hour at the restaurant. They took her back to BGW, where instead of compiling any more reports, she called down to maintenance for a box and sorted through twenty-odd years of personal belongings to pack. By the time she was finished and printed her letter of resignation, all she had to do was turn off the light. The echoing click followed her to her car.

By the time Mark came in a couple of hours later, she'd worked herself into a good lather while pacing the kitchen. She pounced on him when he came in through the garage, indignantly pouring out her news.

"So, that was it? No farewell party, or anything? No general company announcement? No exit interview or the press?"

Mark's nonplussed reaction made the situation more real to Ann. "I sound like a washed up diva or something, don't I? Well, at least they didn't fire me. And the main thing is, they'll keep Gene's name."

■ ■ ■ ■

Mark stood in the hallway looking at the front door. She wrapped her arms around him from behind and rested her face in the hollow between his shoulder blades. "Waiting for someone?"

He turned and gathered to her his side. "What would you think about buying a different house?"

"Oh." Now that it was spoken into reality the echo of Ritchie's feet pounding on the stairs, Gene's shower running and the smell of breakfast mocked her.

"Ann?"

Ann pushed herself away from Mark and went to stand just to the right of the big front door. "I always wait here for you. When I know you're coming, I stand here and watch. When you leave . . ." Mark's warmth soothed her as she felt him move close to her. "I stay here as long as I can, watching the taillights of your car disappear down the driveway and wonder and wait for the time when you'll come again." Ann turned and put her hand on his cheek. "Those are the memories I'd take with me. Yes, I think buying our own home is a very good idea."

"What about Ritchie?"

"Ritchie's got his own house."

"Yeah, I'm already the bad guy. I don't think I can make it worse."

They moved arm in arm to the living room. "You know he doesn't think that way, anymore. It's not like you'll be a father figure to him, or anything."

Mark laughed.

"But you'll find things to do together."

"Like fishing. It helped him to see Gene, too, didn't it?"

"Yes, sad, but helpful. He could say goodbye. I'm glad Linda let them meet. You never seem interested in seeing your old house."

Mark shook his head. "All the best memories of those years were right here."

"I thought about asking if we should sell this place when you first proposed."

"You did? So, you're okay with this?"

"Might as well change everything all at once. New husband, new house." She smiled. Mark kissed her.

Soon after, the Clayton house was shown to a prospective client. Ann and Mark signed the papers making them owners of their new house in Madison, a bi-level with cedar siding and a beautiful yard on a quiet circle in

Madison's west side.

Ann stood with Mark in the driveway and contemplated the "sold" sign with the feeling too many good things were happening way too fast. The quick sale of her home, the purchase of this house, the upcoming wedding to the perfect man — surely that was too much happiness all at once.

She squeezed her eyes shut and prayed for God to ignore a man named Murphy and his law.

CHAPTER
TWENTY-THREE

It was one week before the wedding.

"Ann." Mark hated to wake her, but he had to go and he was worried. This headache had come on the night before without any apparent cause — not inclement weather, no abject tension that he was aware of, no unusual food. She'd clutched her head, gulped her pills and went to bed. He'd stayed on the couch, but traveled up and down the staircase every hour or so, checking on her.

He touched her clammy forehead. "Annie, honey, I'm leaving now."

"Mmm, okay." She rolled on her side and clutched her ears.

Mark lowered himself to the bed. "Are you all right? Should I call your mom or Rachel? I don't want to leave you here alone if you're not better than you were last night."

"No, don't call anyone. It's just an ugly one. I'll be fine." She groaned. "Eventually."

Mark snatched a couple of minutes from a lunch meeting to call Ann. "Hey, how are you?"

"Oh, man, better until the phone rang. You're killing me."

"Sorry, I think you need to make an appointment to see the doctor."

"They just give me more drugs. It would be a waste 'cause it'll be over soon. And I don't want to go out. I'm gonna —"

"Annie, I'll come get you — Ann? Hey!"

Mark could hear her in the background. It didn't sound pleasant. He hung up and returned to the conference room. "I have to step out, take Ann to the doctor. I apologize. I should be back later."

"Sure, sure," Todd Jung waved. "Take good care of her."

"I'll be back," Mark repeated. He talked to Jennifer, then walked to his car and sped to her house. Maybe they should head for the emergency room.

He wound his way around the packing boxes stacked in the garage. She'd been sorting books and dishes, saving out things she thought Ritchie and Colleen would want. Urgency forced him to move faster, though uncustomary dread made him feel like he was lost in a maze from which he'd be too late to do anything.

In the house, he raced up to her room.

"Ann, come on, I'm taking you to the doctor."

Ann tried to lift herself out of the sheets. "I think there's something wrong. It hurts. I hurt." She closed her eyes and flopped back. "Never mind. I just want to sleep some more. Maybe more pills."

"Mark?"

"Shh. You'll be all right. Shh."

Cold. She felt so cold. Where were her slippers and socks? Mark should bring her slippers and a blanket. Something covered her mouth. Where was Mark?

Ann blinked. She tried to talk. Mark? There, Ann could see him. She must be dreaming, for it looked like he was dressed as a doctor. She shook her head. She really did not like this dream.

But dreams didn't usually hurt. Ann couldn't remember a dream with this much pain.

Anti-stars, the night prickles of ancient black holes pierced her eyes. Ann tried to call out again. She dreamed she was a caterpillar and wove herself inside a chrysalis.

Mark gripped his cell phone; the edge bit

into his palm. He'd dream-walked out the intensive care waiting room into the hall and around a quieter corner to make his call. "Tiffany, can you put Dad on, please? I need to talk . . . I need him."

"Mark, he's outside. What do you want?"

"Ann had a ruptured brain aneurism. And a stroke." His voice wouldn't rise above a gargling, painful whisper.

Tiffany's tinny voice echoed through the speaker. "I'm sorry to hear that."

"Can you just call Dad, please? I want to talk to him." Mark's voice gained a decibel. He pinched the bridge of his nose. "Tiffany? Get Dad."

"Just a minute. Wait. I think I hear him. Here."

Mark gripped the phone with both hands. "Dad?"

"Yes?"

"Ann's sick. It doesn't look good."

"Well." Mark heard throat-clearing. "Well, that's too bad."

"Dad? I need you. Can you come? You and . . . Tiffany?"

"Talk to Tiff. She keeps the schedule around here."

With his head feeling like it was spinning, Mark leaned against the rail in the bright hospital corridor outside of Ann's glassed-in room. He tried to find objectivity, to pretend this was a simple deposition in the big conference room at Royce and Jung, not here in a hospital corridor.

". . . that's too bad." Tiffany's voice whistled in echo to his father. Mark heard the telltale sign that she put a hand over the mouthpiece and said something in the background. Her voice returned.

Mark slid to the floor, gripping the phone with both hands. Someone stopped in front of him, but Mark mouthed, "I'm okay." After the white pants and feet disappeared around the corner. Mark spoke into the phone. "Can you and Dad come?"

Silence

"Tiffany?"

"Mark, I don't know." Her voice became impatient, like during his childhood when he or Trey asked one of them to chaperon a field trip or come to open house, or do anything other parents did with their kids. "Why don't you call us when she's better?" she said. "Your father has a golf tournament this weekend. For charity."

Mark severed the connection by holding the button down until his hand went numb. The family he'd needed all his life was a fantasy. Dad and Tiffany's rejection was real. Ann's family would reject him, too, once they knew he'd waited too long to get her proper medical care.

Mark got to his feet, feeling more like an eighty-year-old man with aches deeper than skeletal, and went back into the room where Annie lay. In his mind he saw the things they had done to her, terrible things under the brilliant light that gleamed on blood and steel instruments. There was only one person here now. Mark moved closer to Ann. Blue showed through her eyelids. A machine recorded the lines of her existence while a tube snaked from her mouth. She was still here, just not with him.

The nurse finished whatever she'd been doing to Annie and gently folded the sheet along her still form. With the white gauze wrapped around her head and her ashen color, she looked terribly fragile. He would never again chide those who claimed to have an out of body experience, for surely this was it. He hovered against the wall and watched the solid Mark stare at the bed. He was glad the solid Mark could hear, because the sound of the ocean in his own ears was so loud, it drowned out any other.

When floating Mark saw Ann, he let out a breath and rejoined the solid Mark.

In six days they were getting married. Mark snagged a stool and drew it close to the bed. He traced the line of her brow over her sunken, bruised eyelids. He leaned in to whisper the things that he planned to tell her, about how much he adored only her and not to be afraid. Particularly not to be afraid that he would ever, ever leave her. A faint spark of anger seared the back of his throat, but Mark cauterized it for now. Anger would come later, at its appropriate time.

Phone calls. It was time to call Alice and Ray. And Ritchie.

Ritchie would kill him. He hoped.

Mark went to the waiting room again. He flipped through the directory on his phone, managing to hit the right button on the third try. "Alice? It's Mark. I'm at the hospital." He cleared his throat. "With Ann."

A few minutes later, Mark opened the cell phone again. People want details. He couldn't recall any of them right now, but he had to tell Jim Parsons about bills and insurance. Ann wasn't officially on his insurance, yet. Of course he'd take care of everything. The answering machine at the office picked up. He left his message in a voice that came out only slightly raspy.

Oh, God.

Mark bowed his head once more over his

failure to keep Ann safe and beat his useless faith into pulp. God had done nothing, despite his desperate prayers. What kind of God would do nothing? He walked down the too-bright hall to the elevator.

Where was his car? He began to walk in the cold sleet that began sometime while he was busy watching Ann convulse, then stop breathing, and calling an ambulance. At the icy shore of Lake Monona he stopped, paralyzed with indecision. He could keep going and let the waters take him in, or he could stand perfectly still, invisible like a deer in the woods.

A car stopped behind him. Headlights went off. He heard the car door open.

"Mark? Mark, I've been driving all over. Alice told Rachel what happened and Rachel called me."

Mark let Elle take his arm. He went to her car, sure everything that happened now was one of Ann's weird nightmares she told him she sometimes had when she had her headaches.

"You're so cold, Mark. How long have you been standing there? Let me drive you home."

"No!"

Elle started the engine and cranked the heat. "Don't worry, Mark. My home, I'm taking you to my home."

Once there, she pushed him into the bathroom and turned on the water. Mark stayed numb all during the hot shower. Elle found him a robe and made him sit in a recliner. She covered him with a blanket.

A telephone buzzed him awake. Elle answered then hung up. "Mark, you're up. Good. Here's your cell phone."

Mark's numb hand wouldn't reach for the phone. "I don't want it," he said. "You keep it."

"Okay."

"Whose robe is this?"

"My husband, Art's."

"He's been dead a long time, hasn't he?" The word "dead" burned on Mark's numb lips.

"Some things you keep around. Some things you let go. What about some breakfast?"

"What about it."

"I'll feed you, then take you to the hospital when you're ready."

"I don't think I can do this, Elle." Mark pulled the blanket around his head. "Let me sleep."

"Sure, Mark. There's no hurry. We'll go together later, okay?"

Mark lowered the blanket. "Do you think

she'll come back to us?"

"I know she will. Just rest. I'll wake you later."

"I don't know if I can sleep."

"That's okay."

The only way Mark could function was to let the solid Mark walk and talk, listen, pretend to understand and try to interpret for Ray and Alice. The floating Mark hovered. Rachel was on her phone, talking, talking, talking. Must be to Maeve. Ritchie paced back and forth, like a caged tiger. Back and forth. Hypnotic.

The doctors wanted to talk to Mark. Granger. That was his name. *Focus, Mark.*

The solid Mark and the hovering Mark heard words that echoed around the impersonal room. Coils. Grafts. Too much pressure. Cold therapy. Convulsions and more bleeding. A cerebral vascular accident — accident? Granger induced a coma to keep down the damage. Damage? Mark focused on Granger's comment: "We'll wait and see, Mark. Ann is a strong woman with a will to conquer anything." The solid Mark nodded. His arms were folded and he looked concerned. Good. They wouldn't guess, then, that the Mark who loved Ann was separate. He forced himself to nod and speak.

"So, we won't know anything for a while, Mark," Doctor Granger said. "Until we bring her back. I've called for the neurologist. He should stop in this afternoon yet. You understand?"

"Yes. Thank you," he told the doctor, who went off somewhere else. Everything was either too early or too late. Too young, too old. Balance. There needs to be a balance somewhere.

Mark blinked and was back on the ground, one whole mass of raw flesh and soul.

Elle gathered the others. "We should let Mark alone now. Come, all of you. Let's go."

Mark watched Ann's son, seeing her features stamped in the shape of his eyes and nose. "I just can't believe it. She was so healthy. Colleen and I . . . We just . . . We're all praying, okay?"

Mark nodded and bit the inside of his lip to keep the scream inside. Is healthy. Is. Get it?

Ann slept.

Mark went back and forth between the hospital and Elle's house where he did not question how fresh clothes appeared daily for him or what went into his mouth. On the morning before the wedding he arrived in Ann's room to find Gary St. Clare holding her hand. How dare he bring his religion now, Mark thought. Words wouldn't make any difference. Why say them? Touching her . . . He should not touch her, either, if his words wouldn't help.

"Get away from her. In fact, get out," Mark told him.

"Mark. I want to pray with you."

"Already going on, I believe. Not that anything will change. Talking about what you want to happen won't make it so. Wishing won't . . . Why do you do that? How can you live with yourself? All the lies, the phony talk?"

"Mark, I know you're upset —"

"What would I have to be upset about? No worries, right? All things work together for those who love Him, or something like that, right? Give thanks in all circumstances, right?" Words poured out from Mark. He should have been angry, yet despair colored everything, like the blue apartment he'd left to move into the Madison house.

"I don't think our Lord expects you to be thankful —"

"Damn right! Not today. Get out."

"Mark, sit with me, won't you?"

"I did everything I was told to do! Everything you said God wanted from me. I did it all for him, and look what happened. He took her spirit and left me the shell. He did! I . . . We didn't even have a chance to . . . Ann . . . Ann. I can't. . . . Just leave. Leave!"

St. Clare straightened. "You have every right to be upset. I'll be in prayer, Mark. We all love you and Ann. I'll check in later. See if there's anything you need." He left the room.

Even Mark's shouting hadn't disturbed Ann's rest.

Granger tried to wake her up on Sunday, the day they were to promise each other forever before God and everyone.

Mark knew Ann just wasn't ready, but they wouldn't listen.

Five days after they should have married, a hospital social worker came to Ann's room to talk about something called "options."

Mark told her to call Parsons, and then he went back to Elle's house with its comfortable chair and no pressure.

He was wrong about the no pressure part. Apparently, they'd gotten to Elle. Why couldn't they just wait?

"It's time, Mark," Elle told Mark. "It's time to move Ann to a better place. Ray and

Alice have agreed. Please, try to understand."

"But she's not ready, Elle. I told them. I
told them I'd pay. If it's money, I said I
would pay."

"It's not money. Mark, it's what's best for
Ann. She needs rehabilitation. She needs
the special help they can give her at Solomon House."

"Are you sure?"

"Yes. I'm sure. Shall I make the calls?"

"Yes. You call. Flowers. I have to buy flowers."

"You go buy flowers, Mark."

Ritchie rode with him to Solomon House.
Ritchie did not try to talk to him, or offer
to take anyone else with them. When Mark
saw the building, his hands slipped on the
steering wheel. He missed the turn to the
parking lot, and drove around the block.

Ritchie didn't comment on the extra lap.

"I could have stopped him," Ritchie said.
"Trey — you know. That night he died. But
I didn't. At least, I didn't try hard enough.
And I was afraid." Ritchie turned sideways
on the seat. "If I knew then, if I had an idea
how it would feel to watch someone you
love suffer. I don't know. I don't know. I
would have found a way to make him stop."

Mark drove around the block again. So what if Ritchie needed to assuage his own guilt? He should confess to someone who cared. It meant nothing to him. No confession would make a difference to Ann or to Tiffany now. Tiffany's words echoed. "You don't know what it's like, to lose someone you love. You never forget — never forgive."

He stopped at the curb. "I can't."

"Mark —"

"Later. I promise. I just have to check on something. Get her something. From the house. Then I'll come. Promise."

Ritchie got out. "Okay, man." He slammed the door.

Mark drove north.

Although it was prime tourist season in the great north woods, midweek left a resort cabin free. He slid his credit card across the counter at a horse-faced woman with straw for hair who chewed on an unlit cigarette. He was grateful for her lack of curiosity.

He drove through the dark to park near the door of the cabin. He automatically reached for the briefcase he kept in his car and took it inside. He locked the door behind him and collapsed on the couch. Minutes, hours, days later, Mark opened the briefcase. The case was not his, but Ann's laptop computer. She must have left it there after their last trip to the new house.

Mark turned it on and opened folders at random. A file marked "Ann" turned out to be her diary. Torrents of emotion rushed through him as he read parts of their life. Joy, passion, and, finally, pain made him long for release.

Mark Roth is back. He makes me remember what it's like to be alive. I should be declared incompetent, or at least insane. He's never far from my thoughts, it's as if I can feel him right here, next to me, sitting on the couch, or the next chair in the kitchen. We just ordered takeout and talked, but after he left, I imagine his clothes in the closet next to mine, his scent on my pillow. I ache.

His eyelashes are incredible, so long and thick. I can't stop staring at him. I feel this marvelous rush of heat and energy like light, like a swift current. He kisses me. I am new. He loves me. I am so broken, how can he love me? I don't think I ever felt this way about anyone. I'm afraid, but delirious.

Rachel thinks I'm sick. She doesn't know what it's like to have the luxury of touching a man's wrist. Soothing the hairs, watching the muscles work as he moves, or feeling the pulse. I am fascinated by the little pieces of Mark. He lets me take his hand so I can examine his fingers, his knuckles, his nails, the whorls, the scars. He tells me the white line on his thumb came from a fishhook. I kiss it. His palm grows moist and I know it's because he wants me.

I imagine a wedding. I am delusional. I don't know what to do. Mark will leave me, too, I know it. Ritchie whispered it at Christmas. Elle is the only one who believes, and she's crazy.

It's Mark's birthday. I compress a decade and pretend we're closer in age. Maybe I shouldn't want that, after all. I don't think I could have been mature enough to love a man like him at that age.

I have no memory of being alone or frightened or sad. There was never anyone else beside Mark breathing the same air, completing my thoughts. I can't give him a child. My womb has withered and I long for things I can't have.

When had the sky grown black enough to

match his heart? Mark stared through the windows of the cabin. Emotions played out. Paralyzed with apathy, he couldn't make himself move from the lumpy bed. He might be hungry, he couldn't tell. For a while he wondered if he still breathed, or whether his blood had settled in his back like a great pool, waiting until he needed it again. Would it scab over, or gel, if he didn't move soon?

Where was Annie? Floating somewhere, watching them all? He was alone. Weightless, too. The jet pitch outside wasn't night, it was the river current that caught up, buoyant on white-crested waves, crashing, caressing, pushing him somewhere. Surely this was the hardest place of all. What direction would the curving river route take next? Mark gave up and let the emotional riptide tear the soul from his body.

"Quiet, Noah. I told you, don't bother him."

Mark felt a feather touch on his toes. He felt? Was he . . . ?

He made his chest expand. Just a little. He tried to pry open his eyes, but the attempt was more than he could muster.

"Shh! What are you up to, now?"

He felt his lip twitch.

"Maeve! He moved!"

"I told you, stay out of here."

A door closed off the world once more, but not before Mark realized he could smell. Putting a name to the scents overwhelmed him. Did he know a Maeve? Who was Noah?

The next time Mark surfaced from oblivion, a shaft of sunshine across his cheek made him blink and move. The iron bedstead creaked, which resulted in the immediate opening of his bedroom door.

"Hey, Mister Roth? Are you awake? How you feeling?"

The words felt like metal stakes poking his eardrums. Mark grimaced and frowned. He tried to shake his head.

"You been sick, or something. I dunno. We're taking care of you. Maeve made soup."

Mark winced at the cacophony of sounds and motion. His stomach lurched, bringing a rush of adrenaline. He struggled to sit upright and failed, flopping back the two or three inches he managed to lift his head.

His door slammed open again. "Noah! Be quiet. Mark, are you really awake this time?"

Mark blinked the sand from his eyes and forced himself to an elbow. He came face to face with a green-eyed child who stood beside him.

"Noah, what did I tell you? It's not nice to stare. Help him with the pillow, now."

The three of them managed to get Mark settled against three pillows. "Here, Mark. I made your favorite."

A spoon appeared in front of him. Mark took it, but his hand shook so much he couldn't transfer the hot liquid from the bowl to his lips.

"That's all right." The bed sank beneath her weight. "I'll help. Just a little bit at a time. That's right." Her voice lulled him. "Don't worry. You're gonna be just fine."

He tried to tell Maeve that no, he wouldn't, but she was already gone.

Mark woke again to the beloved face of his dreams. "Ann? Ann, you're all right? I knew it. Hey, I'm sorry. I don't know what happened. I just freaked out. Oh, Ann, you're back. I knew you would make it." He patted her cheek and tried to bring her mouth close.

The face pulled back. "Stop it, Mark."

That was not Ann's voice.

"I'm not Ann. I'm Maeve. Remember? Ann's niece. My mom is Rachel."

"No. I . . . I'm sorry. Where's Ann?"

"She's in Madison, Mark. Remember?"

"Why are you here?"

"The woman from the resort cabins called. When she couldn't wake you, she called me first, from the number on your phone. She thought you might be drugged up, or something. She was going to call the police next, but I said I'd come and get you. You're here, in my apartment in Cottage Grove."

"I'm tired."

"Go back to sleep, if you're not going to eat anything."

"Who's Noah?"

"My roommate's nephew. Why?"

"I just wondered."

"Sleep, Mark. It will be all right soon."

After Maeve closed the door behind her, he closed his eyes again. Why did she keep telling him that?

When Mark came fully conscious, he knew that God was dead.

Where was everyone? Didn't they know he was awake? He wiggled his feet.

If Maeve cared, she would be here. Maeve . . . would every woman from now on look like Ann? Surely this was hell. He deserved eternal punishment for running away again. For hating his father and Tiffany, and for letting Trey run wild with Ritchie. For not being there when Ann needed him most.

Clanging noises came from outside the shrunken world of the bedroom. Maybe he would get up and check it out. He pushed back the quilts and sat up. He set his numb feet on the floor. He looked at his hands to make sure they were still attached. He sniffed. Coffee. He went to the door. Time to explore this godless realm where he felt nothing. If he could see and smell, what about taste?

O, taste and see that the Lord is good . . . Mark stomped on the deceitful versifying.

The first thing he saw was Ray's skinny haunch in the air as he was searching the floor in front of a hideous plaid sofa. Mark thought about laughing, until he remembered that nothing would ever be funny again.

"Why aren't you with Ann?" Mark's voice sounded guttural to his ears. Ungrateful. Since he had nothing to be grateful for, he did not care. He repeated himself.

Ray must have found what he was seeking, for he stood and turned around. "Good morning, Mark. Glad to see you on your feet." He waved his hearing aid. "Changing batteries. Dropped it."

Mark swayed. "Where's Ann?" He staggered to the couch and collapsed.

"It's good to see you up, son."

The surge of rage almost sucked Mark from the couch. "I'm not your son! I belong to nobody!"

The old man turned to the side and clasped his wrists behind his back. He rocked on his heels.

"Not my what?"

"Son!"

"Okay. You're an independent feller who doesn't need anyone."

Mark jerked a fleece throw from the back of the couch around himself. He made himself ask his question again. Didn't the old man care about his daughter? "Where's Ann?"

Ray hooked the aid around his ear. "Ann? You know where she is. At rehab."

"She okay?"

"She's in the Lord's hands now."

Mark sat up. His heart took two weak flops, then seemed to stop. "She . . . She's not —"

"She's still with us. Fighting. Unlike you. You hungry?" Ray asked.

"I don't know." Mark's heart convulsed again.

"Mind if I help myself, then?"

"Fine by me."

Ray returned to sit on the chair near the couch. He held a fork and plate. "Coffee cake's pretty good. Let me know if you want a piece. I'll heat it up for you."

Mark's stomach churned, although he felt

hunger underneath. Maeve's spoonfuls of soup were a long time ago. Watching Ray continue to behave as though nothing was wrong fed his anger. He tossed the blanket aside and sprang up. He put his hands on his hips. "Why are you here?"

"Maeve asked me to come."

"I don't need a baby sitter."

"A what?"

"Baby sitter!"

"Colleen's with the baby."

Mark picked up a cheap ceramic mug with the Hellstrom and Company logo and threw it against the wall. The crash was jarring. Ray took another bite of his breakfast.

Mark sailed a plastic cereal bowl after the mug. It did not break.

Ray set his fork and plate down. "Feel better yet?"

"She wasn't supposed to get sick! Not before I was ready. Not so soon. How could she love me, and then go and do that?"

"Son —"

"I told you, don't call me that!" He sent a thick textbook of some kind flying after the dishes. It dented the drywall.

Ray crossed one thin ankle over a sinewy thigh. "My daughter loves you, Mark. She would never hurt you."

Mark grabbed a pillow from the couch

and punched it. "You're wrong. Annie's gone somewhere I can't follow." His legs gave out. He plopped onto the floor.

"Ann would never leave you."

"But she did," Mark whispered. "And now I can't feel anything."

"When I thought I might lose my Alice I wondered how I was going to make it. Sorta felt like nothing mattered. And I was kinda mad, too. But I had my faith and you folks to help me see it through."

"You didn't lose her, Ray. God let you keep her."

"How's that?"

"Faith is just a pack of lies!" Mark shouted. "Lies they tell children so they won't be afraid when their mothers die." Except that no one had told him about God when his own mother died. He had to find it out for himself when he became a man. Still, he hadn't been smart enough to realize that God was some huge joke. And he told Ann about it. And Ann fell into the same hole.

"Another thing I've come to learn about you," Ray said in his resonant hard-of-hearing voice, "is that you are one of the most faithful men I have ever known. I admire that. How can you drop your faith in God so easily?"

"He abandoned me first."

"Is that really what you think?"

"If I needed to discuss theology, I'd call the good reverend."

"You aren't going to abandon Ann. If I have to dress you, hogtie and carry you to the rehab center, you will not leave her alone. Ann needs you. Especially now."

"She's got you," Mark shouted. "She's got a family who loves her." Unlike me.

Mark might have lost consciousness at that point. He wasn't sure. He went back in time to hear himself ask Ritchie at a long-ago Christmas, "Tell me, what do you love about your wife."

The dream Ritchie looked at him with pity. "The way she knows I'll take care of her."

"Would you recognize love if it came in another package?" Mark had asked.

Ritchie's voice faded. Ann's voice mocked him next. "You made me come alive. You made me feel necessary. I would die if anything happened to take you away from me."

"Who is it that you're angry with? God? Ann? Yourself?" Ray said. "If you decided there is no God after all, then you can't be mad at him. Ann loves you so much it hurts me to watch. You know this is not something anyone planned. If you're mad at yourself, then I have this to say. Real men don't abandon their women when the going gets tough. You don't have to be a man of any particular faith to know that much."

Mark had loved Ann since he'd been in high school. Certainly before she could know and return that love. Before he could even express it. What could change that love? In her present state, if she could not know that he loved her, why would he act differently? He would never stop loving her. Everything he'd become was ultimately because of her support, her willingness to put her family before herself. Even that short year of living next door to her and subsequent summers, watching how she tried so hard to keep her family together, influenced his life choices. All of the things that went into making Ann special, her ease of manipulating numbers into columns like child's play, her family, but most of all, her love for him.

Ann would not have abandoned Gene after he'd been so hurt, despite her misgivings. Mark could never abandon Ann now, no matter what she'd said to him that night in Wausau, before they went to see Donna for the last time. He could no more leave her than he could order every cell of his body to leave him. They cried out when he tried to close his heart. Would God still take him back? Would Ann?

"I'm not sure I can face her, Ray, after I ran away. Why bother, if she doesn't even know me? She needs someone much better than me. I don't think I can pray anymore."

Mark felt Ray's compassionate hands on his head. The shame of his guilt flowed out in dirty streams.

"I think you might be surprised by what Ann knows and what she needs. You have to go and see for yourself. And as for praying," Ann's father said, "there's nothing hard about that. The old ways are best. Say it with me. *Our Father, who art in heaven . . .*"

Mark didn't turn on any lights when he got to Ann's room in Solomon House. In the dimness from the lamp at the nurse's station near the door, he leaned over to kiss her forehead and then her lips. Did they cling to his? She smelled of lily of the valley. He settled beside her gently on the bed and took her hand in both of his. He held it to his cheek, then, with his eyes closed, drifted his lips over the pad of each fingertip. No matter what part of Ann came back to him, he would cherish every breath she took. Her hand fluttered.

Was he dreaming? He opened his eyes to find her staring back.

"Mark?" she whispered.

"Hi, Ann. Remember me? I'm Mark and I've loved you forever."

ABOUT THE AUTHOR

A graduate of the Christian Writer's Guild's Apprentice Course, now multi-published author **Lisa J. Lickel** was first a top ten finisher in the First Operation: First Novel contest. She has written and produced for radio theater and performed live. She holds a bachelors of science in history and RECES and edits for local historical societies, freelances for local newspapers and the occasional magazine. She enjoys membership in local book clubs and writing groups, as well as American Christian Fiction Writers and Wisconsin Regional Writers. She lives in a hundred and fifty-year-old house in Wisconsin filled with books. Married to a high school biology teacher, she enjoys travel and quilting.

www.LisaLickel.com

The employees of Thorndike Press hope you have enjoyed this Large Print book. All our Thorndike, Wheeler, and Kennebec Large Print titles are designed for easy reading, and all our books are made to last. Other Thorndike Press Large Print books are available at your library, through selected bookstores, or directly from us.

For information about titles, please call:
  (800) 223-1244

or visit our Web site at:
  http://gale.cengage.com/thorndike

To share your comments, please write:
  Publisher
  Thorndike Press
  295 Kennedy Memorial Drive
  Waterville, ME 04901